THE BERMUDA TERROR

A DETECTIVE PETE NAZARETH NOVEL

R.H. JOHNSON

OTHER BOOKS BY R.H. JOHNSON

Widow-Taker, 2015

A Measure of Revenge, 2016

Hunting in the Zoo, 2016

The Kirov Wolf, 2017

Eyes in the Cave, 2017

Sailing the Gates of Hell, 2018

The Charleston Assassin, 2018

Hollow-Point Diplomacy, 2019

The Jericho Option, 2019

Books written as Alastair Flythe

Noblest Love, 2018

King of the Vultures, 2018

1.

SHE STILL THOUGHT OF IT as her secret beach, a narrow strip of pink-tinged sand hidden between a pair of massive limestone outcroppings.

Ten years hadn't changed a thing.

A brilliant moonbeam lit up the turquoise water as gentle waves splashed over her bare feet, and she was utterly and wonderfully alone for the first time since returning to Bermuda. Temporarily abandoning the crowded outdoor bar for a quiet stroll had been the right decision, one that paid the extra dividend of getting her away from that leering waiter and his suggestive comments about her backless halter top and lace cover-up board shorts.

Chloe's mother had taken her to this quiet spot on Horseshoe Bay one morning in 2009 while Dad, who had never been much for beaches anyway, was back at the hotel attending the large and undoubtedly boring business meeting that had brought the three of them here in the first place. How odd, she remembered thinking at the time, that Dad's company had chosen such a fabulous place for a business gathering when most of the attendees would be stuck indoors the whole time. Typical adult silliness.

But she and Mom had taken full advantage of the trip, dosing themselves with sunshine and crystal-clear water as often as they could. When they had grown tired of the crowded main beach, they had wandered off to more secluded areas: Butts Beach, Middle Beach, Water Rocks Beach, and Angle Beach, all of them less than a half mile from the parking lot where the hotel van had dropped them off. And that's when she had found her special place, the very same spot where she now stood alone, happy, and slightly drunk after two rum swizzles and a frozen margarita.

While her mother had relaxed on a large blue-and-white towel reading *Jane Eyre* for at least the fifth time, Chloe had built a sand castle. No, more than that. A sand kingdom! A moated palace surrounded by majestic rivers that wound lazily through hillside villages.

Lost in her fantasy that day, she had blocked out the world and all its people, sounds, and cares. She had been aware of nothing but the Bermuda sun on her shoulders until her mother's soft voice called to her, telling her it was time to go back to the hotel. She smiled as the memories of that day came flooding back one by one, like waves lapping the shoreline, and for just a moment she wished her mother were with her instead of back home in Virginia.

But the thought passed quickly. She was all grown up now. Twenty-one, beautiful, just out of college, and ready to take on the world. This Bermuda cruise, her first solo vacation, was meant to be her personal declaration of independence, and she planned to get a little crazy over the next few days. In fact, after she walked back to the bar, she might go ahead and hook up with that hot guy who had bought her the margarita. He was traveling on the same cruise ship, so why not?

One last look at the full moon, and she turned away from the sea.

At first she felt only a strange tingling sensation in her throat, as though she had breathed in too much salt air. Then came the pain. Horrific, paralyzing pain unlike anything she had ever experienced.

A thirteen-inch knife, its deadly edge sharpened to the width of a surgeon's scalpel, had in one swift motion severed the carotid artery on the left side of her slender neck, passed through the muscles and cartilage below her chin, and sliced the right carotid artery as it exited her throat.

Then, like a matador driving his sword into a bull at the end of the bullfight, the killer thrust his blade into Chloe Pedersen's heart as she collapsed to the sand.

He stood over her and watched her long blonde hair rise and fall in the wavelets. He was fascinated by the way her blood mingled with the waters of the Atlantic, swirling away like a summery cloud in a stiff breeze. Then he noticed something important: his hands weren't shaking this time.

Yes, his skills were improving.

2.

EVEN FOR AMERICA, WHERE MASS shootings and assaults on police had grown numbingly commonplace, it was a shocking crime spree. Over the space of five late-April days, thirty-year-old Kyson Bitters had entered the South Bronx apartments of six different women, forced them to place phony domestic-violence 911 calls, and then strangled them with the leather belt from his ripped jeans. After that he murdered a total of eight responding officers with a silenced Beretta 9mm pistol. All of the officers had been killed execution-style: on their knees, hands fastened behind them with their own cuffs.

The police knew who they were after because a security camera outside a Mott Haven bodega had captured his smiling face as he left the apartment building where he had just gunned down his latest victim, Detective Jeff Greeley, a twelve-year veteran of the force and one of the 40th Precinct's most decorated officers. But the NYPD's top brass had no idea how to stop Bitters from killing again. In a city that logs nearly seven hundred 911 domestic-violence calls every day of the year, it was impossible to know which one might be an invitation to assassination.

Greeley's murder proved to be a crucial development in the investigation. He was killed on May 2nd, the day before his first wedding anniversary, and the fellow detective who had served as his best man insisted on being assigned to the case. It wasn't Pete Nazareth's style to demand special treatment from the department's higher-ups, but in this particular instance he was adamant, and no one was about to stand in his way.

He was a star performer who had earned the right to call his own shots now and then.

At 3:30 p.m. on May 4th, Nazareth was cruising the South Bronx in a silver unmarked Ford Fusion when dispatch reported that Bitters had been seen entering an apartment building on 3rd Avenue near East 141st Street a few minutes earlier.

"I'm two blocks away," he told the dispatcher as he hit the gas. "Any idea who called it in?"

"Just someone from the neighborhood," the dispatcher said. "I'll have other units joining you within ten."

"Tell them I'll be inside the building when they get there."

Though acutely aware he could be walking into a trap, Nazareth wasn't about to wait for backup. Waiting meant one of two things: giving Bitters time to break into an apartment and kill someone, or allowing him to escape as soon as he heard sirens approaching. Neither option was acceptable, especially when the suspect in question was Jeff Greeley's murderer.

Greeley and Nazareth had been close friends for nearly twenty years. They had been track teammates at Fordham, had joined the Marines within a week of each other, and had graduated together from the police academy. Then eighteen months ago, when Greeley and fiancée Susan set the big date, the first person they told was Nazareth, who was overjoyed at being asked to serve as his friend's best man.

"I figure my toast will take about two hours," Nazareth had joked at the time. "There's an awful lot of ground to cover, Jeff."

"You disclose any dark secrets," Greeley had laughed, "and you'll need around-the-clock protection, friend."

"You recall that my wife is a cop, right?"

"Oh, yeah. Good point. And Tara's a hell of a lot better shot than you."

"Can't disagree."

The wedding had been fabulous, and Nazareth's brief but deeply moving toast had been something neither man would ever forget. But all the fond memories were now DOA, destroyed by the bullet Kyson Bitters had put in Jeff Greeley's head for no reason other than his hatred of police.

Nazareth swung to the curb alongside the Patterson Houses and eyed the thirteen-story building where someone had reported seeing Bitters.

Or perhaps it had been Bitters himself who had placed the 911 call, hoping to kill the first cop on the scene. That was a strong possibility, and there was only one way to find out.

As Nazareth's left foot hit the pavement, Bitters came out of the building holding a large blue pocketbook he had just snatched from an ex-girlfriend. He reached in, removed her red wallet, and tossed the pocketbook into a cluster of overgrown bushes alongside the main entrance. Then he pulled out all the bills and dropped the wallet on the sidewalk. He was about to walk off when he noticed the overly interested and obviously extremely fit young man standing next to the silver Fusion, and he recognized the look immediately. It was a look unique to New York cops, a stare that guys like Bitters understood instinctively.

Major-league trouble had just reported for duty.

Bitters spun and bolted through the building's front door with Nazareth in pursuit. Four men who had been passing a joint by the entrance scattered when they saw the well-dressed guy with the Glock 19 in his right hand sprinting toward them. The slowest of them, seventy-three and badly overweight, was shot in the head and killed instantly by the second of two rounds Bitters fired wildly through the front door's glass window. Nazareth didn't bother to stop and check for a pulse because the right side of the guy's forehead was missing. He simply stepped over the body as he moved cautiously through the doorway.

At the far end of the empty lobby, several feet beyond an elevator bank, the stairwell door was still closing as Nazareth entered the building. Bitters was racing to the upper floors, and Nazareth had no choice but to go after him immediately since any delay might give Bitters enough time to force his way into someone's apartment. And at this point the worst possible outcome would be a hostage situation involving a thug who had a taste for killing.

Taking the stairs three at a time, Nazareth speed-dialed the man in charge of his home precinct, Captain Eric Jensen, and told him where he was. It was a short conversation.

"I'm following Bitters up the stairwell," Nazareth told him. "Whoever gets here first needs to block all exits."

"Understood, Pete. Watch your back."

"Will do."

It wasn't his back that worried Nazareth. It was his chest. He never wore a bulletproof vest unless he expected trouble, and the present situation had come totally without warning. So he found himself alone and far more exposed than he wanted to be. Bitters could be waiting for him on the next landing, ready to squeeze off a few deadly rounds. Or maybe he had already slipped into one of the upper-floor hallways and was waiting for his pursuer to open the door. Either way, a 9mm round fired at point-blank range would be more than enough to add one more name to the killer's growing list of dead police officers.

Two shots rang out as he approached the eleventh-floor landing, and one of the bullets that Bitters had fired down the stairwell ricocheted off the cinderblock wall and grazed Nazareth's left thigh. His new slacks were ruined, but his leg was only scratched. Then he heard the slamming of a heavy door, which meant conditions were about to get extra dicey. Bitters had finally stopped running and was waiting in ambush. But which floor had he run to, twelfth or thirteenth? This was hardly the time for guessing games.

The door to the eleventh floor caught his attention. It was heavily dented and covered with several layers of spray-painted graffiti. He opened it, gauged its weight, and then slammed it shut as hard as he could. The sound it produced was markedly different from the one he had heard above him — a sharp crack more than a dull thud — and he caught its meaning: hallway doors are lighter and weaker than roof-access doors.

Bitters was now atop the building.

This was good. Unless Bitters planned to jump, he was trapped. All Nazareth had to do was guard the stairwell until backup arrived.

But gunfire erupted from the roof less than a minute later, and a few seconds after that Nazareth's cell phone rang. It was Captain Jensen.

"We've got officers outside," he said, "and Bitters is firing on them. One man is already down."

"What's Bitters' position on the roof?"

"Hold on." Jensen spoke with one of the officers outside the building, then said, "east side of the roof overlooking 3rd Avenue. Damn, now he's shooting at people outside a deli across the street!"

Nazareth had heard enough. He ended the call and gathered his thoughts. He had entered the building through its east-facing lobby entrance and then gone into the stairwell. Had the stairs been turned ninety degrees from the lobby entrance? He thought so. This meant that the stairs alternated north and south as they rose from the ground floor to the roof. In that case, the door to the roof should be facing north.

He looked up the stairwell and saw that the door handle was on the left. This was positive. When he opened the door, he would have some steel between him and Bitters. But there was also a huge negative: his gun would be in his right hand, which meant he would have to expose his entire body in order to get a clean shot off if Bitters chose to fight rather than surrender.

According to Nazareth's calculus, a positive and a negative cancel each other out, so he chose to trust his instincts. He climbed the final stairs, grabbed the handle, and put his shoulder into the heavy steel door.

As soon as his feet were firmly planted on the roof, he dropped into a shooter's crouch and yelled for Bitters to drop his weapon. Had Bitters done so, he would have lived long enough to stand trial.

Instead, he turned and squeezed off one last round that whistled past Nazareth's right ear. Nazareth fired twice, and both bullets caught Bitters in the center of his chest, driving him backwards over the wrought-iron fence that guarded the roof's perimeter. A young woman on 3rd Avenue captured the killer's thirteen-story fall on her cell phone, and the video had gotten nearly a half million views even before being shown on ABC's 6:30 p.m. national broadcast.

Exactly why Bitters had gone to the building's roof would remain a mystery. Some officers thought he had simply been stupid, and that was always a possibility. Others, including Nazareth, assumed he had wanted to die in a shootout with the police. But the answer didn't matter to Susan Greeley or the other wives and parents whose men had been murdered. Good cops had been lost forever while dozens of thugs just as bad as Kyson Bitters, and maybe some who were even worse, still roamed the streets of New York.

It was a losing battle.

3.

TARA GIMBLE WAS HALF OF the NYPD's most successful homicide detective team. Together she and husband Pete Nazareth had closed some of New York City's highest-profile cases, but in the process they had each danced with death more times than any reasonable person would want. In their quieter moments, when they had time to share their deepest concerns and fears, they agreed they were like trapeze artists working high above the arena floor without a net.

Theirs was a great act unless one or both of them fell, and they both figured it was only a matter of time before that happened.

The thought of dying on the job, as uncomfortable as it was, became downright intolerable when they factored in daughter Kayla, who had just celebrated her second birthday. Losing one parent would be difficult for her. Losing both would be horrendous. So Nazareth's latest brush with death had pushed the subject back onto the front burner.

"And you thought that following him up the stairwell by yourself was the only option?" she asked.

She had waited until Kayla was asleep for the night before revisiting her husband's takedown of Kyson Bitters a few hours earlier. She and Nazareth had traded only a few words about the incident when he got home that night at 6:30, but they both knew the conversation was far from over. So after dinner they joined each other on the living room couch, grateful for everything they had but intensely aware of how fleeting it all might be.

"I'm not being critical," she added. "I'm just trying to understand what was going through your head."

He shrugged and said, "This was the guy who had murdered Jeff Greeley, and I wasn't going to lose him."

"But let's say you had taken twenty seconds to pull on your vest before running into the building. Twenty seconds wouldn't have made much of a difference, right?"

"Actually, the vest was in the trunk, so it would have taken a lot longer than twenty seconds."

"So a minute maybe? Would one minute have mattered?"

"For someone who's not being critical," he grinned, "you seem just a little bit critical."

"More fatalistic than critical, Pete. I know what adrenaline does to you, and I doubt you'll ever change."

"For the record, I've seen what adrenaline does to you as well, Tara."

"Okay, that's fair. We both react the same way to certain threats. In the heat of the moment we don't always allow ourselves to consider reasonable alternatives."

"And most likely never will. I'd like to think that maybe I would handle today's incident slightly differently if given a second chance, but I probably wouldn't. I see something, my gut tells me what to do, and I do it."

She studied his face. He would soon turn thirty-seven, but he looked younger despite all the attacks he had survived, some of them just barely. His square jaw, boyish smile, and piercing gaze made him look a bit like a Hollywood star. And at five-ten and one hundred and sixty-five pounds, he still looked as though he could run a sub-4:00 mile, as he had in college, though his athletic claim to fame was now taekwondo and a long string of major fighting championships.

What struck her most, though, was that even now, after having risked his life once again on his community's behalf, he seemed perfectly at peace. His ability to maintain a calm exterior at home despite all that was going on inside his head was one of the things she loved most about him. It was also one of the things she would miss most if he were killed by the next Kyson Bitters to cross his path.

"Today a bullet only scratched your thigh. But it could have been your head."

He didn't bother telling her about the 9mm round that had whizzed past his right ear. Too much detail wouldn't be helpful in this situation.

"Cops sometimes get shot at, Tara."

"I agree. Which is why I think we need to revisit Bill Johnson's offer. It's time we gave him our answer."

He nodded despite not really wanting to go there. They were still miles apart on the issue, and he had hoped to postpone the discussion a little longer. But here it was.

The previous fall, while working a case in Charleston, South Carolina, Nazareth and Gimble had become friends with "Dollar Bill" Johnson, a self-made billionaire who had asked them to join his staff. They would each have cushy, low-risk jobs with big pay, and Kayla would be able to grow up on a fancy estate lined with magnolia trees instead of in an apartment on East 24th Street in Manhattan. Johnson had told them the offer had no expiration date. If or when they wanted to accept, their jobs would be waiting.

They had half-heartedly tossed the idea around several times over the winter. The thought of raising their daughter in a safe, genteel environment had some appeal, as did the low-risk nature of the work they would be doing. No longer would they need to fly above the circus crowd without a net.

They had asked themselves whether two native New Yorkers could ever feel at home in Charleston. Yes, they thought so. Great pizza would be in short supply, but life would go on. The chief sticking point, and the reason they had never reached a decision, was whether they could ever be truly satisfied with the work Johnson was offering them.

Gimble thought so.

Nazareth did not.

"Here's the problem," he said. "I've seen guys in their sixties who can't figure out what to do with their lives once they retire. They shuffle from one day to the next doing meaningless things, and they age twice as fast as they're supposed to. I guarantee you I'm not ready to retire at thirty-six."

"You wouldn't be retiring."

"Technically, no. But the reality is I would no longer be making a difference. I'd be paid more to do less, and how I did the job wouldn't matter to anyone on the planet. How do you compare that to getting someone like Kyson Bitters off the street?"

"I understand the feeling, Pete, and I'd also like to keep contributing to society's welfare. But for Kayla's sake I'd be willing to stop letting thugs try to kill me."

Nazareth shook his head slowly and turned toward the living room window, which overlooked a city whose vast potential for good was being undermined every minute of every day by violence and corruption. He understood only too well that the NYPD wasn't winning the war against crime, but he didn't see how he could abandon the effort after having invested so much of himself in it.

"I don't think I could do it, Tara. I wouldn't want Kayla to have a father who chose the safest, most lucrative path over the right path. If I stop being part of the solution, I become part of the problem. And, yeah, that's a cliché. But just because it's a cliché doesn't mean it's wrong."

It wasn't the flat rejection Gimble had half expected, but it was close. So she moved on to what she believed was a compromise they could both live with. Over the past year they had frequently talked about her taking a lower-risk position within the department, and with that in mind she had recently taken the sergeant's exam. Not surprisingly, she had scored a ninety-nine.

"Then let's consider this," she said. "I take a sergeant's position so that I'm primarily a supervisor. The job certainly isn't riskless, but it cuts the risk way down."

"Perfect."

"But I would also like to move out of Manhattan so that Kayla can grow up with some trees around her."

"I'm ready."

"You are?"

"What, you thought I wouldn't be?" he laughed. "I'm a Staten Island kid, remember? I can't wait to teach Kayla how to climb trees and catch frogs."

Gimble rolled her eyes and said, "In other words, I'll have two kids on my hands?"

He thought about that momentarily, then said, "Yeah, pretty much."

"We're both off tomorrow. Want to go take a look at what's out there?"

"I'm always up for a tree-hugging expedition," he laughed.

She began googling realtors before he could change his mind.

4.

BILL JOHNSON GRABBED THE PHONE on the first ring. The only people who knew he would already be in his office at the Charleston golf course were his key staff members, all of whom had learned long ago not to call him at this hour unless the news was either exceptionally good or exceptionally bad. Otherwise, they could call back at 10:00, after he had gotten in his first round of the day.

When you're worth more than $30 billion and own golf courses all over the country, you get to play a lot of golf. On most days, Johnson managed to squeeze in two rounds — one before lunch, one after.

He recognized the main number of his Bermuda estate. Odd, he thought, since the estate's resident manager, Melanie Seaward, always called on her own phone.

"How's everything in Bermuda, Melanie?" he asked.

"This is Chelsea," came the meek reply.

Johnson's stomach did a quick flip. Chelsea Butterfield was the chief housekeeper, and not once had she ever called him. He sensed that bad news was about to spoil what had started out as a highly promising spring day.

"Melanie is missing, Mr. Johnson. She went out for her usual walk before dinner last night but never returned. The entire staff was out looking for her until almost midnight, but we found nothing. So we called the police."

"And what did they say?"

"They said they couldn't do anything because by then we were having heavy storms. But they arrived shortly after sunrise this morning, and they managed to find one of Melanie's sandals on Windsor Beach." Chelsea began sobbing. "They showed it to me, Mr. Johnson, and it's definitely hers."

"Does she usually walk on Windsor Beach?"

"No, sir. She usually stays on Shore Lane and Tucker's Town Road. But she does like going down to the beach now and then."

He didn't bother asking the usual dumb questions, like would she have spent the night with a friend and not bothered telling anyone. She was too smart and far too dependable for that. The likeliest explanation was one he didn't want to contemplate.

"So what are the police saying, Chelsea?"

"They seem worried, Mr. Johnson, because this is the second time in less than a week someone has gone missing from up here."

The *up here* in question was Billionaires' Row, an incredibly exclusive area of Tucker's Town situated high on a peninsula over-looking Castle Harbour on one side and the open Atlantic on the other. This was a place where only the world's wealthiest individuals could afford to live, and Johnson was one of them. He had named his forty-million-dollar estate Windfall as a tribute to his stunning rags-to-riches story. Once a lowly salesman for a cosmetics manufacturer, he had partnered with a staff scientist to launch a start-up company whose first product was a wildly successful anti-cancer drug. The money had begun rolling in, and now his investments generated more than two billion dollars annually.

The Bermuda home was his favorite foreign property, and he visited frequently throughout the year because the travel time was just under two hours by private jet. Now and then he stayed for a couple of weeks, but generally he simply popped over for long weekends with golfing buddies. He had last seen Windfall three weeks earlier and hadn't planned to return until mid-May.

But he could tell that his travel plans were about to change.

Fifty-year-old Melanie Seaward was more than just an estate manager. She was his first cousin, the daughter of his favorite aunt. Her husband had died three years earlier, leaving her both heartbroken and deeply in debt because of his huge medical bills. Johnson had ridden to the rescue by covering the debts and then offering her one of the world's sweetest jobs: babysitting his Bermuda mansion so that she could, as he put it, "make sure everything is okay."

Nothing at Windfall was ever merely okay. In fact, all eight thousand square feet of the mansion were flawless, and the scenery matched. The home had been meticulously designed to provide its residents with unforgettable views from every room. Look out any window, and you'd see either the Bermuda-blue ocean or lush tropical gardens worthy of a magazine cover.

Although Melanie lived in the guest cottage — a chic two-story home with three bedrooms, four baths, and its own infinity pool — she spent much of her time in and around the main house itself, making sure the five-person staff kept everything in fine order. When Johnson arrived in Bermuda, as he sometimes did unannounced, he expected Windfall to be perfect, and she made sure it was. Even though Chelsea Butterfield and the other full-time employees had performed admirably prior to Seaward's arrival, Johnson liked the idea of having a family member watching over the place in his absence.

From Seaward's perspective, of course, the situation couldn't be better. She had gone from being a flat-broke widow in Danbury, Connecticut, to the highly paid overseer of a Bermuda estate that even the island's other billionaire residents envied. For someone who enjoyed reading and painting, this was as good as it got. She still missed her husband, who had died way too young at fifty-six, but her life was otherwise unbelievably right, and she had no desire to change a thing.

"Someone else disappeared recently?"

"Yes, sir. Mr. Redin just down the road."

"The old guy who lives out near the end of the peninsula?"

"That's the one. His wife said they had gone to Frick's Beach, and he stayed on to watch the sunset but never returned home. Some people around here thought he might have gone into the ocean to commit suicide because he was extremely ill. But now," she said softly, "I think maybe there's more to it."

Johnson had known the old man only well enough to wave when he saw him, which was infrequently. A transplanted Canadian who lived on the island year-round, Liam Redin was in his mid-eighties and had always appeared to be somewhat unsteady on his feet. Why his wife had chosen to leave him alone on the beach was a question the police had probably already asked themselves. She was decades younger, Johnson recalled, and maybe she had … well, who could say? Perhaps the phrase *'Til death do us part* had finally given her an idea about how to improve her social life.

"How long ago was this?"

"Four days."

"Chelsea, did the police say anything about possible kidnappings?"

"No, sir. But why would anyone want to kidnap Melanie?"

On the surface, at least, it was a fair question since Seaward wasn't rich. On the other hand, she lived at one of the island's most spectacular estates and might have been mistaken for its owner. Beyond that, it was possible someone knew she was related to Johnson and assumed he would pay handsomely to have her returned safely. But the fact that he and Seaward were cousins was something only the people working at Windfall would have known. And why would they have told anyone?

He answered his own question: people love to gossip, especially about rich people and their families.

"They probably wouldn't, Chelsea. I'm just struggling to understand all this."

"There's more," she said tentatively. "Two days ago a young tourist woman was murdered on the beach at Horseshoe Bay, and the police apparently think all three incidents are connected."

"That's what they told you?"

"No, but that's the impression I got when they were here. I heard one of them say that this is more than a series of coincidences."

Coincidences, indeed. For two people from one of the world's most exclusive gated communities to disappear without a trace in less than a week would be more than enough to raise eyebrows. Add a beach murder to the mix, and the odds against this being a matter of coincidence were astronomical.

"So how did you leave it with the police, Chelsea?"

"Well, sir, that's partly why I'm calling. The officer in charge said he would like to speak with you. I told him you weren't here, but he wants to speak with you anyway."

Johnson jotted down the officer's name and phone number while scanning the open calendar on his laptop. There were a couple of board meetings and working dinners coming up but nothing he couldn't skip for something like this. If the Bermuda police wanted to speak with him, they wouldn't need to do so over the phone.

Johnson had always believed that the only proper way to handle important business is face to face.

"Please call the officer and let him know I'll be arriving today before noon, Chelsea."

"I will, sir. Right away. Do you want to meet him here?"

"Doesn't matter to me, Chelsea."

In fact, the only thing that mattered to Johnson was getting to Bermuda as fast as he could.

His home in paradise had been attacked, and he took it personally.

5.

HOUSE NUMBER THREE WAS A knockout.

After deciding it was time to look for a place in the suburbs, Nazareth and Gimble had spent the morning with a real estate agent in Westchester, one of the counties where NYPD officers were allowed to live. The first home she showed them was too modern for their taste, and the second had almost no property at all. But the third house, a gleaming white-brick colonial in Hastings-on-Hudson, was checking off all the right boxes.

Kayla agreed. First she tried to chase down a rabbit that had just hopped into the red azaleas that lined the side of the house. Then she turned her attention to the hundreds of daffodils that framed the long rock wall adjacent to the woods. Before reaching them, though, she paused under a large cherry tree and stared up into the pink blossoms, hands outstretched.

"Those are cherry blossoms." Gimble told her.

"See the pretty bird, Mommy?"

A brilliant red cardinal, the object of Kayla's fascination, flew off a low branch and headed for the woods.

"This is definitely the kind of yard I had in mind, Tara," Nazareth said. "Cherry trees are great for climbing."

"Is it okay if we see the house before buying it?"

"Plus we have the woods right next door."

"Yes, and there's even a nice big rock wall for you to fall off," she teased.

"I've never done that, but I bet it's fun."

"That wooded lot is part of the property," agent Jill Sheppard said as she walked over to them. "It's buildable, but the current owner liked having the extra privacy."

"You'd have to be crazy to give up something like that," Nazareth said.

"Unless you had to for financial reasons," Gimble replied. She already knew the house was at the top of their price range, and she found the prospect of a big mortgage payment more than a little intimidating. There was no way they would consider this place unless the inside was nearly perfect.

It was.

A pair of mahogany doors with etched glass panels led to a large foyer that featured gleaming maple floors and a matching staircase. To the left was a huge living room roughly the size of their Manhattan apartment. To the right was a formal dining room that connected on one side to a large breakfast nook and on the other to a family room with a stone fireplace. Rounding out the first floor was Gimble's dream kitchen outfitted with granite countertops, a huge island, and natural-stone floor tiles. The walk-in pantry was large enough to double as a guest room.

"Do you like the first floor?" Sheppard asked.

"A little too much," Gimble confessed. She had been right. There was no way they could afford this place.

"Then let's head upstairs."

Oversized windows in the master bedroom offered gorgeous views of nature to the north and west. The windows were open, and the only sound to be heard was the wind whispering among tree branches. No cabs, no motorcycles, no sirens. The adjoining master bath was an oasis of understated elegance replete with a jetted tub, an extra large shower with stacked-stone walls, and a granite double-sink vanity. Three other second-floor bedrooms provided ample space for guests or a growing family.

Downstairs again, Sheppard opened the back door to the tigerwood deck, a sprawling beauty that looked out on an expansive yard surrounded by a six-foot privacy fence that had obviously cost the current owner a bundle. It was precisely the sort of fence Nazareth and Gimble had wanted. Hastings-on-Hudson wasn't Manhattan, but it wasn't heaven either. A yard that was essentially invisible from the street made perfect sense.

"So that's the full tour," Sheppard said. "What do you think?"

"I'm in love," Gimble replied, "but I don't think we can handle the price tag on this one."

"Actually," Nazareth said gently, "I think we could swing it because our apartment is worth a whole lot more than I paid for it. We'd probably want to come up with more up-front cash to keep the mortgage payment down, but I'm pretty sure we could make this work financially. I'm more concerned about who'd take care of Kayla up here."

It had taken them months to find the right daycare center in Manhattan, and they were extremely happy with the current situation. In addition, Gimble's parents lived in Brooklyn and were always eager to take charge of Kayla when the opportunity arose. So moving to Westchester held the prospect of shaking up their daughter's finely balanced world.

"You'll find absolutely first-rate daycare centers and preschools here," Sheppard assured them, "and they cost less than in Manhattan. If you want, I'll take you by a couple of them right now."

"There's something else," Gimble added enthusiastically. "I just found out yesterday that my father has been offered an adjunct faculty position in the criminal justice program at Pace University in Pleasantville. But he told my mother he wouldn't accept it because they would have to move away from us."

"When did this happen?" Nazareth asked.

"My mother called yesterday afternoon, but you and I had other things to talk about last night."

"Pleasantville is probably less than twenty minutes from here," Sheppard noted helpfully.

"Which is a lot faster than my parents can get from Brooklyn to our apartment in Manhattan," Gimble said.

Nazareth felt the sun, moon, and stars coming into perfect alignment, and he wasn't one to squander such moments.

"I think we should make an offer," he said.

But Gimble didn't hear him. She was running after Kayla, who was chasing a squirrel toward the woods.

6.

JOHNSON'S GULFSTREAM G280 TOUCHED DOWN at L.F. Wade International shortly after 11:00 a.m., and a few minutes later he was in the back seat of a limo zipping over the narrow causeway that crossed Castle Harbour. By all appearances it was just another perfect Bermuda day: turquoise water, clear skies, and pink houses dotting the distant hillside. But he was deeply aware of how much had changed since his last visit.

Old Mr. Redin: missing and presumed dead.

Cousin Melanie: missing and presumed dead.

A young tourist from Virginia: slain on the beach only a few hundred yards from a crowded outdoor bar.

Johnson had lived long enough to know that bad things can happen anywhere. But for these three incidents to occur in less than a week in Bermuda was still virtually incomprehensible. Worse, he deduced that the police were apparently nowhere in the investigation, which explained why they wanted to speak with him. If they had any worthwhile leads, he reasoned, they wouldn't be interviewing a billionaire who had been in South Carolina when all three crimes occurred.

But he was willing to cooperate if that would increase the chances of finding Seaward and bringing her abductor — or was it her killer? — to justice. Inspector Earl Trott had told Chelsea he would come to Windfall in order to spare Johnson the discomfort of visiting police headquarters. Johnson, in turn, had told Chelsea to invite the inspector to discuss Seaward's disappearance over lunch. He expected it to be the oddest working lunch ever, but he considered it the best way to handle a bad situation.

When Johnson's limo pulled into Windfall's circular drive, Chelsea was standing at the front entrance alongside Jacob Brangman, the estate's head groundskeeper and all-around handyman. Brangman opened the limo door for Johnson, welcomed him home, and grabbed the small suitcase from the trunk.

"I'll bring this to your room, Mr. Johnson," Brangman said.

"Thank you, Jacob. I appreciate that." Then he turned to Chelsea, whose eyes were red. "How are you holding up?"

"As well as can be expected, Mr. Johnson. I'm worried about Melanie, and I'm trying to understand how these things could be happening here."

"Well, let's wait and see what the police have to say."

"Yes, sir. Oh, and Shaun said he'll have lunch ready whenever you and the inspector want it."

Formerly the sous chef at one of Bermuda's finest restaurants, Shaun Lightbourne had wisely agreed to come work for Johnson two years earlier in order to decrease his workload while doubling his salary. He now had enough free time to coach his son's football team and volunteer twice a week preparing meals for the homeless. Lightbourne had a standing offer to start his own restaurant with Johnson's generous backing should he care to do so, but for the moment life was more than good for the thirty-year-old chef and his family.

Johnson walked into his home away from home and momentarily abandoned all his cares. Windfall had a way of doing that. The front door opened onto an expansive foyer highlighted by a magnificent spiral staircase leading to the upper floor. This area featured priceless originals by Monet, Renoir, and Pissarro, his three favorite French Impressionists.

To the left of the foyer and down the hallway past the game room and bar was the living room, whose floor-to-ceiling windows looked east to the Atlantic. To the right were Johnson's private office, a massive dining room, and, finally, the kitchen, where Lightbourne was busy adding the finishing touches to his secret recipe for Bermuda fish chowder. In addition to the customary rockfish, he added lobster, red snapper, and conch.

"That smells wonderful," Johnson said as he walked over to the fifty-thousand-dollar range where the chef worked his magic.

"And I hope it tastes even better, Mr. Johnson," Lightbourne smiled. "It's the least I could do for you under the circumstances. I wish I could do more."

"Your friendship and great food are all I could ever ask for, Shaun. Thank you for both."

"Would you like to have lunch out on the deck? It's lovely out there today."

"That sounds wonderful. Might as well give Inspector Trott the full treatment, eh?"

"I couldn't agree more, sir."

The rear deck overlooked two acres of pristine greenery alongside one of the world's most spectacular Atlantic panoramas. A gentle breeze from the east brought with it the scent of Bermudiana blooms and clean salt air, a combination that went a long way toward refreshing Johnson's spirits. Having thought about nothing but the problem of Seaward's disappearance since daybreak in Charleston, he was now ready to turn his attention to the solution. If Inspector Trott had a solution, wonderful. If not, Johnson would come up with his own.

• • •

Johnson had changed into light blue golf shorts and a pale yellow knit polo shirt by the time he greeted the inspector at the front door. Trott wore the customary Bermuda Police Service uniform: a white shirt with black tie and trousers. The two diamonds on his epaulettes signaled his senior rank as did his overall bearing. Ramrod straight and six-three, he carried about two hundred pounds on his athletic frame. His face was expressionless, neither friendly nor hostile, but he made it clear this was no social call. Twenty-three years as an officer had taught him how a proper investigation should be conducted.

Their handshake was an even match. Trott was the far younger man, but Johnson had the powerful grip of an elite golfer and gave as good as he got.

"Thanks for offering to meet with me here," Johnson said warmly. "I don't mind police stations, but this is more agreeable under the circumstances."

"My pleasure, Mr. Johnson. I appreciate your flying in on such short notice."

"If you don't mind talking over lunch, the chef tells me everything's ready."

"Lunch isn't necessary, but I don't mind in the least."

"Good. I have a table reserved for us."

As they walked toward the doorway to the deck, Trott spotted Lightbourne in the kitchen.

"Is that you, Shaun?" Trott's expression immediately changed from neutral to lights-out happy. "By God, it is."

Johnson immediately felt the ice thaw.

"Inspector Trott's son and mine are football teammates," Lightbourne told Johnson. "That's *our* football. What you'd likely call soccer."

"And I don't mean to brag," Trott said, "but they're the two best ten-year-old players in Bermuda."

"In the world, you mean," Lightbourne laughed.

"I stand corrected. And you're the world's finest coach. But I didn't know you worked here."

"This is why I left the restaurant and now have time to do things like coach. Best job I've ever had, Earl. I sure hope you can find Melanie for us."

The look on Trott's face didn't offer much encouragement.

"Well, we're certainly going to try, Shaun."

As soon as Johnson and Trott had taken their seats at the linen-covered table on the deck, the inspector slipped back into steel-jawed police mode.

"Are you sure you want to do this over lunch, Mr. Johnson? I appreciate your hospitality, but ..."

"But you need to ask questions about Melanie's disappearance. I'm accustomed to working while I eat, inspector. Besides, you'd never be able to face Shaun again if you walked away from his seafood chowder."

Trott cracked a hint of a smile.

"Yes, I suppose that's true. Then let me begin with the most difficult questions first. Had you and Melanie Seaward been having any difficulties lately?"

"The only difficulty in my life at the moment is her disappearance."

"So there were no personal disruptions of any kind?"

"Give me an example of a *personal disruption.*"

"Okay, well, what I mean is some sort of infidelity."

Johnson grinned and said, "Inspector, were you aware that I hired Melanie because she's my first cousin?"

Trott looked as though he had been caught stealing the silverware.

"No, I wasn't. I had been under the impression that you and she were a couple."

"Someone told you that?"

"Not explicitly, but I believe it was implied by one of the people I interviewed when I was here earlier this morning."

Johnson took his time processing what he had just heard. Had he been wrong in assuming that everyone on the staff knew that he and Melanie were cousins? If so, it was possible someone had misconstrued their relationship. On the other hand, it was also possible someone had deliberately hinted at impropriety in order to complicate the investigation. But for what reason?

"I assume you can't tell me who."

"No, sir, I cannot. But I'll certainly take a closer look at that person's comments."

By the time Johnson finished giving the inspector a quick history of how Seaward had come to be Windfall's property manager, Lightbourne showed up at the table with two immense bowls of chowder and some freshly baked rolls.

"A taste of Bermuda to help keep you going, gentlemen. I would normally serve this with a white Burgundy," he told Trott, "but I'm assuming you won't have any while on duty."

"Sadly, no. But please," Trott said to Johnson, "don't let me stop you."

"Water is fine for me as well," Johnson said. "Shaun's seafood chowder doesn't need any help at all."

"Then please enjoy," Lightbourne said. He walked off and left the two men to their lunch.

"Spectacular!" Trott declared after the first taste. "You know, that restaurant hasn't been quite the same since Shaun left. He wasn't the executive chef, but he was obviously a key player."

"I'm hoping he'll open his own place one day, but I'm extremely fortunate to have him here in the meantime."

After a short break from the Q&A, Trott circled back to business.

"Did Melanie ever mention having problems with your household staff?"

"Not at all. Is it possible someone resented having her show up here to keep an eye on things? Sure. That's human nature, right? But Melanie has a talent for getting along with people, and I find it impossible to believe anyone on the staff would have wished this on her. Do you suspect otherwise?"

Trott shook his head slightly.

"I believe one or two people may have found her somewhat overbearing, but I don't think that has anything to do with this case."

"Before Melanie arrived, the place was *well* cared for but not *flawlessly* cared for. All I can tell you is that she has made a good staff better, even though not everyone may appreciate her role. Now can I ask you a question?"

"Absolutely."

"Are you connecting any dots between Melanie, Mr. Redin, and the young American woman who was murdered a few days ago?"

"It's tempting to do so simply because these sorts of things rarely happen in Bermuda. And for two of them to have occurred in quick succession in this particular neighborhood," Trott added, "is rather mind-boggling. But if you're asking whether we have any serious leads, the answer is no."

Johnson went back to his seafood chowder. He appreciated Trott's honest answer, but it was highly unsatisfying nevertheless. A dark force had crept onto the island, and so far the local police had no idea who or what that force might be.

It occurred to him that they could probably use a helping hand.

7.

NAZARETH AND GIMBLE AGREED THEY were doing the right thing. They would both remain with the NYPD, but they would buy a home in the suburbs so that Kayla wouldn't have to grow up in a city. The place in Hastings-on-Hudson was going to be ideal, and somehow they would make the numbers work. So the only remaining loose end was a conversation with Bill Johnson. It was time to tell him unequivocally that they couldn't accept his amazing job offer. The idea of moving to South Carolina was officially off the table.

"Great minds really do think alike," Johnson laughed when he answered Nazareth's call. "Or maybe you and Tara are just psychic. I was just about to pick up the phone and call you two."

"I'm sorry we've been dragging our feet, Bill. But your offer gave us a lot to think about. Can I put you on speaker?"

"Absolutely. Good morning, Tara. How's everything up there?"

"Going really well, Bill. Among other things, we've made some important decisions over the past day or two."

"You both sound a little hesitant, so I'm guessing you've decided not to come to Charleston. Am I correct?"

"You are," Nazareth said. "If we both live to be a hundred, we'll never get another offer like yours. But it seems as though Tara and I have NYPD blood running through our veins and aren't willing to walk away from our jobs."

Johnson's momentary silence suggested he was either disappointed or angry. In fact, he was neither.

"I admire that in both of you," he said, "which is why I'm not at all surprised by your decision. New York City is lucky to have you, and I really appreciate the fact that you thought seriously about my offer."

Nazareth and Gimble breathed easier. Johnson's offer had been beyond sweet, and they were heartened by his gracious response to their decision. The guy was one of a kind, no doubt about it.

"I'm going to be moving into a supervisory job," Gimble offered, "which should pretty much take me out of harm's way. So it'll just be Pete on the street trolling for danger."

"Until they force him to move up the ladder, Tara. It's inevitable you'll both be senior people in the department. I have friends up there," Johnson said cryptically, "and I know you're both on your way to bigger things."

"Your sources must be better than ours," Nazareth chuckled. "Care to share any names?"

"Not a chance, Pete. All I'll say is the right people have their eyes on you."

"Oh, and we've also decided to move to Westchester," Gimble added.

"Wow, now that's a surprise. Listen, a really good friend of mine is a realtor up in Westchester. If you need help, I'll call him for you."

"We're already pretty far along. The agent we're working with — Jill Sheppard is her name — has been terrific, and we've already made an offer on a place in Hastings-on-Hudson."

"I know the area well, Tara. It's wonderful. Your little girl is about two now, as I recall, so it's about time for her to be out in the country climbing trees."

"Oh, my God!" Gimble howled. "Are you and Pete secretly brothers? What's with you guys and trees?"

"Hey, I'll bet my last nickel you climbed plenty of trees as a kid, Tara." Johnson challenged.

"A few times maybe."

"There you go. We humans came down from the trees millions of years ago, and we've been wondering why ever since. The trees are a lot safer than the streets nowadays." He paused, then added, "Which leads me to why I was about to call you. I'm in Bermuda, where things have recently become uncharacteristically unsafe."

He shared the unsettling details. Two people had disappeared from Bermuda's safest gated community. One of them was his cousin, who had gone for a pre-dinner walk and never returned. In addition, a young American woman had been brutally murdered on the island's most popular beach. This might be business as usual for two New York homicide detectives, but for any Bermudian it was unfathomable.

"Now here's the interesting part," Johnson explained. "The Bermuda police are wonderful in many ways, but as you might imagine, they don't have a highly experienced homicide team. And I'm wondering if you would do me a great favor and come down here to have a look at what's going on."

"I can't imagine the Bermuda police would think that's a great idea, Bill," Nazareth said. "All cops are pretty uncomfortable about sharing their turf with outsiders."

"The police commissioner here has already given his approval."

"You're serious?"

"I am. And with one more phone call I can have you both assigned here temporarily. What I propose is having you stay at my place for however long it takes you to reach some conclusions. It's possible these cases will never be solved, but at least I'd like to know we had the world's best team working on them."

"You really think the NYPD would agree to having us go there?" Gimble asked.

"No question about it, Tara. And, by the way, being here will be like the best vacation of your life when you're not actually working. I have plenty of room and a full-time staff at the cottage. I'm heading back to Charleston, so the place will be yours for however long you can stay."

"It couldn't be long, Bill," Gimble said. "Between Kayla and the house we just bid on, we'd be limited to maybe two weeks at most."

"At most," Nazareth agreed.

"Whatever time you two can give will be enough, and I'd be extremely grateful for it. I owe it to my cousin as well as to this wonderful island to try to make something good happen."

"Tell you what," Nazareth offered. "How about we run this past our precinct captain before we give you an answer?"

"That's a good idea, Pete. Let's see what he thinks."

Johnson smiled as he hung up. He already knew what Captain Eric Jensen's answer would be.

8.

HE HANDLED THE THIRTEEN-INCH medieval dagger like a holy relic, lovingly passing its eight-inch blade over the sharpening stone at a precise twenty-degree angle. Forward and back, forward and back, again and again and again. The entire process would take nearly forty minutes, every one of them intensely stimulating for him. He knew from experience that no woman could excite him the way this knife did whenever he held it in his hands.

It was actually much more than a knife. It was the gleaming steel embodiment of his righteous indignation, his commitment, and his invincibility.

The story of how the medieval dagger had come into his family's possession was a matter of dispute. His father had told his mother it was a gift from a grateful tourist. But the tourist in question, a British dealer in medieval antiques, claimed it had been stolen. The only verifiable fact was that his father, once a well-paid and much respected bellman at one of the island's top hotels, had been fired over the incident, then promptly committed suicide rather than die destitute and homeless.

Twelve years had passed, and he had kept the knife out of sight until the other night, when he had come across that young American slut wandering Horseshoe Bay. Yes, killing her had erased a small portion of his family's suffering and shame. But it wasn't nearly enough. Much work remained, and he felt greatly blessed to be the instrument of his parents' salvation.

Immediately following his father's suicide, he and his mother had gone to live with an aged aunt who after only a few months tired of having a seven-year-old boy in her tiny home. Then began the long, dehumanizing cycle of living in homeless shelters, abandoned homes, and even caves while his mother worked two full-time jobs as a hotel room attendant to keep them both fed.

When he was fifteen, his mother was accused of stealing ten dollars from the opulent two-bedroom penthouse suite of an American couple. His mother had tearfully claimed the couple left money on the bathroom vanity as a tip. The couple denied it, arguing that the maid's tip was already included in the hotel's daily rate. Rather than offend wealthy repeat guests, the housekeeping manager had fired her on the spot. She collapsed and died of a heart attack while walking to the bus stop down the hill from the hotel's glittering main lobby.

He had been on his own ever since, at first begging or stealing, later holding down a series of dead-end jobs that barely kept food in his belly and clothes on his back. But he had a roof over his head now — a basement roof, but a roof nevertheless — and a knife sharp enough to slice a single strand of hair lengthwise. Above all, he had a lifetime of anger that needed to be purged like the poison it was. Tourists had destroyed his life, and the time had finally come to make them pay.

He paused when he heard the old woman's loud footsteps above him. Was she moving toward the basement door? No, she entered the kitchen, her hard-soled sandals slapping on the wooden floor like so many rifle shots to his brain. She did it deliberately, he knew, because she didn't like him and didn't want him anywhere in her home. The noise got louder and more unbearable every day, and he hated her for it. How he'd like to climb the stairs, walk up to her from behind, and run the knife across the front of her neck.

She dropped a heavy baking pan on the floor, and it sounded like a lightning strike directly above his head. Yes, that was also deliberate. Every day now she dropped something when she thought he was sleeping down below. It was part of her plan to drive him out.

She hadn't wanted him there in the first place, but her husband had insisted. "He's my cousin's boy, for God's sake!" he had argued. "And it's just until he gets on his feet."

But he wouldn't leave the basement apartment now even if someone else would have him. No, this place was perfect for what he had in mind, and he wasn't going anywhere.

If anyone left, it would be her. One way or the other.

He wiped the blade on a hand towel and admired its fine edge. Without question, his was the deadliest knife in Bermuda.

9.

KAYLA CLIMBED INTO THE CAR seat and sat still while her grandmother strapped her in. Then she gave Nazareth and Gimble a brief wave and immediately began jabbering to her grandfather, who was behind the wheel of the Ford Expedition. An eight-passenger behemoth that weighed nearly three tons was a lot more vehicle than Bud and Joan Gimble needed, but they had bought it hoping they would frequently have their granddaughter in the back seat.

What a fortuitous move that had been.

Completely out of the blue, both families had decided to move to Westchester. Nazareth and Gimble had already found their dream home in Hastings-on-Hudson, while Bud and Joan were about to look for a place in Pleasantville. They were taking Kayla house hunting with them for the day, then heading up to their vacation home on Lake George. Meanwhile, Nazareth and Gimble would be flying to Bermuda at Bill Johnson's request.

"Be careful," Gimble called from the sidewalk as the SUV pulled away from the curb. "Kayla has expensive taste in homes."

But she knew it was a lost cause. If Kayla fell in love with any of the houses they looked at, Grandma and Grandpa would almost certainly make an offer. Both of them had basically made spoiling Kayla their life's work. Besides, Kayla would probably be spending as much time in their home as in her own once both moves were completed. Having Gimble's parents living only twenty minutes away in Westchester was an unexpected and thoroughly amazing gift.

An hour later, a private car dropped Nazareth and Gimble off at Teterboro Airport's executive terminal, where Johnson's plane was parked. A beaming young flight attendant dressed in a smart navy-blue pant suit and a collared white silk blouse greeted them as soon as they walked in.

"Bill Johnson sends his regards, detectives," she said warmly. "I'm Faith Greene, and I'll be making sure you enjoy your short flight to Bermuda."

"It's already off to a perfect start," Nazareth said. "Not having to wait on a TSA line for an hour is as good as it gets."

"No," she smiled knowingly, "it really does get quite a bit better."

Her comment began to make more sense as the three of them walked across the tarmac to the waiting aircraft, a gleaming white Gulfstream G280 that had set Johnson back slightly more than twenty-five million dollars. The twin-engine business jet could seat ten passengers comfortably, but today it would have only two. A trim uniformed pilot was standing at the foot of the entry staircase to meet the VIPs. He shook their hands.

"Welcome aboard, Detective Gimble and oorah, Captain Nazareth! I'm Clint Sheffield."

Gimble grinned and said, "Just a wild guess here, but you're a former Marine."

"Yes, ma'am, but technically ..."

"Once a Marine, always a Marine," Nazareth added. "When did you serve?"

"About the same time as you but with far less distinction. I flew an AV-8B off the USS Bonhomme Richard during the Iraq War while you were doing your thing in Afghanistan."

As a young Marine captain in a Special Operations Battalion, Nazareth had been awarded the Navy Cross, the nation's second highest military honor, for his actions while leading troops on a high-risk mission among the caves of Eastern Afghanistan. In an area known as the Valley of the Shadow, Nazareth had gone hand-to-hand with a group of Al Qaeda hostiles who were dragging off one of his injured team members. His bravery had resulted in a small scar on his chin and three very dead bad guys.

"*All* Marines serve with distinction, Clint," Nazareth said, and it wasn't false modesty speaking. He truly believed that everyone who had worn the uniform had done his or her part in eradicating evil in the Middle East. In fact, this helped explain his strong feelings toward those who carried NYPD badges. They all shared a bold and necessary mission that outsiders couldn't completely understand.

"But not all of them get to wear the Navy Cross," Sheffield countered. "When Bill Johnson told me who our passengers were today, I recognized your name right away. And yours as well, Detective Gimble. You would have made a great Marine."

He was right about that. An All-American soccer player in college, Gimble held a judo black belt and carried one hundred and twenty pounds of well-toned muscle on her five-seven frame. She was also known to be pretty good with a gun. Several times, in fact, she had won gold medals at the national police pistol competition in St. Louis while up against the country's top marksmen.

During her career as an NYPD detective and a presidential special agent, she had put her life on the line countless times and taken down nearly as many bad guys as her husband. But Nazareth often joked that she had an advantage: perps often didn't take her seriously because she was beautiful. She had gleaming blonde hair, captivating blue eyes, and perfect skin that needed no help from makeup, which explained why she rarely used it. The fact that she now doubled as a tough cop and a mom made her even more impressive.

"How on earth did you hear about me?" she laughed.

"Bill Johnson told me all about you both," he said. "It's an honor to have you on board."

Sheffield introduced them to copilot Amanda Elliot as they passed the cockpit.

"Amanda is former Air Force," he noted. "Former B-1 pilot who did some of her best work in Afghanistan."

Gimble was plainly intrigued.

"How do two former military combat pilots end up flying a corporate jet for one of the country's richest men?"

"As far as I can tell," Sheffield explained, "Bill just likes to invest in people. He caught some major breaks in life, and now he wants to help create some lucky breaks for others. But I understand you guys won't be signing on with him."

"No, we've decided to stick with the NYPD," Nazareth said.

"I also said no at first because I had what I thought was a great job with a major airline. But the industry just kept getting worse, and one day Bill called and asked whether I would reconsider his offer."

"And here you are."

"And here I am. Best career move of all time. And if you ever change your mind," he added, "I'm willing to bet his offer will still be there."

"How did you meet him to begin with?" Gimble asked.

"I was deadheading from Chicago to Charleston, and there was room for me in first class. Bill was sitting next to me and noticed my Naval Academy ring. Before you know it, he's getting my life story: Academy, Iraq, and all the rest. He was especially interested in my combat experiences and the fact that I had received a couple of DFCs."

Before Gimble could ask, Nazareth said, "Distinguished Flying Cross. It's a really big deal."

"Not nearly as big as the Navy Cross," Sheffield told her, "but big enough to hold Bill's interest. For whatever reason, he figured I deserved to catch a break, and the rest is history."

"Had he bought his own plane before hiring you?" Nazareth wondered.

"Nope. When I decided to join him, he told me to find the right copilot and the right aircraft. So that's what I did. I had met Amanda at a DFC Society reunion and gave her a call."

"Wait. Amanda also has a DFC?"

"And when we get married next month," he added, " I think we'll become the only husband-wife DFC recipients. Anyway, make yourselves comfortable. Time for me to go up front. I'll check in with you later."

"That's amazing," Nazareth said to Gimble. "Husband-and-wife DFC pilots."

But she wasn't listening. She was instead scrolling through a text message that had just arrived.

That's when Faith Greene walked up to their seats with a glass of champagne in each hand.

"Bill said that since you won't be working today, he hoped you would consider a champagne toast to help start your Bermuda working vacation."

"I'll gladly toast our first trip to Bermuda," Nazareth said as he accepted one of the glasses. "As for the vacation part, only time will tell."

Gimble didn't reach for the offered champagne.

"Thanks, Faith, but I'd like to stick with water," she said pleasantly.

"Of course," Faith said. "I'll be right back."

Nazareth was surprised. He and his wife had never been big drinkers, but Gimble rarely said no to champagne under the right circumstances. If this didn't qualify, what did?

"Day off, private jet, Bermuda, expensive champagne. What's wrong with this picture?"

"I can't have alcohol," she grinned.

His jaw dropped, and she held up her cell phone so that he could see the lab results her doctor had just sent.

He made a great show of counting the months on his fingers and said, "January?"

"Uh, huh. Another winter baby on the way."

He leaned over, hugged her, and planted a kiss on the top of her head.

"Teaching two kids how to climb trees will be a challenge," he said seriously, "but I'm up to it."

She groaned softly. Tending two babies and one adult kid was going to be a serious challenge.

10.

JENNA TUMBRIDGE WAS WAITING FOR Nazareth and Gimble when they cleared Customs and Immigration in Bermuda. Thanks to Bill Johnson, the guy who always seemed to think of everything, she would be their personal driver for as long as they were on the island. She walked over and introduced herself when she matched them to the photo on her cell phone.

"Welcome to Bermuda, folks. Non-residents can't rent cars, and Bill didn't want you riding around on scooters while you're here. So I'll be at your disposal 24/7."

"That sounds like a pretty heavy commitment," Gimble said sympathetically.

"Any commitment is fine by me when it involves Bill. I have ten other drivers on staff, but Bill asked me to take care of you myself. And I'm glad to do so."

"You have your own limo company?"

"For three years now, yes. Thanks to Bill."

Neither detective was surprised. Johnson was obviously on a mission to help people he liked.

"Did he happen to mention why we're here?" Nazareth asked.

"After swearing me to secrecy, yes. That's why I didn't hold up a sign with your names on it. Thank you for coming. What's happening here," she said ruefully, "isn't at all normal for Bermuda."

"We'll certainly do the best we can."

"From what Bill has told me, that will be enough."

Nazareth and Gimble appreciated Johnson's confidence in them but feared he was guilty of building false hopes for people like Jenna. After all, it was impossible to draw a straight line between being the NYPD's top homicide team and cracking three major cases in a country they were visiting for the first time. In fact, they had come to Bermuda believing that if the cases got solved, it would be through the efforts of the local police. They figured that the best a couple of New York detectives could do was offer helpful insights along the way.

They had another nagging concern. No one had told them exactly how this temporary assignment had gotten approved in the first place. When they had asked Captain Jensen about the possibility of going to Bermuda at Johnson's request, he had immediately given them a green light. He hadn't even asked how long they might be there. How odd was that?

Answer: extremely.

"Here we are," Jenna said as they approached the black Mercedes S550 sedan. She popped the trunk and helped them stow their two small carry-on bags. "It's a short ride to Bill's, but it's quite scenic."

She wasn't kidding. As soon as the vehicle rolled onto the causeway that linked the airport to the mainland, they were surrounded by pale turquoise water so gorgeous is almost looked fake.

"Looks a little cleaner than New York Harbor," Nazareth joked.

"I haven't seen any test comparisons," Jenna laughed, "but I suspect you're correct. The water is our most precious natural resource, so we take good care of it."

Gimble, meanwhile, was momentarily focused on the traffic. It was her first time in a country where vehicles traveled on the left side of the roadway.

"Thank God you don't allow tourists to drive here," she said, "because I'm not sure I could do it."

"It would take some time, but you'd get the hang of it. Unfortunately, many tourists who rent scooters end up in the hospital before they learn how to ride safely."

"Are there a lot of scooter accidents?"

"Every day, yes, and many of them involve hospital visits. Deaths aren't common, but they do happen."

"I like having lots of steel around me."

"As do I. There's far less risk of something bad happening."

The words were scarcely out of her mouth when Nazareth yelled, "Pull over, Jenna!"

They had just left the causeway, and she swerved onto a grassy strip near the entrance to Blue Hole Park, one of the island's most popular nature preserves. It was a sprawling area featuring picturesque beach views, winding jungle trails, and a pristine swimming lagoon.

At the moment, however, it was also a crime scene. From his position in the rear of the limo, Nazareth had spotted a robbery in progress. A burly man had grabbed an elderly woman's purse, slashed her husband with a knife, and taken off into the preserve.

"What's wrong?" Jenna screamed. The urgency of Nazareth's voice had left her shaken.

But he was already out the door. Even in street clothes, he would have had a distinct advantage over the younger perp since he had been a sub-4:00 miler in college and still had blistering speed over short distances. Dressed in Bermuda shorts and his favorite Nikes, though, he basically had no competition. He overtook his quarry within twenty seconds.

When the guy realized he couldn't outrun his pursuer, he turned and charged, frantically swiping his blade back and forth. Nazareth's response was automatic. He calmly waited for the guy to get close enough, then drove a powerful sidekick into his rib cage. It was the same kick Nazareth had frequently used in taekwondo tournaments to flatten his opponents. The EMT who eventually treated the perp said he had seen rib damage this bad only once before, when an old man was hit by a speeding bus.

Once the police had taken the robber into custody, Jenna resumed the drive to Windfall.

"Well, that certainly got my heart pumping," she laughed. "Does your husband do this sort of thing often, Detective Gimble?"

"If you mean every day, no. Otherwise, yes."

"Ah, I see. I'll keep that in mind next time we're out and about together."

"I apologize for startling you, Jenna," Nazareth said gently. "But I knew we'd lose him if he got too far ahead in all that greenery."

"No apology necessary. You haven't been here for twenty minutes, and you're already making a difference. Bill Johnson was right."

Nazareth and Gimble traded knowing glances in the back seat. Running down a robber wasn't nearly the same as solving a string of homicides, but the difference was probably lost on most civilians. This wasn't the time to tell Jenna why success with one enterprise doesn't guarantee success with the other.

A succession of narrow roads lined with rugged limestone walls, orange hibiscus, and pink oleander brought them to the gate guarding the private Tucker's Town community that Johnson and other billionaires called home. Three minutes later, Jenna turned into Windfall's long driveway.

"This is it," Jenna said.

Nazareth and Gimble thought she was talking about the imposing guest house on the right. It was a lovely home in a spectacular setting. But when Jenna kept driving, they realized she had been talking about the massive hillside home behind the carefully tended hedge. This, they would later agree, wasn't how the "other half" lived. This was how the other one-tenth of one percent lived.

Gimble summed up their feelings with a simple but heartfelt, "Oh my God!"

New York City this was not.

Chelsea Butterfield opened the front door to greet them. A short, sturdy woman in her mid-fifties, she seemed genuinely glad to see the detectives. She had been fonder of Seaward than some other members of the staff, and she hoped the young detectives would succeed in solving the mystery of her disappearance.

"Good afternoon, Jenna," she said. "I see you've brought us our two special guests."

"I have indeed. Detectives, this is Chelsea Butterfield, the head housekeeper," Jenna said, "and I'll leave you in her capable hands. You have my business card. Please call whenever you want to go somewhere, even on short notice. My company and I are at your service."

"Please come inside," Chelsea said warmly, "and let me show you around. I think you'll be quite comfortable here."

The detectives tried and failed not to gape. They had been inside nice homes before, but they had never seen anything like this.

"Maybe our investigation could take a few months," Nazareth deadpanned.

"Years, even," Gimble added.

"I'm sure Mr. Johnson would be fine with that, detectives. He's told me he's a very big fan of yours."

"As we are of him," Gimble said.

"And I can tell you he's extremely upset by all this. What's going on here is offensive to all of us. People like Melanie simply don't disappear without a trace, and tourists aren't murdered on the beach."

Until they are, Nazareth thought.

He was keenly aware that no amount of wishful thinking would change one of life's most basic principles: evil goes wherever it chooses.

11.

CHELSEA GAVE HER GUESTS A twenty-minute grand tour of Windfall's breathtaking interior, including the vast master suite that Johnson had insisted they use. The guest suite was nearly as large, but the master had a slightly better view of the beach, so that's what they got. They would eventually learn that their room had been featured in *Architectural Digest* as one of the most outstanding bedrooms of 2017.

When they all returned to the foyer, they were met by Jacob Brangman, who had come to give Nazareth and Gimble a walking tour of the estate's grounds. Brangman, fifty-eight and clearly quite fit, was officially the head groundsman, but he was also a highly skilled jack of all trades who could subdue a leaky faucet as easily as an overgrown shrub.

They began by kicking off their shoes and following a sandy trail that snaked from the back of the property down to a small unspoiled beach.

"Some people argue about which is the best beach in Bermuda," Brangman noted, "but I don't. This is it. It's compact but perfect. It's also quite private. Although even private beaches can be accessed by boaters, I have never seen an outsider here."

"And Bermuda really does have pink sand!" Gimble exclaimed.

"It does. And you'll see more of it on this beach than anyplace else."

"Does the beach have a name?"

"Not officially, but I call it Windfall Beach. And why not?"

He gestured upward to the mansion, which clung to the side of a one-hundred-foot hill seemingly in defiance of gravity.

"Back in California," Nazareth observed, "places like that sometimes get washed right down the hill in heavy storms. I'm guessing Bill had this one built on steel pilings."

"You're close," Brangman nodded. "The home is definitely anchored to the hillside, but traditional steel pilings wouldn't be good here." He explained that Bermuda's limestone bedrock can be extremely tricky to work with and might not support massive steel structural beams. So for Johnson's home, the architect specified the use of micropiles. "Basically, you drill deep into the limestone and insert a steel tube. Then you place a threaded steel rod into the casing and fill the whole thing with high-strength cement. It's an incredibly strong system perfectly suited to the conditions."

"In other words, we won't wake up at the bottom of the hill tomorrow?" Gimble laughed.

"You can sleep easy here, ma'am. Windfall was built to last for a very long time."

On the way back up the hill, Gimble stopped to smell the lovely pink oleander flowers she had noticed during the drive to Johnson's home earlier that day. The blooms had a strong and highly appealing fragrance similar to apricots. But when she reached out to cradle one of the flowers in her hand, Brangman placed his hand gently on hers.

"That's not a good idea," he cautioned. She pulled her hand back and gave him a curious look. "The plant is deadly poisonous if you eat any part of it, and the sap can be extremely irritating to the skin. You're best off just enjoying the smell."

"But they seem to be growing everywhere."

"Yes, the shrub does quite well in Bermuda, which explains why people plant it. It's extremely dangerous, however."

"You certainly wouldn't know by looking at it, would you?"

"No, you would not. It's one of Mother Nature's extremely devilish tricks."

The three of them strolled Windfall's grounds for another fifteen minutes before heading over to the guest cottage where Melanie lived. As they approached the front door, Nazareth looked to his left and noticed a young man in workman's clothes standing alongside a large workshed set well back from the residence. Even from a distance it was obvious his eyes were glued to Gimble's body, but he was so interested in what he saw that he didn't notice the threatening look Nazareth was giving him.

"Who's that?" Nazareth asked Brangman.

Brangman looked and saw his junior groundsman, Dwayne, who waved unenthusiastically though it was clear he would have preferred to slink off into the shadows.

"Come say hello to our guests, Dwayne."

On his way over, Dwayne was unable to resist sneaking a few additional looks at Gimble. He was a sullen, dust-covered youth of nineteen, and discretion wasn't his strong suit.

Brangman introduced Gimble first. Dwayne shook her out-stretched hand and mumbled hello to her chest. Since his eyes were fixed elsewhere, he didn't see the fierce look on her face, but Brangman did. He and Dwayne would talk about this later.

"And this is her husband, Detective Nazareth."

Normal grip force for a man Nazareth's age was about eighty-eight pounds. His was closer to a hundred and sixty, or roughly that of a pro hockey player, and he treated Dwayne to max power. The junior groundsman winced and was barely able to keep from crying out.

"I'll see you when I'm finished showing the detectives the guest cottage," Brangman told Dwayne cryptically, then walked off with the detectives. But when he turned around abruptly, he caught his junior partner studying the snug fit of Gimble's pale-blue Bermuda shorts. Was this a new deficiency in the young man's behavior, Brangman wondered, or was it something he had simply missed earlier?

Gimble eased the tension by returning to the business at hand. "Do you know whether the police have searched Melanie's home?"

"I suppose it's possible," Brangman answered, "but I really don't know."

Odd, Nazareth thought. The guy can explain in detail how Windfall is anchored to the limestone bedrock and knows every square inch of the property, but he doesn't know whether the police have been inside the guest cottage.

"How much interaction do you and Melanie normally have?" Nazareth asked.

It was a harmless question that nevertheless seemed to unsettle Brangman.

"I'm not sure what you mean by *interaction*," he replied somewhat defensively. "I have my jobs, and she had hers. Her primary role, as far as I can tell, was making sure the household staff met Mr. Johnson's expectations. She really didn't have much to say about the grounds-keeping."

Nazareth noted Brangman's exclusive use of the past tense when talking about Melanie but didn't read anything into it since most people probably assumed Melanie was already dead.

"Would you say that she mostly keeps to herself?"

"No, I would say she spent a great deal of time checking on the work of the two housekeepers and the chef. She wouldn't have needed to watch over Dwayne, since he's my responsibility, and she rarely commented on my work one way or the other."

"Do you and Melanie get along well?"

Brangman hesitated. "We didn't *not* get along. She really never had much cause to supervise me the way she did the others."

Whatever other questions Nazareth had, and there were now several, he chose to hold them until he could speak privately with other staff members. It was obvious Brangman found the probing uncomfortable.

The front door of the guest cottage was unlocked when they arrived, and Gimble considered that odd under the circumstances. She hadn't necessarily been expecting yellow crime-scene tape, but she also hadn't expected the home to be totally unsecured. Even if the police had already searched the place, which was not at all certain, the front door should have been locked.

"Do you know whether Melanie usually left the door unlocked?" she asked.

"I don't think so. I used a key whenever I went in to fix something."

"Is that something you did fairly often?"

"No more than twice a year, I would guess. Several times she had a problem with a sluggish kitchen drain, and not long ago I had to replace a ceiling fan in her bedroom because she said the old one was squeaking. I couldn't hear it myself."

Gimble quickly reached the same conclusion her husband had: Brangman planned to say no more about Melanie than absolutely necessary.

"Would you like us to lock the door when we leave?" Nazareth asked.

"Oh, well, uh, if you don't need me to stay," Brangman said hesitantly, "I suppose you should lock up, yes."

"Okay, we'll be sure to do that." Nazareth put his hand out. "And thanks for the fine tour. We both enjoyed it."

"It was my pleasure, detectives. Please let me know if there's anything I can do to make your stay more pleasant."

As soon as Brangman left the guest house, he walked quickly to the workshed and motioned for Dwayne to go inside. He slammed the door behind him, but his yelling was still loud enough for Nazareth and Gimble to hear.

Before Gimble said anything, Nazareth pointed to the vase of wilted flowers on the foyer table. Next to it, scarcely noticeable among a half dozen framed photographs, was a wireless security camera the size of a salt shaker.

The green light was on.

12.

GIVEN THE PRESENCE OF A partially concealed security camera, Nazareth and Gimble said nothing to each other about Brangman's ill-disguised nervousness in the face of what they considered extremely gentle questioning. They didn't necessarily believe he had something to do with Melanie Seaward's disappearance, but his evasiveness definitely invited further scrutiny.

Beyond that, the fact that he had his own key to the guest cottage's front door seemed slightly odd to them. Why would he have a key if Seaward needed something repaired perhaps only twice a year? Why wouldn't she have simply opened the door for him on those rare occasions instead of allowing him to have his own key?

And then, of course, there was the foyer security camera, which did nothing to diminish their curiosity. Had Melanie placed the camera there herself? If so, why? And if not Melanie, who? They had seen no evidence of a whole-house alarm system, so why did someone feel it was necessary to detect and record what happened at the front door?

"How about I take upstairs and you take downstairs?" Gimble suggested.

Nazareth gave her a thumbs up and walked toward the kitchen at the far end of the first floor. They didn't need to discuss what they would look for since they had been down this same road countless times. If the home hadn't been tampered with — something that was by no means certain — they might be lucky enough to detect one or two tiny pieces of the puzzle out of place. Luck wasn't their favorite go-to technique, but they were willing to accept help from any quarter.

The kitchen was perfectly ordinary in every way except for the outrageous view of the Atlantic. A small dining table by the rear window featured an attractive centerpiece of three votive candles in clear-glass cups. The granite counters were brightly polished and held nothing more than the usual chef's items, including a walnut block containing an expensive set of thirty-six Wusthof knives of various sizes. The eight-thousand-dollar dishwasher was empty save for two glasses and several small plates that had been carefully rinsed before being placed inside.

Nothing suggested that Seaward had been preparing dinner before taking her evening walk, but Nazareth wondered whether she would have cooked dinner for herself anyway. Given her role as Johnson's stand-in, perhaps she had her meals brought over from the main house. Or maybe she ate over there. He would find out.

The dining room and living room also gave up no secrets. They were in perfect order, free of clutter, dust, and anything that seemed even remotely out of place. The most unusual item was an immense agave plant that spilled out of a large terracotta planter in the farthest corner of the living room. To Nazareth's eye it seemed like something that belonged outdoors, but he had never pretended to know much about gardening.

He briefly wondered why the large agave was the only live plant on the entire first floor. Most people who enjoy caring for plants have several, usually small ones set on tables and window sills where they can catch the sun. Seaward had only this one monster.

Gimble came downstairs and found her husband looking out the living room window toward the workshed. The shed door was open, but Brangman and Dwayne were nowhere to be seen.

"Come across anything worthwhile down here?"

"Nothing that means much. How about you?"

She held out Melanie's laptop computer.

"This was on the night table in the master bedroom," she nodded. "It was plugged in and fully charged."

"As though she had planned to use it when she came back from her walk."

"That's my guess."

"Have you opened it yet?" Nazareth wondered.

"I have. And guess what: it's not password protected."

50

"You said *not?*"

"Yep, as in we can have a look at this." She pointed to the icon for the wireless security camera that watched over the front entrance.

Nazareth took a seat on the couch, and Gimble settled next to him. She clicked the camera icon and instantly saw herself on the screen. It was a still photo of her walking into the living room less than a minute earlier. When she clicked the forward arrow, the app replayed the video sequence that began when they entered the guest cottage with Brangman. The scenes were choppy because the motion-activated camera recorded only when someone was in its line of sight, but the video quality was otherwise excellent.

"No sound," Nazareth observed, "but I assume that's fairly common for this type of device."

"Actually, the system is able to record sound, but that feature was turned off."

"So all she cared about was the video?"

"Assuming she's the one who put the camera there. Wait, let me check something." She opened the app's history file and scrolled to the first entry. "It only goes back seven days, but that's better than nothing, right?"

"Absolutely. Let's see what we've got."

The video footage for the first three days showed nothing more than Seaward coming and going through the front door, sometimes with groceries or freshly picked flowers. Otherwise, the camera switched on only when she passed by the foyer throughout the day. In most scenes she wore a casual long-sleeved shirt, loose beach pants, and suede moccasin slippers. At approximately 5:00 p.m. on all three days she walked from the kitchen side of the home to the living room with a blue sapphire martini in hand. At about 6:00 on all three days she left the cottage dressed for a walk: lightweight sweatshirt, Bermuda shorts, and New Balance walking shoes.

"A blue sapphire martini is hardly your typical pre-exercise drink," Gimble noted, "but I suppose we all have our quirks."

"She doesn't look like much of a fitness nut. Fifty, a touch overweight, very tan. I'm guessing she walks more for relaxation than for exercise. So a blue martini and a pre-dinner walk are probably fine."

"Especially on very safe roads."

"Which is all you have up here."

The video for the fourth day produced two small additions to Seaward's relatively boring schedule. At 7:15 p.m. the front door opened, and a smiling young man walked in carrying a large tray covered with a white linen cloth. He said something to Seaward and went toward the kitchen. A few minutes later, he left carrying the empty tray.

Then at 9:00 p.m. Seaward opened the front door again, this time for Brangman. They smiled and spoke to each other briefly before walking into the living room. The camera didn't begin recording again until 10:25, when Brangman let himself out. At 11:02 Melanie entered the foyer, checked that the front door was locked — it was — and went upstairs for the night.

"He's there for nearly an hour and a half," Gimble began, "then leaves and locks the door behind him. They were discussing what kinds of flowers he should plant in the front yard maybe?"

"Highly doubtful."

"Agreed."

They moved on, but the remaining footage was brief.

The video for the fifth day ended with Melanie leaving for her evening walk. Possibly her last walk she would ever take.

On day six Brangman entered the guest cottage at 8:15 a.m., appeared to call out for Seaward, then went upstairs. At 8:17 he returned to the foyer and left the home.

The day-seven video had only one surprising sequence. At 5:03 a.m. Dwayne entered the guest house and went immediately toward the kitchen. At 5:08 he left carrying a brown paper bag filled with unknown items.

Nazareth and Gimble looked at each other in disbelief. They knew what they had just seen, but they had absolutely no idea what it meant.

Except, of course, that Brangman and Dwayne had just become persons of interest.

13.

RALPH AND KATRINA SHIPMAN WERE cruising to the dive site in a sleek sixteen-foot Boston Whaler outfitted with a peppy forty-horsepower Mercury outboard. The four-hour rental had set them back two hundred and fifty dollars, but that was chump change compared to the cost of their penthouse suite at the ritzy Hamilton Princess. Besides, how many times throughout their marriage would they get to go scuba diving in the spectacular waters of Bermuda?

Both newlyweds had earned their Advanced Open Water Diver, or AOWD, certifications a year earlier after graduating from Boston University and were eager to dive without an instructor for the first time. Although they were qualified to go as deep as one hundred feet, they had agreed to stick to shallower water just to be safe. The first stop of the day was the Cathedral, a popular dive site near the opening of Castle Harbour, where they could explore caverns, archways, and canyons in the company of tarpon, crabs, and assorted other local sea creatures. The maximum dive depth at the Cathedral was roughly fifty feet, well short of their limit.

"You're sure you know where you're going?" Katrina was nervous but tried not to show it. Ralph had handled plenty of small boats back home, but this was his first attempt in foreign waters.

"Piece of cake!" he told her. "The biggest risk here is scraping the bottom. The water's pretty shallow."

She found his answer comforting. Since the water was shallow and land was in sight, she began to relax. Diving on their own had been Ralph's idea, not hers. She had voted for a professional dive cruise in the company of local experts, but Ralph wouldn't hear of it. They were perfectly capable of going out alone, he had insisted, and he wouldn't let anything bad happen to her.

Katrina had actually been more worried about Ralph than herself. A normally level-headed guy with a degree in physics, he had a tendency to overreach his physical abilities. He had been a competitive athlete all his life, and he believed that pushing yourself to the limit was the only way to get good at anything. More than once she had seen him limp out of the gym after "going for it," and she didn't want to see anything like that happen while they were out on the water. But he had promised not to dive beyond forty or fifty feet today, and the Cathedral had a reputation for being a safe location.

They anchored near the dive site, and Ralph was first in the water. He rolled backward off the side of the boat like a pro and waited for his wife to join him.

"The water's amazing, Kat. Really warm. And it's so clear I can't believe this is actually the ocean."

"It looks more like pool water."

"You bet. Man, this is heaven!"

As soon as his bride joined him, Ralph led the way below. He pointed to a large school of brilliant parrot fish that flashed orange, green, and neon blue in the shafts of morning light, then waved for her to follow him into a relatively narrow limestone tunnel some thirty feet below the surface. She shook her head emphatically. Even though the darkened passage was no more than twenty-five feet long, she wanted no part of an enclosed space whether under or above water. Katrina had always been mildly claustrophobic.

She motioned with her hand that she would go around and meet him on the other side. Seeing that she was adamant, he blew her an exaggerated kiss and swam in alone.

The tunnel walls grew uncomfortably close at the narrowest point, then immediately opened onto a magnificent cathedral-like space with towering coral walls and eerie half-hidden caves. He saw Katrina waiting for him in front of the opening, and he waved for her to join him. When she refused, he shrugged and turned his attention to a large spiny lobster as it scuttled into a dark hole. Was it legal to grab a lobster here? He doubted it. But he considered risking a fine anyway. As far as he was concerned, nothing beat the taste of fresh-caught lobster.

Katrina's heart rate spiked as soon as she saw the massive light-green shape collide with Ralph's left thigh. Half a heartbeat later came a second shape, this one more blue than green. It streaked into his right shoulder, and his blood began coloring the water. He was waving his arms frantically when the third shape, this one nearly thirteen feet long, took his left hip in its jaws and began shaking him violently from side to side.

Katrina looked on helplessly as three huge tiger sharks savaged her husband.

He was gone in less than a minute.

An elderly local fisherman found Katrina in the water screaming hysterically. He got her on board his own vessel, radioed the police, and towed the rental boat back to the harbor. Along the way, he did his best to console her, but nothing anyone did was going to matter. Not ever.

A young police officer was waiting for them, and he helped the fisherman lift Katrina onto the dock. Since she was in shock, he got nothing more than a few sketchy facts before she was taken away by ambulance. He had plenty of questions for her, but asking them now was pointless. So he turned to the fisherman instead.

"What do you think really happened out there?"

The old man looked puzzled. "You don't believe her husband was eaten by sharks?"

"When's the last time that happened here?" the officer scoffed.

"Today, I'd guess."

"We're surrounded by reefs, as you well know. Sharks can't swim past them."

"If cruise ships can sail past the reefs into Hamilton Harbour," the fisherman huffed, "so can sharks."

It was a fact the officer hadn't considered until that moment.

But he would keep it in mind next time he took his wife and kids to the beach.

14.

AFTER CELEBRATING THEIR FIRST MORNING in Bermuda with a vigorous sunrise run along Tucker's Town Road, Nazareth and Gimble hiked down the winding trail at the back of Johnson's estate. Except for a squadron of Bermuda longtails that soared overhead, they had the entire beach to themselves. And since they didn't know how much more vacationing they would be able to squeeze in once they began working Seaward's case in earnest, they took their time exploring the exotic shoreline.

The pink-sand beach swept upward to broad, steep dunes dotted with low shrubs and grassy areas alive with Bermuda buckeye butterflies. Tall casuarina trees, their elegant feathery branches swaying in the brisk onshore breeze, provided safe accommodations for dozens of small birds, some of them brilliant red-and-black scarlet tanagers about to migrate to the U.S. for the warm summer months.

As always, the beachscape's star attraction was the turquoise water, but on this particular morning it was the craggy limestone cliffs that spoke loudest to Gimble. They rose like castle walls at the ocean's edge, imposing sentinels guarding the island's darkest secrets.

"There's something ancient and frightening about them," she remarked. "They remind me of dinosaur skeletons."

"You might get scraped up pretty badly if you tried to climb on them, but aside from that," Nazareth smiled, "I think you're safe."

She wasn't convinced. "They just give off a strange vibe."

"Tara the Psychic rides again."

She back-handed his upper arm. "No, it's just my incredibly fine-tuned detective's sixth sense," she laughed.

"Speaking of which, my own sixth sense says I'm hungry. Why don't we head back and raid the refrigerator?"

"This is something we agree on."

It was 7:45 when they reached the top of the hill, and the sun was high in the clear-blue sky on what promised to be another warm day. The closer they got to the house, the stronger the aroma of freshly baked bread became. Chef Shaun Lightbourne opened the kitchen door and walked out onto the deck high above them. He was wearing a long white apron and matching cap.

"Good morning, detectives," he called down. "I'm Shaun, and I hope you came back hungry."

He had caught them off guard.

"We did," Gimble said, "but we certainly didn't expect anyone to be fixing breakfast for us. We're used to grabbing whatever's in the refrigerator."

"You wouldn't want me to lose the best job I've ever had, would you?"

"No, we certainly wouldn't want that."

"Then come on up whenever you're ready."

After quick showers, they joined the chef in the kitchen and got the introductions out of the way. Then Lightbourne began filling a wicker basket with fresh multi-grain rolls. A metal tray on top of the stove held assorted fruit pastries he had just pulled from the oven.

Nazareth was dumbfounded. "What the heck time did you get here this morning?"

"Not too early. I saw you two running down the road when I arrived."

"And you've done this already?"

"I always make some dough the night before, so the morning prep is quite easy. Now, what would you like this morning? Lobster Benedict, steak and eggs, blueberry pancakes?"

"Shaun," Gimble said earnestly, "you don't have to go to all this trouble for us. We appreciate it, but ..."

"But cooking is what I love to do, Detective Gimble, especially for Bill's infrequent guests."

"Tell you what. If you'll call me Tara, I'll go with the pancakes."

"And if you call me Pete," Nazareth added, "I'll try lobster Benedict for the first time."

"My pleasure, Tara and Pete. Just have a seat on the deck, and I'll get things moving."

They lingered over breakfast for nearly an hour, which was fifty minutes longer than usual. Back in Manhattan they each typically had nothing more than a piece of fruit, a cup of lowfat yogurt, and some coffee. As much as they enjoyed the feast, it wasn't something they would replicate often. Staying in shape was automatically getting harder as they got older, so they weren't going to accelerate the process by chowing down on eight-hundred-calorie breakfasts during their entire stay.

"Will you be here for lunch and dinner today?" Lightbourne asked as he topped off their coffee mugs.

"Definitely not for lunch," Nazareth answered, "because we'll be going into town." He looked at his wife. "Dinner?"

"Dinner would be great," she nodded, "as long as nothing strange comes up. Our lives tend to be unpredictable."

"Never a problem. Call me when you have a better idea, and I'll be ready."

Before he could leave the table, Gimble switched gracefully into NYPD mode. "Can I ask you a couple of questions about Melanie Seaward?" She smiled, but her eyes said she wouldn't take no for an answer.

Lightbourne's mood changed perceptibly from upbeat to despondent. "My wife and I are in shock over this, Tara. Melanie has been extremely kind to us, and we're praying the story ends well."

"So are we," Gimble assured him, "but I'll be honest with you. Disappearances that aren't accompanied almost immediately by ransom requests don't usually have happy endings."

"Understood. But we'll keep on praying."

"Let's begin with her evening walk. Is that something she does regularly?"

"Oh, yes. Unless she's sick, which isn't often, she walks every evening. She goes out before dinner and generally returns around sunset."

"Is it usually dark when she returns?"

"More twilight than dark, I'd say. Even though this neighborhood is quite safe, she's not one to take chances."

"And do you know whether she normally goes down to the beach during her walks?"

"Not normally, I don't think, but upon occasion, yes. The beach is lovely at both sunrise and sunset."

"Do you usually cook for her?" Nazareth wondered.

"Breakfast five mornings each week and dinner several nights a week."

"Does she eat here at the main house?"

"Breakfast, always. Dinner, sometimes. There are times when she prefers to have dinner at her place, so I bring it over."

"You said breakfast five times a week. So you don't work here every day?"

"No, only five days unless Bill is in town. When he's here, I work seven days. That's my rule, by the way, not his. Given all he's done for me, I refuse to let him fend for himself in the kitchen when he's on the island."

"Last question. How well would you say Melanie gets along with the Windfall staff?"

Lightbourne looked past Nazareth toward the sea, as though something out there might help him phrase his answer properly. The right words were slow in coming.

"She's demanding," he finally said, "as she should be. Working here is a distinct privilege, and you should therefore do your job as well as it can be done. I know everyone on the staff feels that way when Bill is in town, but I'm not sure everyone does when it's only Melanie. I'd say there are times when her presence is underappreciated."

It seemed a studiously tactful way of saying she wasn't well liked by everyone.

"Would you go so far as to say some people don't like her?" Gimble asked.

"Not at all. And I can tell you categorically there's no possibility anyone here had anything to do with her disappearance. All I'm saying is that she's not always valued for what she is, which is Bill's stand-in.

As far as I'm concerned, when Bill's not here, it's Melanie who enables me to have this fabulous job."

Nazareth wanted to ask whether one particular staff member might "underappreciate" Melanie more than the others, but he felt they had pressed the young guy enough.

Besides, Brangman and Dwayne had already raised their hands and practically begged to be considered suspects.

15.

NAZARETH AND GIMBLE WERE ON a bench in the front garden waiting for their car, having arranged to spend some time at the police headquarters in Hamilton. As they sat there soaking up the abundant morning sunshine, they each wondered what great mysteries lay ahead of them. And, just like that, one small mystery got solved.

Housekeeper Chelsea Butterfield came outside with the house phone and handed it to Nazareth. "It's Neville Whitmore, the Bermuda police commissioner."

After introducing himself, Whitmore said he was pleased to inform the detectives that their status as liaison officers had just been formally approved. Bingo! They finally began to understand exactly how their presence in Bermuda had come about.

In 2003 the NYPD launched the International Liaison Program, a counterterrorism effort through which it began posting officers in key overseas locations like Paris, Tel Aviv, and Singapore. Prior to this morning there had been fourteen liaison officers assigned to foreign countries.

Nazareth and Gimble became numbers fifteen and sixteen.

The liaison program was funded by private donations to the non-profit New York City Police Foundation, whose top donor was none other than Bill Johnson. So it was easy to see why a phone call from Johnson would have set the wheels in motion in New York City.

But why would the Bermuda Police Service go along with the idea? The liaison program was focused on terrorism, and absolutely no one thought the recent murder and disappearances might be terrorist acts.

Whitmore provided the answer. "I must be frank with you, detectives. I do not believe we need outside help in dealing with our own problems. But the premier of Bermuda decided otherwise after speaking with Mr. Bill Johnson, who as you may know donates many millions of dollars to local charities each year. So here we are," he continued, trying hard to sound more cheerful than he felt. "I pledge to you my full support. Feel free to call me on my private number if you need help of any kind."

"So that's how the wheels of progress get greased," Gimble said wryly when the call ended. "A few million here, a few million there, and pretty soon the machine works just fine."

"That's how the whole world operates, Tara. At least this time it's not some corrupt politician or lobbyist doling out the money. It's a good man who's simply trying to make good things happen."

"Can you imagine how much money Bill must donate?"

"Probably more than you and I make in a year … combined," he laughed.

She feigned shock. "Impossible."

"Sorry to burst your bubble. And, for the record, I hope it's money well spent as far as our investigation goes. Bill has obviously gone out on a limb to get us involved, and I'd like not to screw things up."

"Do we usually?"

He shrugged off the question, keenly aware that the NYPD wasn't paying them for previous accomplishments. While it was true that he and Gimble had cracked every major case they had been handed, it was also true that elite performers like them were only as good as their next show. Everything in the rearview mirror was meaningless.

Their private car pulled up at 10:30, and Jenna Tumbridge got out to open the door for them.

"Good morning, detectives," she said brightly. "Will we be chasing down any criminals on the way to Hamilton this morning?"

Nazareth grinned. He still felt guilty about scaring her the previous day. "I promise to be on good behavior this morning. If I see any bad guys up to no good, I'll look the other way."

"Don't you dare! What you did yesterday was wonderful, Detective Nazareth." She took a deep breath then added, "And I am almost fully recovered from the experience."

The short drive to Hamilton was uneventful except for the stunning scenery. Most of the trip was along South Road, and Tumbridge pointed out some of her favorite places along the way. The sixty-acre Spittal Pond Nature Reserve, the Palm Grove Gardens, and the Bermuda Botanical Gardens passed by in rapid succession, while some of the island's most breathtaking beaches were over their left shoulders the entire way, just beyond the manicured lawns and fine pastel homes in pink, yellow, and pale blue.

"How much do homes along here cost?" Gimble wondered.

"A small fortune," Tumbridge answered. "But even if you had millions, you wouldn't be able to buy most of them. Only about five percent of all homes in Bermuda can be purchased by non-residents."

"Makes sense to me," Nazareth observed. "If you allowed rich foreigners to buy whatever they wanted, they'd end up owning the whole place."

"Well said, detective. It's already difficult for the average wage-earner here to own a small home. It would be absolutely impossible if we had to compete with all the foreign money that wants to come in."

Tumbridge turned right onto Trimingham Road at a busy round-about, headed into downtown Hamilton, and a few minutes later pulled in front of the large white building on Victoria Street that the Bermuda Police Service called home.

"I'll be nearby whenever you're ready," she told them. "Just call."

She was on her way before they could protest. They felt guilty about monopolizing her entire day, but apparently this was how it would be during their stay.

"I sure hope Bill is making it worth her while," Gimble offered.

"I'd say there's zero chance he's not. But still, I hate having her on call the whole time. Besides that," he added, "you know it's only a matter of time before we're involved in something."

"By *something* you mean another episode that scares her half to death?"

"I suppose."

"She'll be fine, Pete. I'm sure she would have sent one of her other drivers if she felt she couldn't deal with another of your improvisations."

"An *improvisation*. I like that. Sounds artistic, doesn't it?"

"It certainly sounds better than *blunt force trauma*."

Inspector Earl Trott met them at the front desk and ushered them to a conference room down the main hallway. "Can I offer you something to drink? Coffee perhaps?"

He was polite but reserved. Nazareth wondered whether this was his customary manner or rather a reflection of his irritation over having two outsiders invading his turf. There was only one way to know.

"We spoke with Commissioner Whitmore earlier today," Nazareth began, "and he made it clear that having Tara and me here was not his choice. I want you to know that we fully understand his sentiment and are reluctant intruders. But we're here under orders and have no choice but to see if we can help you in any way."

"I appreciate your concern, Detective Nazareth, and thank you for putting the issue on the table. This arrangement is highly unusual, of course, and it's not something the commissioner and I would have asked for. But as you've said, we're here under orders, all of us. So let's see what we can accomplish together."

"As Tara and I understand it, there are three separate cases. Melanie Seaward and Liam Redin have disappeared without a trace, and a young tourist, Chloe Pedersen, was murdered on the beach. All within a matter of days."

"Yes, well, let's begin with the disappearances because I think we can pretty much put those investigations to rest. Have you heard about yesterday's fatal shark attack?"

Since they had not, he filled them in on the tragic death of newly-wed Ralph Shipman. Police divers had succeeded in locating some of the young man's badly damaged gear at the Cathedral dive site, and a marine biologist had confirmed that the bite marks on the equipment were consistent with those of tiger sharks. The evidence suggested the presence of at least two sharks, possibly three. If sharks had indeed killed Shipman, it would be the first fatal shark attack in more than a hundred years.

"So what you're suggesting," Gimble interjected, "is that Melanie Seaward and Liam Redin were eaten by sharks?"

He nodded confidently. "Mr. Redin was by all accounts both ill and suicidal. I think it's reasonable to assume he entered the water and encountered the sharks that killed young Mr. Shipman yesterday. As for Mrs. Seaward, we have evidence she was on Windsor Beach when she disappeared, and I don't think it's too much of a stretch to assume she met the same fate as Mr. Redin."

"You think she decided to go swimming while on her evening walk?"

"Not necessarily swimming. You see, when I met with Mr. Johnson, he told me that Mrs. Seaward had been rather depressed after losing her husband. This is why he invited her to come stay at his estate here in Bermuda. I've done a bit of reading on the subject, and it seems that the suicide rate among widows is quite high."

"Wait. You think she and Mr. Redin both decided to commit suicide by drowning themselves on a Tucker's Town beach within days of each other?" Gimble found the logic absurd and struggled to find words that wouldn't offend her host. "That would be quite a coincidence, wouldn't it?"

"I understand your skepticism, detective," Trott said coolly, "but consider this. It's likely that Mrs. Seaward and Mr. Redin knew each other and perhaps even spoke to each other now and then. So it's not at all farfetched to believe they had even discussed their unhappiness with life. It's therefore possible that the suicide of one prompted the suicide of the other. I haven't completely ruled out another explanation, by the way, but I'm getting closer."

Nazareth believed Trott was guilty of torturing the facts until they fit a convenient explanation that would get the cases off his desk, but he declined to join the debate. He simply moved on. "If, for the sake of argument, we assume that there is another explanation, do you see any connection between the two disappearances and Chloe Pedersen's murder?"

The smirk on Trott's face revealed what he thought of the question.

"We don't have a problem with serial killers here in Bermuda, detective. We do, however, often have problems involving passengers from the same cruise ship. Not murders, mind you, but there's a first time for everything, correct? My colleagues and I believe Miss Pedersen was killed by someone from the ship. And now that the ship has sailed on, there's not much more we can do."

"Have you formally closed the case?" Gimble asked.

"No, but we probably will before long."

"I understand there's an outdoor bar close to where she was murdered."

"Just up the beach, yes."

"I think Pete and I should take a ride there."

Trott's eyes flashed something between annoyance and anger, but he was under orders to be pleasant. "That's perfectly fine with me," he lied. "I'll take you myself if you'd like."

"We have a car waiting outside," Gimble said sweetly, "and I'm sure this will be nothing more than a fishing expedition. But thanks for the offer."

"As you wish, detective. But please let me know if you would like me to help in any way. The commissioner is eager to have all this wrapped up as quickly as possible, as I'm sure you can understand."

What Nazareth and Gimble both understood was that Trott seemed to be in a big hurry to close all three cases. Was it merely that he felt the heat from up top? That was certainly possible.

A stronger possibility was that he simply wanted the two out-of-towners to butt out.

He didn't know them well enough to realize how ridiculously unlikely that was.

16.

TUMBRIDGE PULLED INTO THE DOWNTOWN Hamilton traffic. "Where are we off to now, detectives?"

"To the outdoor bar on Horseshoe Bay Beach," Gimble laughed, "but not for drinks."

"Oh, that's too bad. I thought you might have a little free time on your hands. You're going to the perfect spot to enjoy a rum swizzle."

"You've been there before, I take it?"

"Many times, yes. Will this be your first visit to Horseshoe Bay?"

"It will."

"Then you're in for a treat." A twenty-minute drive, most of it along South Road with its glorious ocean views, brought them to the small parking lot at Horseshoe Bay Beach. After parking the Mercedes, she said, "Here, I'll show you the way."

She guided them along a wide, sandy path to the beach's main entrance. High season was still a couple of weeks away, so the place was sparsely populated. But a half dozen adventurous local kids were scrambling up the trails of a towering limestone cliff that sat alongside a shimmering cove. The detectives watched as one by one the kids leapt from the cliff into the sparkling water.

"Looks like fun as long as you live through the experience," Nazareth commented.

"Most of them do," Tumbridge assured him, "but to get up that trail you have to walk past a huge warning sign that mentions how unstable the limestone is. They might as well take the sign down, though, since everyone ignores it. Besides, it helps provide jobs at our local hospitals."

"And let me guess," Gimble said to her husband. "You'd like to try it."

"Wouldn't you?"

"Not particularly. And neither would Kayla, in case that's what's on your mind. If we come back here with her sometime, both of you will stay off the stupid cliffs."

He shrugged noncommittally. They could fight that battle another day.

"And over here," Tumbridge said, pointing to her right at a large thatched-roof building, "is the place you're looking for."

"Looks like a giant tiki bar," Gimble joked.

"It does, yes, but I stand by my earlier comment. They make excellent rum swizzles here."

As they approached the building, a short heavyset man in a gaudy Hawaiian shirt shouted from behind the bar, "Hey, Jenna, welcome home."

"Oh, my goodness," Tumbridge said loud enough for the man to hear, "there goes my reputation."

"Such as it was," he called back. "Three rum swizzles, is it?"

"No, I'm afraid it's business only today." To Nazareth and Gimble she said, "This is my good friend Leonard, who is also the owner. Leonard, Pete Nazareth and Tara Gimble are New York City police detectives."

A young waiter who was clearing a table near the bar stiffened when he heard the word *detectives*. He placed the remaining glasses on his tray and disappeared inside the limestone-block building that stood next to the outdoor bar.

"I'm prepared to vouch for Jenna, detectives. She's not guilty." Leonard was a loud, friendly sort who gave every sign of not taking anything too seriously. "What did she do?"

"Good luck trying to get a straight answer out of this one," Tumbridge snickered. "I'll be at the car whenever you're ready, detectives. Oh, and by the way, Leonard here is my brother-in-law."

"Have you tried a rum swizzle, detectives?" Leonard asked. "It's Bermuda's national drink, and you can't get a better one anywhere. Best of all, your first one is on the house."

Gimble was about to decline, but Nazareth interrupted. "What's in it?"

"Dark rum, amber rum, pineapple juice, orange juice, and a bit of grenadine. I have my own secret ingredients as well, but you'd have to torture me to find out what they are."

"I guess we should pass right now," Nazareth reluctantly concluded. "But how about a rain check?"

"You bet. I'm good for two rum swizzles whenever you care to claim them. Now, I'm assuming you're here to ask about that poor American girl, aren't you?"

"We are," Nazareth nodded. "The local police tell us she was drinking here the night she was murdered."

"That's certainly possible, but I can't say for sure. I'm not sure anyone can, for that matter. I know the police interviewed people on the cruise ship, but if those folks drank here that night, it's a safe bet their memories weren't all that keen. Cruise ship passengers tend to party rather hard."

"So you don't remember seeing her that night?" Gimble prodded.

"I wasn't working that night, but I wouldn't have remembered anyway. Basically I see bottles and glasses the whole time. When I'm here, I'm the mixologist-in-chief."

"Is there anyone working here this afternoon who was also working that night?" Nazareth asked. "We're very early in our investigation, and it would be really helpful to speak with someone who has first-hand knowledge of that evening."

Leonard looked around and said, "Yes, Eddie Simons was here that night, and I saw him just a minute ago. Uh, let me go into the main building and have a look."

He returned alone a few minutes later. "Yes, well, Simons is here and I'm happy to have you speak with him. But could you do that inside? It would be better than out here."

The detectives were fine with that, so Leonard guided them to his tiny office, where Simons was waiting for them. He looked to be in his early twenties, stood well under six feet, and had the lean, well-muscled body of a sprinter. He sported a fashionable stubble beard and a jumble of badly executed black tattoos on both forearms.

Leonard invited the detectives to take as much time as they needed, then closed the door. The only chair, an ancient wooden swivel rocker, was behind the cluttered desk, so the three of them stood.

Simons spoke first. "As soon as I heard you were detectives, I knew you'd be looking for me. Every time a woman gets touched on this island, the police are knocking on my door."

"We don't know anything about you," Nazareth began, "so why don't you give us some background."

"Sure, like the local police didn't tell you all about me already," he replied indignantly.

"They didn't," Gimble said calmly. "We honestly don't know anything about you."

"You know I was working the night that American girl died. Leonard already told you that. So here we are, aren't we?"

"This is just a wild guess," Nazareth continued, "but is there a sex-crime conviction in your record?"

"As though you didn't know that already. And by the way," Simons complained, "a conviction doesn't mean I was guilty. What it means is that a judge took the word of some bimbo tourist over mine. What she and I did was fine with her until she decided it wasn't. Then she called it rape."

"And you served time."

"Five years for sexual assault, and now I'm a registered sex offender. But let me tell you, most of the women from those cruise ships come to the bar panting for it, and the one who accused me was no different."

Gimble was sorely tempted to respond but let the comment pass rather than escalate the war of words. She reached into her purse and showed Simons a picture of Chloe Pedersen that Inspector Trott had given her. "Do you remember seeing this woman at the bar on the night she was murdered down the beach?"

Simons began shaking his head even before he had looked at the photo.

"I never saw her or anyone like her that night. It was crazy busy, and I could hardly keep up. I'm here to make tips, you know, not score with the women."

Nazareth posed a pointed follow-up question: "If the local police decided to give you a lie detector test, would you still not remember seeing her?"

"How do I know whether I saw her?" Simons snapped. "The place was jammed that night, and I could hardly get through the crowd to serve drinks. I saw lots of faces, okay? I'm supposed to remember all of them?"

Gimble decided to go straight for the jugular. "What did you say to her?"

Simons looked as though he had been kicked in the gut, but he recovered quickly and grew defiant.

"Since when do New York City cops get to push people around in Bermuda?" he demanded. "I don't have to answer your questions."

"That may be true," Nazareth countered, "but we can have an inspector here in ten minutes if that would make you feel more comfortable."

It took Simons half a second to conclude that speaking with the local police wouldn't make him more comfortable. He looked from Nazareth to Gimble, then studied the ceiling, and finally looked toward the door. Instinct told him to run through it, but his brain argued for him to stand his ground. The police had nothing on him.

"I chatted up a few women that night," he finally admitted, "and maybe she was one of them. But all I did was talk. I worked until closing and had no time to go off with anyone. I sure as hell didn't have time to go down the beach and murder someone."

"So you were mistaken a few minutes ago when you said you had never seen her or anyone who looked like her?" Gimble pressed.

"Look, I didn't hurt anybody, okay? I talk to lots of girls every night. There's no law against that. But I never did anything more than talk that night."

By the time Simons left the room, he looked as though he had run a marathon. Sweat was pouring off his forehead, and the armpits of his blue T-shirt were soaked through.

"He remembers her," Gimble said, not a hint of doubt in her voice.

"I tend to agree, but I doubt he's good for the murder. I think he's just scared to death of cops now that he's a registered sex offender.

"I'd like to know more about him."

"I'm sure Inspector Trott can fill us in."

Nazareth waited until he and Gimble had been dropped off at Windfall before calling the inspector and asking what he had on Eddie Simons. Trott didn't know offhand since it hadn't been his case, but offered to check. He called back a few minutes later, and Nazareth put him on speaker.

"Edward Simons," he began, "twenty-two years old, high school graduate, no criminal record other than the sexual assault conviction. A cruise passenger from the United States accused him of rape, but he claimed the sex was consensual. A judge ultimately found him guilty of sexual assault and sentenced him to five years. No problems since then as far as we know."

Gimble had a hunch. "Inspector, does the file happen to contain a photo of his accuser?"

They heard him rifling through the papers. "Yes, in fact it does. About twenty, very pretty, long blonde hair."

The detectives didn't need to take another look at the photo in Gimble's purse.

Trott had just described someone who could probably pass for Chloe Pedersen's twin.

17.

THE EPISODES ALWAYS STRUCK WITHOUT warning. He'd be watching TV or riding to work on his scooter or maybe walking along the beach when something set him off — an unpleasant look someone gave him or a turn of phrase that unintentionally gave offense — triggering the release of chemicals that jangled his brain and compelled him to act. He didn't know why it happened. It just did.

There was a time early in his life, his pre-adolescent years, when he had fought the urge, had in fact struggled mightily to remain in control of his own mind and body. But not anymore. Now he accepted the fact that he was little more than a rowboat adrift on an angry sea. When the tsunami arrived, as it inevitably did, he was powerless to change course.

He began with insects and small animals when he was a kid. Now it was people. Killing had always been the only thing that could calm the storm that raged within him. After a kill he would feel completely in control of his demons for weeks, sometimes even months. But that was changing. He could feel it happening.

The urges were becoming more frequent and more intense.

He knew he should be afraid. But he was excited.

Night had fallen over Bermuda, and every cell in his body tingled with anticipation.

Bare from the waist up, he stood before the small cracked mirror hanging on the basement wall next to his cot. He admired what he saw: a taut, well-defined chest; powerful upper arms sculpted by weight training; and a narrow waist highlighted by perfect six-pack abs. In his right hand he held the medieval dagger, and he began slashing it back and forth at an imaginary foe. He could almost feel the cold blade slicing into warm flesh — the face, neck, chest, and soft belly were all at his mercy. He was the punisher, and his father's dagger made him invincible.

He had used the dagger for the first time on the blonde tourist, and the results had been extremely satisfying. It had been a swift, clean job, not like the ones that had preceded it. His other kills, he now saw, had been ugly and primitive by comparison: a large rock to a skull, a length of electrical wire to a neck, a claw hammer embedded in a brain. What's more, in all but one of those murders, the bodies had never been found. He had simply pushed his victims off a cliff, never to be seen again. There was no fame to be had.

So his latest kill was special. It had been surgically precise, more a work of art than a murder. Beyond that, it had made him a star. People didn't know his name, but everyone in Bermuda knew his work.

AMERICAN TOURIST SLAIN ON BEACH
SAVAGE HORSESHOE BAY MURDER GOES UNSOLVED
NO SUSPECTS IN HORSESHOE BAY SLAYING

He kept all the newspaper articles in an old shoebox under his bed, and he read them every night before going to sleep, the way his mother once dutifully read the Bible. The people he met every day thought he was a nobody, but the headlines proved otherwise. He was a man to be feared.

When the pantomime in front of the mirror was no longer sufficiently stimulating, he pulled on a black hoodie and dark-blue jogging pants. The moon was bright in the May sky as he set out on his scooter to hunt.

Twenty minutes into his ride he saw the man foolishly walk into Hog Bay Park, a thirty-acre wilderness whose narrow dirt trails led to a secluded rocky beach. The man moved somewhat unsteadily, a long walking stick in his right hand and a large camera bag slung over his left shoulder. All that was missing was a neon sign identifying him as a tourist. And a stupid one at that. He would not be photographing moonbeams on the water tonight.

He hid his scooter among the bushes near the park's entrance and followed his prey into the park's inner sanctum. Ten minutes later, he was on his way home, a warm, bloody knife in his backpack and a smile on his face.

18.

NAZARETH AND GIMBLE TOOK A slight detour after their pre-breakfast run. They strolled over to the workshed near the guest cottage and opened the door. Morning light was just beginning to slant in through the small side window, but they had no trouble making out the shed's contents. Pruning shears, electric trimmers, shovels, and rakes were arrayed neatly on the side walls. A large workbench at the rear of the shed held a collection of gardening pots, trowels, and bags of fertilizer.

They noticed the large plastic storage boxes under the workbench and began lifting the lids one by one. The first box contained an assortment of standard garden chemicals. No surprise there. The second held open bags of topsoil. Ditto. This continued until they reached the eighth box, the one shoved under the farthest, darkest corner of the workbench. This one, to their amazement, was filled with bottles of expensive liquor. Several bottles — Johnnie Walker Black scotch, Crown Royal Blue Label whiskey, and Don Julio 70th-anniversary tequila among them — were unopened. The large bottle of The London No. 1 blue gin, worth well over three hundred dollars, and the bottle of Contratto dry vermouth were only half full.

"Someone has expensive taste," Nazareth whispered. "This is about five hundred dollars' worth of booze."

"Dwayne would be my first guess," Gimble answered. "I think I know what the video showed him carrying out of the house."

"I'm thinking the same thing. After breakfast, let's have another look inside the guest cottage."

A half hour later they sat down to breakfast on Windfall's back deck. Chef Lightbourne had respected their wishes and prepared a light banquet for their second morning in Bermuda. Fresh fruit and yogurt headlined the menu, but he still provided the customary fresh-baked rolls and pastries.

"I can't let the dough go to waste," Lightbourne said with a straight face.

"We wouldn't hear of it," Gimble smiled. She slathered her second roll with butter.

"Does Bill usually gain weight while he's here?" Nazareth inquired. "I've only been here twenty-four hours, and my belt is getting tighter."

"Belts often shrink in Bermuda," Lightbourne assured him. "Something to do with humidity and salt air, I believe. But to answer your question, no, Bill doesn't gain weight here. He plays a lot of golf, and he paces himself at meals. Unless I make ice cream. He's a sucker for homemade ice cream."

"So am I," Gimble said between bites. "Peach especially."

"I'll keep that in mind, Tara. Bill is partial to strawberry. But except for the ice cream, he pretty much avoids dessert."

Lightbourne left them alone to enjoy breakfast, but a few minutes later Chelsea Butterfield came onto the deck phone in hand.

"I'm terribly sorry, detectives, but Inspector Trott called and says it's important that he speak with you right away."

The news that Trott shared with them promptly dulled their appetites.

"I'm afraid we've had another murder," he said somberly. "I wanted you to hear it from me before you turned on the radio or TV. I'm going to visit the crime scene shortly and wonder whether you would like me to pick you up on the way."

"Absolutely," Nazareth said without hesitation. "We'll be ready when you get here."

"Bad news?" Gimble asked when the call ended.

"A second murder. Trott's driving out to the crime scene and invited us to join him."

"Wow, that's a switch. Yesterday he thought we were intruding. Today he thinks maybe we're worth something."

Nazareth looked at her over his cup as he drained the last of his coffee. "This morning he knows he's got a serial killer on his hands, and I'm guessing you and I are the most experienced homicide detectives in town."

A half hour later they were in Trott's police SUV on their way to Hog Bay Park at the opposite end of the island. Nazareth was up front studying the crime scene photos that the forensics people had taken that morning. He passed them to Gimble in the back one by one. They had both seen worse, but the images were nevertheless unsettling.

The victim had been posed on a flat rock. He was on his back, legs crossed, feet together, arms spread wide. Crucifixion style. The close-ups of his neck showed a gaping wound running from ear to ear just under his chin. A massive blood stain on his polo shirt indicated he had also been stabbed in the upper chest. Left side, near the heart.

"Same MO as Chloe Pedersen," Gimble declared. "Did the local newspapers ever publish photos from her murder?"

"They did not," Trott replied. "So it's safe to say the same person committed both crimes."

"What do you know about the victim?" Nazareth asked.

"Charles Griffin. Aged sixty-three, an American from Detroit, renting a small cottage not far from Hog Bay Park. The landlady told our officers he had been there for just over a week already — by himself because his wife had died a year ago. Apparently he was quite the photographer, so I assume he was thinking more about pictures of moonlight on water than the risks of wandering alone in such a desolate spot."

"Is the body still there?"

"No. It was removed after the photos had been taken."

It wasn't the answer Nazareth had hoped for, but it wasn't his place to second-guess anyone.

"Any signs of robbery?"

"None. A bag filled with expensive cameras and lenses was on the ground not far from where he died, and his wallet was in the back pocket of his cargo pants. Oh, one other thing. The landlady said he had told her about being bothered by a homeless man on the beach near the same spot two or three days ago."

"I'm surprised you even have homeless people in Bermuda," Gimble commented.

"We don't have many, I'm happy to report, but we do have them. Typically their chief crime is squatting in abandoned homes or begging from tourists. Nothing like this, though."

"Who found the body?"

"A young couple visiting from Germany. They were quite upset, as you can imagine."

"Is Hog Bay a popular tourist area?" Nazareth asked.

"Less than some other parts of Bermuda, I suppose, but still popular. But I doubt even most locals would think that hiking in Hog Bay Park at night was a good idea. That said, the worst you would normally expect is a robbery. Not this."

When they reached the park entrance, the first thing Nazareth noticed was the number of police officers. Some were walking into the park while others walked out. Way too many feet trampling the sandy soil, he thought, but he kept the concern to himself.

"Here we are," Trott announced. "The crime scene is well back from the road."

The three of them were about to begin hiking when Nazareth noticed something that struck him as odd. Tire tracks from what appeared to be a motor scooter led away from the entrance and traveled well back into the heavy undergrowth. Careful not to disturb the tracks, he followed them for about thirty feet to an area well hidden from the road.

"Have a look at this," he called to the others. What he showed them was the spot where someone had ridden in on a scooter, dismounted, and then ridden back out the same way. The imprints in the soft earth were unmistakably clear. "Why park a scooter all the way back here?"

Trott seemed to agree this was unusual. "We do have quite a few vehicles stolen each year, but I don't believe I've ever seen anyone exercise this much caution when parking. You're assuming the scooter belonged to the murderer?"

"It's as good a guess as any. Looks as though the rider wore running shoes." Nazareth gently placed his right foot alongside one of the footprints. "I take a size ten. These are a touch smaller."

"But an adult," Gimble noted.

"I'd say so."

Trott called one of the officers over and instructed him to have the area sealed off. "Have someone take pictures of everything, especially the shoe prints. And for God's sake, don't let everyone walk all over the evidence." He looked at the detectives and rolled his eyes. "Some of the young ones are still learning how this works."

When they reached the actual crime scene, it was easy to see why the victim would have come here last night. It was an extremely picturesque spot where from a certain angle the moon would have cast its beam across the water and onto a craggy limestone outcropping at the edge of the cove. Gimble noted the Nikon camera lying a few feet from the man's right hand and wondered whether he had snapped the perfect photo before being attacked. Not that it mattered anymore.

"Have they already sampled the blood on this rock?" she asked Trott.

"Yes, first thing. I assume the blood is all Mr. Griffin's, but there's always a chance some might be the killer's."

Nazareth crouched alongside the flat rock upon which Griffin's body had been posed after death and studied the bloody partial imprint of a running shoe on the side of the rock. It was barely noticeable in the sun's glare, but he had spotted it nevertheless.

"Check this out. If it's what I think it is, we have our first decent clue."

"This is promising," Trott observed, "but I suppose it might have been made by Mr. Griffin himself after he was attacked."

Nazareth shook his head. "The photos show him wearing moccasins. So this was left here either by the killer or by someone who came upon the scene later."

"The German couple," Gimble said.

"I'm told they were badly shaken by what they saw, so I doubt they would have gotten that close," Trott answered. "Which means I must agree it was the killer."

"A killer who was wearing the same sort of running shoes worn by whoever hid the scooter by the park entrance," Nazareth added. "If we're really lucky, your forensics people should be able to tell us whether the prints match."

Trott nodded but otherwise didn't seem terribly impressed with the find. "I'm not sure how much that helps us, though, since thousands of people wear the same kind of shoe." He smiled. "Both of you, for instance."

"It may not help us identify the killer," Gimble reasoned, "but it tells us he came here on a scooter, meaning he's willing to travel in order to find victims. I think that's a really big deal. I was hoping this was someone who confined himself to one particular location that he knew well. If that's not the case, our job just became infinitely more difficult."

Nazareth processed his wife's comments while studying the spot where Charles Griffin had been murdered. Even amid all this natural beauty on one of the world's most special islands, a killer had plotted and executed a savage crime. It had been a hunt, plain and simple, and it had been successful.

But there were questions. Had the killer been after Griffin specifically, or had the American simply been in the wrong place at the wrong time? Was it more than coincidence that both murder victims had been tourists? And what did it mean that this time he had gone after a man instead of a woman?

About one key issue, however, Nazareth had no question. Two nearly identical murders in the space of only a few days meant that the killer enjoyed what he was doing.

Unless they caught him quickly, murder number three was on the way.

19.

NAZARETH BEGAN TAPPING NOTES INTO his cell phone as soon as they were back in the police SUV on their way to Windfall. Only after he had finished and slipped the phone back in his pocket did Trott say, "We haven't had anything like this since 1959, you know. Back then it was three women raped and beaten to death over the space of six months. They caught the killer — a nineteen-year-old local — and sentenced him to death, then commuted the sentence to life in prison. I can tell you I never expected to see anything like it again during my lifetime."

"God help Bermuda if the guy we're after gets another six months," Nazareth warned. "You might have a dozen victims by then."

"Probably more," Gimble chimed in. "Even if he didn't have anything to do with the two disappearances, he's easily on track to become the worst serial killer in Bermuda's history."

"I still believe the disappearances were suicide," Trott countered, "but I fear you're right about the pace of murders. The fact that they took place miles apart from each other is extremely troubling, but I have no idea what sort of warning we can issue. We obviously can't just tell everyone in Bermuda to stay away from the beaches."

"You can warn people to avoid the beaches at night," Gimble replied.

"The Bermuda Tourism Authority might have a problem with that."

"More murders would be better?"

Trott didn't respond immediately. He stared at the road ahead, seemingly focused on the heavy morning traffic, but he was in fact thoroughly preoccupied with murder number three even though it hadn't occurred yet. His long years of devoted service and his sterling reputation would count for nothing if the killings continued. This was a fact. The higher-ups were counting on him to make the problem go away. Yet he was painfully aware that his professional experience wasn't equal to the challenge.

Sitting alongside him and in the back seat, however, were two NYPD homicide detectives who by all accounts were among America's best at what they did. In some ways he resented their presence, yes. He couldn't deny it. On the other hand, he had a responsibility to use every tool available to him to capture a madman who had already taken two lives and was undoubtedly willing to take more.

He couldn't let his pride stand in the way of swift justice.

"As I'm sure you both know," he began, "my experience in dealing with this sort of thing is quite limited. I could request assistance from Scotland Yard detectives, of course, but that would take some time, and time is a luxury we seem not to have. So I wonder if you would care to give me your assessment of this situation."

It was as close as he would get to an outright plea for help, so Nazareth seized the opportunity.

"I'm not a professional profiler," Nazareth replied, "but I'll tell you what I think so far. First, the nature of the attacks — not just slashing the victim's throat but also stabbing him or her in the heart — suggests that this guy is driven by hate. And for the moment, at least, I think it's hate directed specifically at tourists. Second, I believe the killer is young, maybe in his twenties, and probably in excellent physical condition, which is why he had no problem attacking a man this time. An older man, yes, but still a man. Third, he's no genius, but he's smart enough to plan his attacks and execute them without leaving witnesses. I'll guess he graduated from high school but holds a relatively menial job."

Gimble followed up. "The menial job you're talking about may help explain your point about hating tourists. I'm thinking there's a good chance his job puts him into contact with tourists, and he doesn't like what he sees. Maybe they make him feel like a nobody."

"Some tourists treat the police like nobodies," Trott answered, "but we don't go around killing people over it."

"Police everywhere are taken for granted, but you and I both know they're not considered nobodies. People have no choice but to respect the authority we represent. But some people have no authority whatsoever and are not just taken for granted. They're abused."

"I guess I need an example," Trott replied.

"A hotel maid," Gimble fired back. "She works like a dog, gets lousy pay, and is completely ignored when she walks down the hallway."

"Or worse," Nazareth said, "she's criticized for not doing a good enough job of cleaning up the mess some people make."

"Or she's subjected to sexual harassment, sometimes of the most explicit and disgusting kind," Gimble noted. "And if she complains, what happens? It's her word against the word of someone who's paying a small fortune to stay at a fancy hotel. Someone like that could learn to hate tourists in a hurry, no?"

"Enough to commit murder?" Trott wondered.

"I guess that depends upon how the person's brain is wired," Nazareth answered. "Let me ask you something. That guy who killed the three women in 1959. Why was his sentence reduced to life in prison?"

"He was found to be mentally impaired."

"There you go. The person we're after is also impaired. And if he's in a job that constantly reinforces his sense of worthlessness, he's probably always ready to snap. But remember: I said at the outset I'm not a professional profiler. What I'm giving you is a combination of experience and pure guesswork."

"I understand. But I'll tell you something, detective. Your guess-work is worth more than my experience when it comes to working homicide cases. So I appreciate your thoughts. I'll have my people looking for a suspect in his twenties, quite fit, and perhaps dissatisfied with the way tourists treat him. That's not much to go on, but it's something."

"The good news is that Pete just ruled out half of Bermuda for you," Gimble quipped. "You don't need to worry about women."

Trott laughed for the first time since they had met him. He was light-years from solving the case, but he found the two American detectives to be a highly engaging couple.

All things considered, having them here was probably a good thing.

20.

"You have your water bottle?"

"Yes, Mum, I have my water bottle."

"And your phone?"

"Right here, Mum." He tapped the black Nike running belt he wore around his slim waist. It held his cell phone, a couple of tissues, and a twenty-dollar bill.

"Where's the reflective vest I bought you?"

"There are no cars on the beach, Mum," he replied gently. He appreciated his mother's loving concern even though he was seventeen and old enough to use the fine brain God had given him. "And that's the only place I'll be running."

Isaiah Porter still had more than a month to go before summer vacation, and he planned to finish the year with the Bermuda high school record for the two-hundred-meter dash under his belt. To own that record as a junior would be a remarkable achievement, one that virtually guaranteed him a full ride at one of America's top track-and-field universities. The University of Florida was his top choice because it had a great program and was only a short flight from home.

So to make his dream a reality, he worked out twice a day: once with the team right after school, then again in the evening on his own. The evening session on the beach had a special purpose. Isaiah believed that running in the sand helped build the explosive power he needed for a fast start. And a fast start could easily shave three-tenths of a second off his time.

He was smart, gifted, and exceptionally driven for a person so young.

"It's too late Isaiah," his mother pleaded. "Why are you going out so late tonight?"

"I had a lot of homework, Mum."

"It's almost 8:30, and it's getting dark."

"I can run the beach with my eyes closed," he laughed. "You worry too much. I'll be back in a half hour."

Then he was gone.

He was about to cross South Road when Lamont Woodley spotted him from his scooter. Woodley was moderately drunk and in a vile mood after losing his last dime gambling at an illegal club out in Somerset Village. So he did what he usually did when he was flat broke well before payday at the landfill: he took someone else's money.

"Hey, brother," he called pleasantly as he stopped alongside the young man, "do you know where Edgehill Drive is?" Porter looked to his right and was about to point the way when he felt the blade on his throat. Woodley grabbed Porter's running shirt and pulled him closer. "Now take off your running belt and hand it to me, or you die right here."

Hands shaking, Porter unfastened the belt and slowly handed it over. "Please don't cut me," he pleaded.

Woodley laughed as he sped off. He had cut plenty of people in his life, but only if they needed cutting. The kid was smart not to give him trouble.

Twenty minutes later, Woodley had already bought a bottle of cheap wine with Porter's money. So he swung by his girlfriend Kemari's house and told her to grab a blanket because they were going to a beach party. She didn't bother asking whose party or where. Her boyfriend had powerful hands he wasn't shy about using if she talked back.

Kemari didn't hear anyone partying when they pulled into the lot at John Smith's Bay Park, but she wasn't about to complain. It was a lovely night, after all, and the waves splashing on the shore provided enough music for her. Like her boyfriend, she was thirsty.

They followed the narrow path through the dunes and spread the blanket on the sand. The night air was warm. The moon was full. And they had the place to themselves.

After a few minutes of passing the bottle between them, Woodley announced he was heading down the beach to relieve himself. "And don't you go finishing that bottle while I'm away," he threatened. "It's all I've got."

She swore she wouldn't. No bottle of wine was worth another broken jaw.

Ten minutes passed, then twenty, then thirty. The sky began to cloud over, and she heard distant thunder. "Lamont!" she yelled. "Where are you? I think there's a storm coming."

When he didn't answer, she walked the entire length of the beach but saw no sign of him. "Lamont! I hear thunder. We should leave."

Nothing.

She went back to the blanket and took one last pull on the wine bottle as the first drops began to fall. Then she began the long walk home since Woodley had the key to the scooter. She wondered whether he would end up beating her for leaving. Sure, most likely. It didn't take much to set him off.

But she was through playing games for tonight.

At that moment, in fact, she hoped she'd never see him again.

21.

AFTER BREAKFAST NAZARETH AND GIMBLE found Chelsea Butterfield polishing furniture in the living room and told her they wanted to look around in the guest cottage. The housekeeper had a set of keys clipped to the pocket of her simple blue dress, and she removed the one they needed.

"I'm glad to help in any small way I can," she told them. "Have you learned anything more about Melanie?"

"We have a long way to go," Gimble told her. That was a tactful way of saying she and her partner had made no progress whatsoever on the case. So far they had spent more time talking about murders than Melanie's disappearance.

"Then I'll just keep praying for her."

"Have you done any cleaning in there since Melanie disappeared?" Nazareth asked before walking off.

"Only after the police said they were through looking around." She grew concerned. "They didn't tell me I shouldn't. Should I have kept out?"

"I'm sure they would have told you otherwise," Gimble assured her. "Not to worry."

The woman nodded and gave Gimble a forced smile.

Nazareth waited until they had left the main house before saying what he and his wife were both thinking. "So we now know the police did, in fact, go through the guest cottage. I'm glad they did, but I'm still surprised Jacob Brangman couldn't remember that detail."

"Maybe he wasn't here when they searched the place."

"That's possible."

"Or even likely."

He didn't answer. His suspicious nature had served him well throughout his NYPD career, and he wasn't prepared to let Brangman off the hook just yet. He was sure the head groundsman was withholding information, and he was determined to get hold of it one way or the other.

As soon as they were inside the cottage, Gimble left the foyer and walked toward the kitchen. There was a small, panelled study on the right side of the hallway, and in its far corner was a handsome oak liquor cabinet she remembered from their first visit. The cabinet's upper glass doors revealed an array of fancy goblets, flutes, and snifters. But that wasn't what interested her. She opened the heavy wooden doors at the bottom to inspect the liquor bottles.

The space was large enough to hold a dozen bottles, but there were only three, all unopened: sambuca, anisette, and peppermint schnapps. Faint rings of dried liquor on the base of the storage area indicated that other bottles had once stood there.

"All three of those are disgusting," Nazareth frowned. "Among the worst things I've ever tasted."

"I've only tried the peppermint schnapps. Hated it."

"You'd love it compared to sambuca and anisette."

"Which means all the good stuff is gone, especially the blue gin that Melanie apparently drank every evening. And now there's a load of great booze, including blue gin, outside in the workshed. Hardly surprising since the security video showed Dwayne carting it off."

"Yeah, time to have a chat with Dwayne." Nazareth took his cell phone out and began punching in a number. "But first I want to chat with Bill. There's something about Melanie I need to know."

Before Gimble could ask what was on her husband's mind, Johnson answered with a rousing, "Good morning in Bermuda."

"Good morning, Bill," Nazareth replied. "I've got you on speaker for Tara."

"Hey, Tara. So what do you think of Bermuda so far?"

"Gorgeous place filled with mysteries. We have our work cut out for us."

"You and Pete are equal to any task that comes along, Tara. So what's up?"

"I hope you're not on the fifth green," Nazareth said, "because we have a couple of important questions."

"It's raining here in Charleston, but I'd gladly stop playing anytime you needed me. So fire away."

"Okay, then. First, do you know whether Melanie was dating anyone?"

Gimble was only slightly surprised by the question. She had also been wondering about Melanie's private life, but she hadn't known her husband was curious enough to raise the subject with Johnson.

Johnson told them what little he knew. "She was way down in the dumps after her husband died, and she ended up on antidepressants. But over the past month or so her mood seemed to improve. She also looked better the last time I saw her. More color in her face, more energetic, that sort of thing. I asked whether she got out much, and she said she did now and then. She smiled when she told me that. But I never specifically asked whether she was dating."

"Okay, second question: did she ever complain about problems with either Jacob Brangman or Dwayne, the junior gardener?"

"Brangman, definitely not. She always had glowing things to say about his work. As for Dwayne, I think she found him a bit creepy, but she never told me about any problems. Brangman hired him, so he's in charge of what the kid does."

"Last question: did you ever have background checks run on any of your Bermuda staff members?"

Johnson thought about that one, then said, "Only on the three main hires: Shaun Lightbourne, Chelsea Butterfield, and Jacob. They all passed with flying colors. Chelsea hired a number-two named Carlita, and Jacob hired Dwayne. I didn't have background checks run on those two. So now I'm curious. What do you think is going on?"

They told him what the video had revealed: Brangman paying Seaward a late-evening visit and Dwayne carting off bottles of expensive liquor after she had gone missing.

"Ah, okay. Let's backtrack. You're wondering whether Melanie might have been dating Brangman. Am I correct?"

"That's it," Nazareth said.

"Let me put it this way, Pete. She would have no reason not to. He's a bright, attractive guy about her own age, and I'm sure they've gotten to know each other quite well through their jobs at Windfall. I wouldn't be at all surprised if they've dated. But I'd stake my reputation on his integrity. He retired as the regimental sergeant major of the Royal Bermuda Regiment, their home-defense force. He's a class act."

"What about Dwayne?" Gimble asked.

"All I can tell you is this: Brangman once mentioned that Dwayne is somewhat challenged intellectually, but he vouched for him completely."

"Did he use the word *disabled*?"

"No, I would have remembered that, but it wouldn't have bothered me if he had. Jacob hired him, and I trust Jacob. Having said that, though, I guess it's time for Dwayne to go if he's stealing."

"Is it okay if we take that up with Brangman?"

"Sure. Do what you think is best. But if Dwayne's a thief, he needs to leave."

"Understood."

When their conversation with Johnson ended, the detectives went back to the main house, where they found Butterfield in the kitchen across the granite-topped island from Lightbourne. Both wore troubled expressions.

"More bad news, it would seem," Lightbourne announced without preliminaries. "Chelsea just heard on the radio that another person has disappeared."

"Where?" Nazareth asked.

"John Smith's Bay. About a mile and a half from here."

The math was getting worse.

They now had three disappearances, two murders, and zero clues.

22.

INSPECTOR TROTT PICKED NAZARETH AND Gimble up for the short drive along South Road to John Smith's Bay Park and filled them in on the key facts. A young woman reported having been at the beach the prior evening with her boyfriend, a punk named Lamont Woodley, who was well known to the police for a long history of petty crimes. According to the girlfriend, Woodley had vanished after wandering off to relieve himself.

"She ended up walking home in a thunderstorm but rode back to the beach early this morning and got frightened when she saw that his scooter was still there. So she called us. The officer who searched the scooter found a stolen cell phone in the underseat storage area."

"Did you find out who owns the phone?" Gimble asked.

"Yes, it was taken at knifepoint the previous evening from a local boy who was out for a run. Woodley had stolen the boy's running belt, which contained the cell phone and a small amount of money. The boy's mother reported the incident around 9:00 last night."

"And sometime after that Woodley and his girlfriend were on the beach?"

"Exactly. And that's all we know."

"Let's have a look," Nazareth suggested.

The three of them followed a narrow dune trail down to the water's edge, stopping only once for Nazareth to inspect an area where the shrubs and weeds were noticeably flattened. He assumed some local kids had trampled this section of the dunes while horsing around, but there was no way of knowing. Any tracks that might have been there had been washed away by the overnight rain.

About thirty feet down the beach they found the soggy blanket that Kemari had brought with her the night before.

"The young woman said she left the blanket here this morning just in case we wanted to see it," Trott explained. "But a soggy blanket doesn't help much, does it?"

Gimble walked over toward the dunes, studied the area, and reached under one of the large shrubs. She held up an empty wine bottle. "Looks as though they brought some refreshments."

"Most likely bought with the money Woodley had stolen earlier," Trott guessed.

But Nazareth was already running down the beach. Something had caught his attention. A few seconds later, he picked up the large piece of bright yellow cloth that had been floating back and forth in the waves at the water's edge. He held it up for the others when they joined him.

"Looks like part of a cotton shirt," Gimble said right away, "and the material is still in good condition."

"Except for the torn edges," Nazareth noted. "Waves don't rip a shirt apart, do they?"

"They do not," Trott answered. "But sharks do."

Nazareth was reluctant to concede the point but was unable to offer a plausible alternative explanation. He could not dispute the fact that sharks had recently killed a young tourist, and he could hardly argue that Woodley wouldn't have gone in the water last night. The guy was probably drunk at the time and might have decided that a late-night swim was a perfectly fine idea.

But if he had done that, wouldn't he have told his girlfriend? Even a drunk probably knows it's a good idea to have someone watching out for you while you swim.

"What I'm having a hard time understanding," Nazareth reasoned, "is why Bermuda hasn't had a fatal shark attack in one hundred years then suddenly has three of them in rapid succession."

"I'm not a marine biologist," Trott said, "but I assume there's a reasonable explanation."

"But think about it. You have beaches where hundreds of people are splashing around in the water, making more than enough noise to attract sharks. But that's not where the sharks go, right? You want me to believe that in the case of all three recent disappearances a shark was in precisely the right spot when one lone individual set foot in the water? What are the odds that a shark just happened to be waiting out there for Liam Redin, then Melanie Seaward, and then Lamont Woodley?"

"I'm not a gambler, so I can't calculate the odds. But I'm sure they would be high. Nevertheless, three people have disappeared, and for the moment at least I see no reason to believe they weren't killed by sharks."

Nazareth stared out at the sea that stretched before him, glittering and inviting in the morning sunshine. He understood, of course, that beneath the placid emerald-green surface was a world where dark forces were constantly at work. Big creatures preyed on small creatures, then were themselves preyed upon by even larger creatures. This was simply nature doing its thing.

But what Trott was suggesting seemed impossible. Three people step into the water on separate days and on separate beaches, and each one is immediately eaten by a shark. Is that how it happened? Not a chance. It was like saying the creature was out there waiting for precisely the right meal to come along. And to Nazareth's way of thinking, that was pure fantasy.

Gimble's voice interrupted his thoughts. "Anything else you want to do here, Pete?"

He shook his head.

There was one thing Nazareth would *not* do. He wouldn't tell Bill Johnson that his cousin had decided to commit suicide and then promptly been eaten by a shark. Because that's not what had happened.

Now he had to find out what did.

23.

LATE THAT AFTERNOON NAZARETH WENT for a long run — to clear his head, he said — and Gimble chose to stay at the house since her husband's ferocious head-clearing runs were usually well beyond her athletic capabilities. She went onto the balcony off the master suite, settled into a comfortable cushioned chair, and put her feet up on the railing. Then she dialed her parents to see how they and Kayla were doing up in Lake George.

Her mother answered. "Kayla and Dad have been fishing off the dock out back for over an hour," she reported, "and your daughter refuses to leave until she catches something. She definitely has her mommy's tenacity, Tara. You were the same way when you were little. Well, I suppose you still are, aren't you?"

"You have to go after the things you want, Mom. You can't rely on handouts in this world."

"Amen to that. So how are things in Bermuda? Is it beautiful?"

"Which question do you want me to answer first?"

"Uh, oh. That doesn't sound good."

"Things aren't going well with the investigation, but, yes, Bermuda is gorgeous. And Bill Johnson's home — a mansion, really — is beyond anything I've ever seen. I'll send you some pictures. How's everything at Lake George?"

"Perfectly relaxing. The only excitement we've had was the day before yesterday, when a tourist from Ohio claimed he saw a bull shark while out fishing on the lake. But the local newspaper said it was a hoax. Bull sharks are actually capable of living in fresh water," she added, "but they sure as heck can't get to Lake George unless they fly."

Tara had forgotten all about the urban legend of bull sharks swimming up the Hudson River to Lake George, but in light of recent developments in Bermuda, the mere mention of the word *shark* made her edgy. She hoped her voice didn't show it.

"Well, Pete's out on one of his crazy runs," Gimble said, "and he won't be back for a half hour or so. Give me a call when Dad and Kayla get back."

"I'll FaceTime you so that Kayla can show you her fish."

"If she has one."

"Tara, I guarantee you Kayla won't be coming back to the house unless she has one. This could be a very late call."

Gimble laughed and hung up. That's when she noticed Dwayne down below in a grove of fruit trees off to her left. The junior groundsman appeared to be studying her, same as he had done the other day. She wasn't imagining things, and she wasn't happy. She stood quickly, glared at him, and yelled, "Stay right there. I'm coming down."

Dwayne recognized the threatening tone of her voice, and he wanted to bolt. Yet he seemed frozen to the spot. If he disobeyed the woman from New York, she might have him fired. And he couldn't have that. No, that would not be good. So he waited obediently at the edge of the garden. Besides, all he had done was look at her. How was that wrong?

He correctly read the fury in her eyes when she arrived, and he grew tense. His left hand squeezed the dead branches he had just cut from a peach tree. His right tightened around the hardwood handle of the expensive Italian pruning knife. When he noticed her studying the knife's menacing hooked blade, he pushed it closed against his overalls.

"How can I help you?" he mumbled softly. Gimble was caught slightly off guard. She had expected either aggressiveness or defensiveness, but she was getting submissiveness instead. Not that she cared either way. Even though he outweighed her by fifty pounds or more, she had used her judo skills against far larger and far more dangerous opponents. She knew she could snap Dwayne like a twig if she wanted.

"You keep watching me," she scolded. "Why?"

Plainly confused, Dwayne muttered, "Jacob told me to."

"Jacob told you to?" She was incredulous. "And why would he have done that?"

"I don't know. He just did."

"Should I ask Jacob about this?" she demanded.

Dwayne looked past her, and she was tempted to turn. No, it's a clever feint, she thought. He wants me to turn so that he can cut my throat. It now occurred to her that the killer she and Nazareth were looking for had been right in front of them the whole time.

She jumped slightly when Brangman came up from behind and said, "Good afternoon, Detective Gimble."

Rather than escalate the situation with Dwayne present, she simply replied, "I think you and I need to talk, Mr. Brangman."

"Of course. Dwayne, please gather up all the dead limbs and put them in the truck for me. I'll drive everything out to the composting facility later today."

Dwayne nodded and said, "Sure, Jacob," then walked off without another word.

"Is something wrong?" Brangman asked.

"I was up on the balcony relaxing, and when I looked down, I saw Dwayne staring at me. This is the second time it's happened," she fumed, "so I came down here and asked him why he was doing it. He said you told him to."

Brangman seemed not to understand. "What did he say exactly?"

"I asked him why he kept watching me, and he said you told him to."

Brangman grimaced and said, "The other day I told Dwayne that Mr. Johnson wants the entire staff to watch over you and your husband while you're here. The distinction between *watch* and *watch over* was apparently lost on Dwayne."

"That's not the sort of thing most people would confuse."

"But Dwayne isn't most people, you see. He's an extremely hard worker but a very slow learner. *Challenged* is the word we're supposed to use nowadays, I guess. If I asked Dwayne to dig me a hole to China, he would dig until he dropped. But if I showed him a map of the world, he wouldn't be able to show me where China is."

Gimble wasn't buying it. "The other day Pete and I heard you yelling at Dwayne in the workshed. Was that not because he had been staring at me?"

Brangman shook his head vigorously. "No, it's because at that moment he was supposed to be out behind the main house weeding the garden, not at the workshed deciding whether to use a hoe, a shovel, or a rake. He gets befuddled sometimes, and it was wrong of me to yell at him. But I have to confess he exhausts my patience now and then."

Gimble tried to read Brangman's eyes. Was he an expert liar, or was he telling the truth? She couldn't tell, so she moved on.

"There's something else. Pete and I had planned to ask you about it," she told him, "but since you and I are already here, I might as well continue."

"By all means, detective," he smiled.

She told him about the security video that showed Dwayne sneaking out of the guest cottage with a bag of liquor. Brangman seemed to squirm a bit before responding. She apparently had struck a nerve.

"We have two separate issues," he began, "one of which is somewhat delicate. The first is that Dwayne wasn't stealing anything. You saw him carrying out food from the refrigerator, and I'm the one who told him to do that. Melanie had gone missing, and there were things in the fridge that were going to spoil: milk, salad, eggs, uncooked meat, and such. I told Dwayne to bring it home to his wife rather than let it go to waste."

"He's married?"

"He is. She's also a bit slow at learning, and they sometimes have a hard time of it. So I saw no harm in having him take the food. If Melanie had returned, I would have replaced it, of course."

"Pete and I saw the liquor bottles in the workshed," she continued, "but the only person we saw on the security video carrying things out was Dwayne."

"Yes, well, here's the delicate part, and I ask for your discretion in using what I'm about to tell you. On the night before she disappeared, Melanie asked me to clear out the liquor from the cabinet, and I did so. You didn't see me because I used the kitchen entrance. I brought a large plastic container from the shed, filled it completely, and then stored it under the workbench."

"There were still some bottles in the liquor cabinet."

"Swill that Melanie would never have touched, believe me. I didn't have room left in the container, but I would have gotten around to those bottles eventually. And now," he continued, "you're wondering why she asked me to remove the liquor."

Gimble's mood began to soften. "To eliminate the temptation?"

"Precisely. Melanie had become rather inflexible about her drinking schedule. She had certain drinks in the kitchen both at breakfast and at lunch. And before dinner, as you probably saw on the security video, she enjoyed her blue martini in the living room. The reason she installed the security camera, in fact, was to remind herself that her *better self*, she called it, was always watching."

Gimble pronounced herself guilty of having forced the evidence to fit her own conclusions, and she was duly miserable. But it was a professional hazard, something that had happened to her and Nazareth before and almost certainly would again.

"It looks as though I've completely misread the signals, Mr. Brangman, and I do apologize."

"There's no need, Detective Gimble. It tells me you're looking for answers, and I urge you to keep doing that. I would rather have you see things that aren't there than miss things that are."

"That's very well put. Thank you." His graciousness was striking. Not many men would have congratulated her for getting things so wrong.

She had only one more question for him but decided to hold it for another time.

She felt she had embarrassed herself enough for one day.

24.

HE HIT THE FLOOR FOR push-ups as soon as he got out of bed in the morning. Not just some mornings. *Every* morning. Even if he had worked late the night before and even if he felt sick, the day had to begin with fifty push-ups, each done perfectly. Chest to the floor, then arms fully extended. If it wasn't flawlessly executed, it didn't count.

He cut himself no slack.

Then he immediately picked up the pair of thirty-pound dumb-bells — no resting allowed! — and began the curls regimen. Twenty slow reps. All the way up, all the way down. No cheating. How he loved the intense burning in his biceps as he strained against the weight. It made him feel alive.

Now back onto the floor for stomach crunches. One hundred of them, the final ten brutally painful.

Then roll over and do another fifty push-ups. Quick, bounce up for more curls. Now more stomach crunches.

Repeat. Repeat. Repeat.

Years of punishing himself in this way had transformed him from a chubby coward into a slender, magnificently sculpted predator armed with frightening strength. When he walked down the beach in a bathing suit, women snuck a peek and men stepped aside. He was never the biggest guy on the beach. He was simply the one any reasonable person would be least likely to offend. Even when he smiled, he looked ready to damage whatever or whoever got in his way.

But he was always scrupulous about not showing off his strength. That was his secret, a dark power he kept in reserve for those times when the urge took control and whispered things to him. In the meantime, he was content to let people draw their own conclusions about what he might be capable of.

He would, however, be willing to make an exception for Delray Tankard, the man his mother had taken up with for a short time after his father had died. Tankard was a mean one, a nasty drunk who had threatened him more than once. One night Tankard took him by the throat and shoved him hard against the wall. "You cross me, you little sissy," he snarled, "and they'll find your lifeless body in the bay."

That was years ago, and he hadn't seen Tankard since. But he planned to look him up before long. Sometime soon he would wait for him to stagger home from the pub late one night and gut him on his own doorstep, no questions asked. He would plunge the blade deep in his soft belly and rip it up to his chin with both hands.

Then he would taunt him as he bled out. "Who's the little sissy now?" he would ask just before driving the dagger through his heart.

It was a delicious fantasy.

Other than Tankard, he had no particular victim in mind. Today, like most days, he would get along fine with people, tourists included. He might even make it through the entire day that way. If so, fine. If not, so be it. He would do whatever was necessary to quench the flames that burned deep inside him.

When the voices came, he had no choice but to listen.

25.

NAZARETH RETURNED TO WINDFALL HAVING blazed through five miles on the local roads, and he was feeling sky high. Gimble, on the other hand, was about as low as he had ever seen her. She looked up at him disconsolately when he walked into the master suite but didn't say anything. It wasn't at all like her.

"Everything okay at home?" His first thought was Kayla.

"All's well. Kayla and Dad are out fishing. Weather's fine. No problems."

"But."

"But I made a complete fool of myself with Brangman while you were running."

She filled him in on the unsettling episode.

"Sounds to me as though Brangman approved of your thought process," Nazareth argued. "He understands what we do, Tara. We're not the judge and jury. We're the guys who look for clues, assess what we find, and constantly reject or accept theories. It's art, not science."

"I get that, but I should have been more sensitive to what Bill Johnson told us this morning. He said Brangman had once mentioned that Dwayne is somewhat ... I think he used the words *challenged intellectually*. But I blew right past that comment when I saw Dwayne staring at me. Or," she corrected herself, "when I thought I saw him staring at me."

"I'm no shrink, Tara, so I can't tell you what goes on inside Dwayne's head. But I do know he was staring at you the other day when Brangman took us to the guest cottage. That wasn't my imagination. Brangman's excuse is that Dwayne simply doesn't appreciate the distinction between *watch* and *watch over*. Sorry, but I'm not convinced."

"You're not?"

"Why would I be? I trust my own eyes more than Brangman's lame excuse for Dwayne's behavior. I think he was just covering for the guy."

"In that case I feel a little less stupid about rushing to judgment. But at least it's good to know Dwayne wasn't stealing booze from Melanie's liquor cabinet."

"*Apparently* wasn't stealing booze," Nazareth countered. "Brangman says the security video shows Dwayne carrying out food. He probably was. But, again, I trust my own eyes more than someone else's words. And, for the record, Dwayne was leaving the house just after 5:00 a.m. What's he doing here at that time of day, especially if he's married? Why isn't he home having breakfast with his wife?"

Gimble had no answer for that. In fact, she felt herself doing a slow one-eighty on the subject of Brangman and Dwayne. Maybe she had read all the clues correctly and then been sidetracked by a skilled liar.

"I think the only thing we can do," she concluded, "is keep an eye on Dwayne and look for any holes in the story Brangman gave me. In the meantime, though, I think we should both pump him on why he was in the guest cottage for so long a few nights before Melanie disappeared."

"Then let's do it."

"You don't want to shower first?"

"Nope. Let's catch him before he leaves for the day."

A few minutes later they found Brangman tossing fifty-pound bags of fertilizer from the back of his red Toyota Hilux pickup onto the grass alongside a vegetable garden. The guy was nearly sixty, but he didn't look it. He had thick upper arms, a broad back, and a trim waist. His strength and coordination made him look like a man in his twenties. Apparently his military discipline had followed him into his new career.

When Brangman saw the detectives walking toward him, he stopped his work, wiped his sweaty face off on his right arm, and smiled broadly. "How was your run, Detective Nazareth?"

Gimble hadn't told Brangman that her husband had gone running, but it seemed obvious from his attire: a pale-blue T-shirt, dark-blue running shorts, and his Nike Air Zoom Pegasus sneakers.

"Perfect. I love running roads when there's almost no traffic."

"Traffic is one thing you'll never get in this community," Brangman laughed. "You also won't get crowds of tourists, loud parties, or litter. It's quite the sanctuary."

"It definitely is. Tara and I wondered if we could ask you a somewhat personal question." He paused to consider his word choice. "Actually, it's more than *somewhat* personal. It's personal, period."

Brangman looked from Nazareth to Gimble. "Ask away," he said amiably.

Since he was looking directly at her, Gimble spoke first. "When Pete and I reviewed the security video, we noticed that you recently spent about an hour and a half with Melanie one night. We know that you handle some repairs here at Windfall, but on the night in question you appeared to be in the living room the whole time."

"A few months ago I gave Melanie a plant — the large agave you no doubt saw in the living room. It's pretty hard to miss," he laughed. "I'm sure it seems like an odd gift, but she had mentioned to me how much she had loved a trip she and her late husband had taken to Arizona. The desert landscape is what she remembered most, and I surprised her with the agave a few days later. I also told her I would take care of it for her since she claimed not to be very good with plants."

"So you were there taking care of the agave that night?" Nazareth asked.

"No, detective," he replied, "it was a social call. Melanie and I socialized now and then. Dated, if you prefer. We were in the early stages of what I had hoped would be a long-term relationship, but that wasn't to be."

"Thank you for sharing that with us. We're not looking to pry into your personal life, but ..."

"But you're detectives, and detectives cannot ignore facts that beg to be considered. I don't consider it prying at all."

"Have you given up hope of Melanie's return?" Gimble wondered.

"I will gladly accept a miracle if it comes my way, but short of that, I believe she's gone. As you know better than I do, terrible things are happening in Bermuda these days, things that make no sense at all given the island's history and culture. And I fear that Melanie has been swallowed up by them. I pray that you will prove me wrong."

The detectives left Brangman to his work and walked back to the main house. A strong breeze blew in off the ocean, filling the late afternoon with an enticing mixture of salt air and oleander. Everything around them hinted at paradise, yet the island had for some bizarre reason turned hellish.

"So what do you think?" Gimble asked.

"About Brangman and Melanie?"

"And his smooth explanations for everything."

"Yeah, he's definitely smooth and unflappable, isn't he? But why wouldn't he be if he has nothing to hide? He seems like a good man. I can easily imagine Melanie being attracted to him."

"I'm torn, Pete. On the surface, Brangman looks perfectly legit. But I can't escape the feeling that he's holding something back. I wish I could put my finger on it."

Her cell phone rang, and she grabbed the call. It was the FaceTime her mother had promised, and Kayla was on the screen proudly showing off her speckled lake trout. It was too small for her to keep, but that clearly didn't matter to her.

Gimble was heartened to know that someplace in the world life was still gloriously normal.

26.

"YEAH, YOU'VE GOT THE LIFE, Dwayne, spending all day sniffing flowers at a mansion in Tucker's Town while I'm kissing the butts of tourists who parade around like members of the royal family."

The bitterness in Kane Swainson's voice was lost on Dwayne, who always took words literally. The nuances of things like sarcasm, jealously, and humor simply got lost somewhere between his ears and his brain. He had been born without the ability to detect the emotional content of most things that were said to him, and this wasn't going to change. In one way, of course, it was a blessing since he often didn't know when people were being cruel to him. But it often made it difficult — no, impossible — to distinguish between friend and foe.

Swainson was somewhere between the two.

He didn't necessarily hate Dwayne, his friend for the past eight years. But he found it impossible to be happy over Dwayne's good fortune in having been hired as a junior groundsman at one of Bermuda's grandest estates. After all, the job had been handed to him on a silver platter by his uncle, Jacob Brangman, when far more qualified men would have killed for a chance at the position. Swainson certainly would have. Making a lot more money for doing a great deal less was one of his life's goals.

"They want you to kiss their butts?" Dwayne asked between mouthfuls of cheap beer. He doubted he would ever kiss someone's butt, but his friend Kane certainly knew more about such things. After all, he worked among tourists almost every day.

"Yeah, they do." Swainson signaled for the waiter to bring another couple of pints. As usual, he would drink his fill. Dwayne was buying. "The ones from America are the worst. They think they're doing you a favor just by looking at you. Especially the women, who are mostly whores as far as I can tell. As for the American men, all they need is tiny jeweled crowns on their heads. They hand you a five-dollar bill for carrying up ten suitcases, and they expect you to bow down in gratitude. I tell you, Dwayne, I hate Amercan tourists more than any others."

Like most Bermudians, Dwayne had heard about the murders. "But they're dying, aren't they?"

Swainson's eyes lit up. "They're not just dying, Dwayne. Someone is helping them die. Someone is slitting their necks wide open. At least that's what the newspapers say."

"Serves them right, then, if they want you to kiss their butts."

"My sentiments exactly."

Swainson sucked down the last of his mug when the waiter arrived with a large refill. He was a thirsty man whenever he and Dwayne met for drinks at the workingman's pub now and then. Although he earned a decent wage as a bellman at one of Bermuda's finer hotels, he made far less than Dwayne, who clipped shrubs and pulled weeds in a veritable Garden of Eden. Paid more for doing less! It was his dream, but his defective friend was living it. Life had never been fair.

"I don't like American women either," Dwayne volunteered. He was slightly drunk, but it didn't matter since he was within walking distance of his ramshackle home, where his young wife was busy cooking up some of the meat he had brought from Windfall. "One of them is mad at me. I think she wants me to get fired."

Swainson grew intensely interested. "Tell me about her, and don't leave anything out."

Dwayne told the story as well as he could remember. Anger was one of the few emotional signals he could understand, and he had seen the anger on Gimble's face and in her eyes. Yes, her eyes more than anything. He had hated the way she looked at him.

"What does she look like?"

"Young. Pretty. Tight shorts."

"Did she invite you up to her bedroom?" Swainson leered.

Dwayne shook his head emphatically. "She just yelled and asked me why I was watching her."

"Yeah, well, tell her to wear more clothes if she doesn't want you to watch her. But you know something, Dwayne? Maybe she's just after you, eh? Maybe she was just trying to get your attention."

"She's married."

"All the more reason, Dwayne. Her American husband probably isn't man enough for her. Maybe she needs a young Bermuda groundsman."

"I'm only the junior groundsman."

"What difference does that make, for God's sake?" Swainson snapped. "I say she has her eye on you. But why are she and her husband staying at Windfall in the first place?"

"Jacob told me Mr. Johnson asked them to come. They're from New York. Detectives," he said.

Swainson choked on his beer and coughed until his face was bright red and his eyes teared. "Detectives from New York? What are they doing here in Bermuda?"

"Jacob didn't tell me."

Swainson knew it didn't take a genius — something Dwayne wasn't — to figure out why two New York detectives were on the island.

So they weren't just tourists after all. They were even worse.

"Let's have one more," Swainson told the waiter.

"I have to go home now," Dwayne announced abruptly. "Quinnae told me I can't be late tonight."

"And she's the boss?"

Dwayne shrugged. "She cooks dinner."

Swainson considered buying a pint for himself, then reconsidered. Drinking for free was better. Besides, his mood had soured.

Too much talk of tourists and detectives had a way of doing that.

27.

THE TWO GLOWERING AMERICANS WERE the first guests Kane Swainson had the pleasure of greeting that day. He opened the cab's rear door as soon as the driver stopped at the hotel's main entrance and offered the customary — and per hotel policy, mandatory — effusive greeting. But no one heard him.

The husband, a pudgy man with a pink, slightly piggish face, was screaming into his cell phone. His secretary back in the States had allowed his office phone to ring four times when he called in, and he was livid. "First ring! First ring! That's what I expect, Marie. Are you hearing me? Are we clear now? Does this sound at all familiar?"

The wife, meanwhile, was berating the cab driver. "This is the filthiest cab I've ever been in! And if you ruined my new slacks, you'll be paying for them." Then she got out and slammed the door as hard as she could.

They were an unpleasantly mismatched couple: a short, porky man and a tall, emaciated woman whose dieting had rewarded her with a look normally found only in concentration camps. Swainson had already begun hauling their four massive suitcases onto the bellman's cart, but they walked passed him wordlessly.

Swainson glanced at the cab driver, who said, "Feel free to put those two out of their misery, brother."

"I hear you." In fact, he'd just been thinking the same thing himself. This was no way to start his shift.

Fifteen minutes later, Swainson knocked on the door of the couple's suite, and the husband came to the door. He was bare from the waist up, his soft, pink flesh layered with the fat of too many fine meals at expensive restaurants.

"How nice of you to get here the same day," he said sarcastically. "We'd really like to see the beach."

"I apologize," Swainson replied, barely able to maintain his composure. "The freight elevator was busy."

"Oh, right, the busy freight elevator. Of course. Then it's no problem at all for my wife and me to hang around the room instead of enjoying our vacation."

The wife was on the balcony yelling into her cell phone, telling the guest services manager about her cab ordeal. "Filthy, I mean disgusting, and I now have a black grease stain on the new slacks that cost me five hundred dollars."

Swainson set the four bags down where he was told — one on each luggage rack and one on each of the king beds — and asked whether there was anything else he could do for them. Then he paused, expecting the man to reach into his pocket. A ten-dollar tip for four bags was standard, though some folks threw him a twenty if he smiled enough. But he apparently paused too long.

"Something I can do for you?" the guy sneered.

"No, sir. Thank you." Swainson headed for the door.

"Tips are included in the daily hotel fee," the guy yelled from behind. "Or did no one tell you that?"

Swainson gently closed the door without answering. If he said anything other than "yes, sir" or "no, sir," he could lose his job. It wasn't the job of his dreams, but it was a job, and he needed it.

Although he couldn't talk back to the guests, he was free to think whatever he wanted. And what he thought about first was planting an ax in the pig-man's head, then strangling the scrawny wife with an electrical cord. The world wouldn't miss either of them.

When the freight elevator arrived, he stepped aside for Quincy Warner, a fellow hotel employee, who juggled a large load of sheets, pillow cases, and bedspreads in his arms.

"What the heck are you doing up here?" Swainson asked pleasantly. He knew that Warner worked in the laundry and rarely had cause to visit guest rooms.

"One of our new guests complained that the sheets aren't clean," Warner grumbled, "so here I am. I'm dropping this off for the maid. She's on her way."

"Let me guess. Room 648."

"How'd you know that?"

Swainson leaned close and whispered, "Two nasty-ass Americans in that room, bro', and don't bother standing there with your hand out because they'll just spit in it."

"I don't get tips anyway."

"Well then you're going to the right place. Be cool, Quincy."

"Cooler up here than down in the laundry, man."

"Then take your sweet time going back."

As he rode down to the lobby, Swainson pictured himself waiting outside in the shadows when the plump American took a late-night walk. He imagined dragging him into the bushes and wrapping a bungee cord around his bulging neck. He always kept a nice long one in his scooter just in case he needed to tie something down. What better use than to choke the life out of some nasty guest? Hell, he'd be doing the wife a favor. She'd collect the insurance money and live happily ever after without him.

Thank God for pleasant dreams.

Swainson got off the freight elevator and pushed his cart toward the main lobby. As he passed the guest services counter, the well-dressed manager beckoned.

"Did you just come from 648?" he demanded.

Swainson nodded. "Dropped off four bags, yes, sir."

"Okay, then. The wife called me and said her new slacks were ruined in a dirty cab. She said a bellman had seen the whole thing. So I guess that was you."

"I heard her yelling at the cab driver, if that's what you mean."

"Well, what did the back seat of the cab look like?"

"I didn't see it," he lied. He had, in fact, seen that the back seat wasn't at all filthy. If the woman's new pants had grease on them, it was there before she sat in that cab.

"You didn't open the door for her?"

"I opened the door nearest me, and the husband was sitting there. But I didn't study the inside of the cab."

The manager was peeved. "You didn't walk around and open the door for the wife?"

"She let herself out while I was opening the door for her husband."

"So you didn't open the door for her?"

"How could I?"

"Let's see, I suppose you could have looked inside the cab to see which side the woman was sitting on. Would that have worked?"

"Most times everyone just slides out whichever door is open," Swainson replied meekly. Could this conversation actually be taking place?

"Hotel policy is for our bellmen to open car doors for guests. You know that, right?"

"I do, sir, and I did. But I can't open two doors at once."

"Get smart with me," the manager warned, "and you'll be unemployed."

"I'm not trying to get smart, sir. I'm just explaining how it usually works. I open a door, and two or three people slide out."

"From now on, make sure you open both doors so that our guests don't have to slide out. Are you with me?"

"I am, yes, sir. I'll do that every time from now on."

"And look inside the cab to see whether it's filthy. That way I'll know what to say if a guest complains to me about it."

"I'll do that too."

"So is she right?" Swainson looked lost, so the manager helped him out. "Yes or no: was the cab filthy enough to ruin her new pants?"

Swainson considered the choice. If he said yes, a cab driver could lose his job because of a lying tourist who had a chip on her shoulder. If he said no, he might be the one losing his job. This wasn't how the world was supposed to operate, but obviously it did.

"It may have been," he finally answered.

"So that's a yes?"

Swainson nodded.

As he walked off, he heard the manager order one of the desk clerks to get the cab company on the line for him. Someone was going to pay a stiff price for milady's displeasure.

Swainson had read about the recent shark attacks.

With luck, he thought, the husband and wife in 648 would soon be dined upon.

28.

Bridget Hayes had always been a knockout in a little black dress, but tonight she was in a league of her own. She had paid four thousand dollars for the Dolce & Gabbana masterpiece and looked like a million bucks.

Five million, actually. That's how much commission revenue she had generated for her investment firm in the previous year, making her the company's number-one broker. And tonight at the annual awards banquet she would bask in the glow of her achievement. Each of the other forty-nine big producers would get a check for ten grand as an extra pat on the head for helping break the company's annual sales record. And each of them would be consumed with jealousy when the CEO handed her a check for one hundred thousand.

Only one broker could be the best of the best, and Chicago's Bridget Hayes was it.

After studying herself in the mirror and approving of what she saw, she wandered onto the balcony of her sprawling suite. At two thousand dollars a night, it was the best room in Bermuda's best hotel: top floor, fully stocked bar, and panoramic oceanfront views of the beach. She figured she might bring someone back here later to share the amenities, but she had no particular guest in mind. The night was young, after all.

The one person who would definitely not be coming here, though, was Dan Corbett, the L.A. broker who had been hitting on her ever since the group had arrived for the reward trip three days earlier. Every time she turned around, there he was. In her face at meals. Sitting as close to her as he could at the morning business meetings. Constantly eyeing her as though she were a side of prime beef.

She disliked virtually everything about him, beginning with his God's-gift-to-womankind smarminess. And if he started on her again tonight, she would shut him down hard. This was her night, and she wouldn't allow him to spoil it for her.

Thirty minutes later he tried.

She was only halfway through her first glass of chardonnay at the cocktail reception when he was on her, the scent of his liberally applied Yves Saint Laurent cologne enveloping her like a thick Lake Michigan fog. He had already sucked down three beers and a glass of cabernet, so he was feeling courageous and lucky.

"Tonight's the night," he leered, slurring his words slightly. He carried too much weight on his six-two frame, and Hayes found his size intimidating.

She backed up and tried to smile. "Yes, we all get our checks."

"No, I was talking about you and me, Bridget."

"There is no *you and me*, Dan."

She walked away and took her seat at the head table alongside Jeffrey Pierce, the handsome, polished, and enormously wealthy CEO of Pierce Global Securities. He was married, unfortunately, but for some reason his wife hadn't joined him on the trip. Had he seen the suite that the hotel had reserved for his number-one producer? If not, maybe he'd like to.

Even while flirting with Pierce over dinner — and, no, he had not yet seen her suite — she felt Corbett's eyes all over her. The more he drank, the less he cared about being discreet. But even by his low standards, he finally went too far. He began licking his lips when she looked in his direction.

Pierce noticed the lewd gesture and turned to Hayes. "What's with you and Dan?"

"It's with *Dan*, not with *Dan and me*," she replied stiffly. "I can't get him to leave me alone."

"I can."

Pierce got up and motioned for Corbett to join him at the side of the banquet room, then waited impatiently for him to stagger over.

"You have a choice," Pierce told him. "Leave now or be fired on the spot. What's it going to be?"

"W-what did I do?" Corbett stuttered.

"You made a complete ass of yourself by harassing our broker of the year, and now you've got everyone in the room watching you because you're so drunk you can hardly stand up. So I'll ask you again. Are you leaving, or am I firing you and having you escorted out?"

Corbett sneered but somehow managed to keep his thoughts to himself. He stumbled out of the room in the direction of the main bar.

"Thank you for that," Hayes said when Pierce sat down again. "I probably should have complained sooner. He's been out of line since the day we all arrived."

"I'm sorry for that, Bridget, but you won't have any more problems with him."

The remainder of the awards banquet went smoothly and ended with the check presentations, the evening's highlight. Hayes accepted her one hundred thousand dollars graciously and thanked Pierce for all the support he always gave his brokers. And now, she told herself, it's time for Jeffrey Pierce to come upstairs for a nightcap.

But it wasn't meant to be. Before she could seal the deal, Pierce's phone rang, and his wife launched into a lengthy report on their youngest child's sinus infection. The moment and the mood vanished.

Disappointed with the way her special evening had ended, she decided to stroll the beach before returning to her lonely room. She invited her friend Sherri to come along, but the young Phoenix broker and two other honorees were taking a cab to Spinning Wheel, a Hamilton nightclub famous for its four bars and reggae music.

"Why don't you come with us?" Sherri offered. "It'll be fun."

Hayes wavered, then declined. The last thing she needed on her final night in Bermuda was a roomful of anonymous drunks coming on to her. Been there, done that.

She went outside, walked past the bustling pool at the rear of the hotel, and slipped out of her seven-hundred-dollar Christian Louboutin heels. She considered carrying them with her, then placed them instead behind a large terracotta planter at the edge of the patio before stepping onto the sand. And she relaxed for the first time all day.

A ribbon of moonlight on the water and cool sand between her toes proved to be the perfect remedy for earthly cares. Gone were thoughts of Dan Corbett, her manic job in Chicago, and the "almost" moment with Jeffrey Pierce. She waded into the water up to mid-calf and felt nothing but pure bliss. The last time she had felt this good was at Waioli Beach in Kauai, and that had been nearly ten years ago. She wished she had taken this walk earlier in her Bermuda stay, but at least she was here now.

Twenty minutes later she reached the jagged limestone cliffs marking the end of the hotel's long private beach, so she turned back. Only then did it register: she hadn't seen anyone else on the beach since saying hello to that young couple about ten minutes earlier. When the moon disappeared behind some passing clouds, she grew uneasy. Yes, this was Bermuda. But still.

She was a hundred and fifty yards from the hotel when she saw him emerge from the shadowy dunes on her left, and she felt as though a swarm of crazed butterflies had taken flight in her stomach. He was moving slowly and deliberately toward the spot at the water's edge where their paths would intersect. He appeared to be looking straight ahead, not at her, but how could she tell in the dark?

She walked faster.

So did he.

It was Corbett. It had to be. But he wasn't staggering. How could he have sobered up so quickly?

She stopped walking and looked behind her toward the limestone wall. It was impassable. Then she looked up to the dunes. Could she get over them and out to the street before he did? And if so, would anyone be there to help her?

She turned toward the hotel again.

Now he was walking directly toward her. No, it wasn't Corbett. The silhouette was that of a younger, fitter man who moved with an easy animalistic grace that she understood instinctively.

He was a hunter, and she was his prey.

If she had carried her high heels to the beach, she would have had two sharp weapons at her disposal. But she hadn't. So her options were limited.

She could scream, but no one would hear her this far from the hotel while the waves crashed onto the shore.

She could try to outrun him, but she was a poor runner under the best of conditions. And here she was slightly drunk and wrapped tightly in her expensive little black dress.

She could escape to the waves and hope he couldn't swim. But how many people can't swim?

Or she could stand her ground. And why not? She was probably imagining a threat that wasn't actually there. Of course. This was Bermuda. The man from the dunes would say hello, wish her a pleasant evening, and be on his way. Maybe he thought she was someone else, the girl he was supposed to meet here. Not a threat at all!

Suddenly her fears seemed ridiculous.

She walked straight for him. "Good evening. Beautiful night, isn't it?"

His reply was slow in coming. He was only five feet away when he spoke.

"Are you afraid?" he asked calmly.

His deep voice sent chills through her entire body.

"Why should I be afraid?" She laughed nervously, wondering whether she sounded as frightened as she was.

"Because I'm going to kill you."

She blocked his first swipe with her right hand and felt the blade slice through the tendons of her palm.

She froze.

He struck again.

It was over in fifteen seconds.

29.

HE RETURNED TO HIS BASEMENT apartment deeply confused. Killing the American slut in her short black dress should have tamed the fire that burned within him. Instead, the flames were growing higher, consuming him with hate, urging him to do terrible, wonderful things.

"Beautiful evening, isn't it?" she had said. Had she been mocking him? Or had she been coming on to him? Yes, that was it. She had been trolling the beach late at night eager to find someone like him.

But he'd given her more than she'd bargained for, hadn't he?

She was wrong to have spoken to him, wrong to have intruded upon his private moment. Her job had been to die, not wish him a pleasant evening. And then she had actually tried to stop him! She had put her hand up, catching the sharp blade in her palm instead of her neck. What should have been a clean, swift kill had turned ugly. Worse, she had still been looking at her hand, not at him, when the knife passed through her neck.

It was as though she hadn't even seen him.

And there it was, same as always: a tourist ignoring the invisible man whose sole purpose was to be there if or when needed. Even as he was about to take her life, he had meant no more to her than a grain of sand beneath her bare feet.

Was it any wonder his anger hadn't subsided?

He needed to fix this. Now. Before the sun came up.

The clock on the wall said 2:45. There was little chance he could find another tourist at this hour. But someone else was available, someone truly deserving, and his time had finally come. A short scooter ride would make everything right.

Fifteen minutes later he stood in front of Delray Tankard's ragged home on a dismal side street. The only sound he heard was that of the tree frogs calling to each other in the dark. Heavy clouds obscured the moon. An open trash can by the corner of the house stunk of rotten fish and sour milk. And the front door was wide open, no doubt left that way when Tankard had stumbled drunk toward his tiny bedroom.

The intruder gently closed the door behind him, checked that the front curtains were drawn, and walked to the side of the filthy cot. Killing Tankard while he snored wouldn't do, not after all the things he had said and done. No, he wanted to see the flash of recognition on Tankards's face as he realized the "little sissy" had grown up and transformed himself into an avenging angel. Hearing him beg for his life would be a sweet reward after years of waiting patiently for this moment. And, with luck, it would dull the memory of how the American whore had abused him on the beach.

He switched the bedside light on.

Tankard woke from his troubled sleep and covered his eyes with the back of his hand. He was bare from the waist up and drenched with sweat. He was older and greyer than the last time their paths had crossed, but the meanness in his face had not softened or become any less menacing. This was a man who had been born to hate.

"Who the hell is it?" he growled as the vague shape looming over him came into focus. Then he grinned. "Oh, it's the little sissy isn't it? I didn't think ..."

His words were cut short by the steel blade slicing through his trachea, and his face registered fear for one of the few times in his life. He struggled to sit up, but he was driven backward by the force of the dagger being thrust through his heart.

Exhilaration bordering on ecstasy is what the killer experienced as Tankard's blood spilled onto the soiled bedspread, and the excitement grew even more intense each time he stabbed his one-time tormentor.

He was overwhelmed by the great change taking place inside him. He was finally crossing the bridge from childhood to manhood, and he was truly alive for the first time.

Tears of joy filled his eyes.

Yes, this is how he wanted to feel forever.

30.

NAZARETH WAS SOUND ASLEEP BUT still managed to grab the phone before the second ring. A call at 5:45 a.m. rarely brought good news, but since he never considered himself off duty, he answered.

"Sorry for the hour," Inspector Trott said, "but I'm afraid we've got another dead woman. They haven't moved her body yet, and I thought you might want to walk the crime scene with me."

"Absolutely. Tara and I can get a ride and meet you there."

"It's no problem at all for me to pick you up on the way. Is fifteen minutes okay?"

It was. The detectives were at the front door ready to roll when Trott pulled in front of the mansion.

"What have you got so far?" Gimble asked as she slipped into the SUV's rear seat.

"A woman murdered on the beach not far from her hotel. A jogger out early found her. He called 911 and stayed at the scene until officers arrived."

"Any ID yet?" Nazareth wondered.

"No. All we have is the body. I suppose it may be hours before we can speak with hotel guests who might know her."

Trott drove past the hotel's main entrance and parked a hundred yards down the road behind two other police vehicles. Then he and the detectives walked over the dunes to the beach, where the woman lay in the sand at the water's edge. Nazareth was unpleasantly surprised to see that someone had covered her with a green blanket.

"Not a good idea to cover the body," he mentioned to Trott as they approached the victim. "It's really easy to contaminate the evidence that way."

"I'm sure someone was just being respectful, but I understand your concern. It's certainly not protocol."

Nazareth shrugged. "I doubt it will matter much if we're dealing with the same killer. He's smart enough not to touch his victims, which is why we have nothing on him yet. Let's have a look at the wounds."

When Trott pulled the blanket back, the first thing Gimble noticed was the expensive cocktail dress. The deceased had spent a bundle on it. Then she saw the deep wound on the woman's right palm. "She tried to defend herself."

"Yeah, she's the only vic who did," Nazareth responded. "The first two looked as though they had been taken completely by surprise. But she definitely saw it coming."

"Other than that, though, it's the same story," Trott offered. "Neck sliced wide open and a knife wound to the upper chest near the heart. This is one sick person we're dealing with."

"And he's growing more confident," Nazareth added. "He probably snuck up on his other victims, but the self-defense wounds in this case suggest he just walked right up to her. She was out here alone, saw him approach, and had no choice but to meet him head-on since there was no place else to go."

"This was a pretty bold attack," Gimble said. "I mean, we're close to the road and just a short distance from the hotel. If someone had come along, the killer would have been trapped. In New York we have alleys where dirtbags can run and hide, but where do you hide on a beach?"

"There may be no alleys," Trott reasoned, "but I suspect the killer knew exactly how to escape if that became necessary. The dunes might provide enough cover, especially in the dark, but I'm thinking mainly about the caves."

"You have caves in this area?"

Trott pointed to the limestone wall at the far end of the beach. "Bermuda is mostly limestone, Detective Gimble, and the limestone is riddled with caves of all sizes. Some we know about, some we don't. Have you visited any of our caves yet?"

"No, we haven't."

"I'll take you sometime. You'll see how incredibly easy it would be to disappear. I think it would be possible to hide in the right cave forever."

"In that case," Nazareth said, "I'd like to go check out those limestone cliffs up ahead. Let's see if we can find any obvious hiding places."

"Of course. I'll walk with you."

Gimble leaned over and snapped a close-up of the victim's face, carefully avoiding the grim neck wound. "I'm going to the hotel," she announced. "It's nearly 6:30, so someone who knows this woman is probably up and about."

Nazareth could almost read his wife's mind. She and the victim were both beautiful and about the same age, but only one of them was still alive. Life's unpredictability was more than unsettling. It was downright terrifying.

"Okay," he told her. "We'll see you back at the hotel."

A young officer sheepishly approached Trott. "Is it okay to remove the body now?"

The inspector nodded. "If you're finished taking pictures, yes, you can take her away now."

"And, sir," the officer continued, "I apologize about the blanket. I'm the one who covered her. I just felt, well, really bad for her."

"You were being kind, but you now know it shouldn't be done, right?"

"I do, sir, yes. I won't make the same mistake again."

"God willing, you'll never have the opportunity again. We've had enough murders in Bermuda to last a lifetime."

Nazareth said nothing. But he wondered whether he was the only person on the beach who understood that the killer wasn't nearly finished.

If anything, he was just getting started.

31.

GIMBLE SPOTTED THE FANCY HIGH heels as soon as she stepped onto the hotel patio from the beach, and they whispered their sad tale to her: purchased by a young woman to complement an expensive little black dress, then left behind when she took the last evening stroll of her life.

Gimble used a tissue to pick up the shoes. They probably didn't hold any worthwhile evidence, but it cost her nothing to play it safe.

When she reached the lobby, she was somewhat surprised to find more than a dozen people standing around jabbering to each other, most of them with coffee cups in hand. A large collection of luggage near the door suggested the early risers were waiting for airport transportation. She figured they were heading back home after a corporate event, and the accents she heard told her they were Americans.

When Gimble walked over to the front desk, the young woman working behind it studied the high heels.

"Nice shoes," she offered.

"Oh, right, thanks. They're not mine, actually." Gimble put the shoes on the counter and showed the clerk her NYPD shield. "I'm helping the local police with a criminal investigation. Do you know whether all those people over there are part of the same group?"

"Yes, ma'am. They're from Pierce Securities. Last night was their big banquet, and most of them are going home today."

"I need to speak with whoever's in charge of Pierce Securities."

The young woman called the company's account up on her computer and found Jeffrey Pierce's name and room number. He had checked out less than five minutes earlier. With luck, he was still with the others waiting for the airport van.

The woman left the desk and walked over to the waiting group. "Excuse me, everyone!" She waited for the noise to die down. "Is Mr. Pierce here?"

"I am," Pierce replied. He walked over to her looking every inch the vacationing Wall Street CEO. Tailored blazer and slacks, tasseled loafers without socks, and a five-hundred-dollar haircut. "Can I help you?"

"There's a New York City detective at the desk," she said softly, "and she would like to speak with you."

"Okay, sure." He went to the desk, introduced himself, and glanced at Gimble's ID. He wondered why an NYPD detective was working in Bermuda but correctly assumed this wasn't the time to ask. "How can I help you?"

"I need to ask whether you can identify this woman." She showed him the photo on her cell phone. Even though he couldn't see the neck damage, the lifeless eyes and pallid skin told him what he was looking at. "Good Lord. That's Bridget Hayes, our broker of the year. What happened to her?"

A uniformed driver entered the lobby and invited the Pierce Securities group to board the van. People began moving toward the door.

"I'm afraid she's been murdered," Gimble told him. "Any chance you can book everyone on a later flight so that I can interview a few people?"

"Yeah, sure, no problem." He summoned his executive vice president, Tom Evans, and made it fast. "Bridget has been murdered. Get everybody off the van. We all stay here until the police say we can leave."

Evans did a double take. "You said murdered?"

"Show him," Pierce said to Gimble. She did.

"God, no." He stared at the image. "Are you sure it's Bridget?"

"Get everybody off the van!" Pierce repeated, this time more forcefully. Then to Gimble, "Tell me how you want to do this, and everyone will cooperate. But, just to be clear, you're not thinking someone from my firm is involved in her murder, are you?"

"Not unless you can think of someone who might have wanted her gone." She pounced when she saw his eyes widen. "What? Talk to me."

"Bridget told me last night that one of the other brokers had been making a pest of himself, so I asked him to leave the dinner. I mean, I told him he could leave or be fired. So he left."

"What had he been doing?"

"Hitting on her, you know. Making off-color comments and, uh, gestures."

"Is he here in the lobby now?"

Pierce shook his head. "I'm almost positive he flies out later today. He's from L.A."

"I'd like to speak with him."

"Yeah, sure. His name is Dan Corbett. But listen, he was so drunk last night he could hardly walk out of the dining room. Besides, he's a jerk, not a murderer."

"You'd be surprised how many jerks are also murderers," she told him. "I'm going to speak with Mr. Corbett, but I'd like you to make sure all these people stay in the lobby. Other officers will be here shortly."

"Okay, but are you sure you don't want me to go with you?"

"I'm sure, but thanks."

She got Corbett's room number from the desk clerk and took the elevator to the fifth floor. His room was at the far end of the hallway on the ocean side of the building. On the floor outside his door was a tray holding an empty bottle of top-shelf cabernet. Had he drunk that before or after being ejected from the previous night's banquet? If after, he certainly would have been in no condition to murder anyone on the beach. But she needed to question him anyway.

She rapped on the door. No answer. Rapped harder. Then rapped again before she heard the muffled voice from within: "Goddamn, all right, I'm coming!"

Corbett yanked the door open and stood there dressed only in boxer shorts. Red with little white hearts. His paunch hung over the elastic waistband.

"Now this is what I mean by a wake-up call," he grinned. His breath had distinctive hints of stale beer, red wine, and Cuban cigars.

She showed him her shield and ID. "I'm Detective Gimble, New York Police Department, and I'm investigating a case involving someone from Pierce Securities. I'd like to speak with you, Mr. Corbett."

"Hey, no prob."

He stepped aside so that she could enter. As she walked by, he lowered his large right hand to her butt and squeezed. In one fast, fluid motion, she spun away from him and swung her right elbow one hundred and eighty degrees to the center of his gut. He slammed against the wall and then collapsed to the floor.

"Want to try this again?" she asked when he was finally able to breathe. He nodded and slowly began to stand. She tossed him the slacks he had thrown over the back of a chair the night before, and he pulled them on. She motioned to the couch. "Have a seat."

He sank into the soft cushion and closed his eyes. His stomach would be hurting for days.

"What do you want?" he whimpered. He didn't like her standing over him like a prison warden, but there was no longer any doubt about who was in charge. "And why are New York police in Bermuda anyway?"

"We've been asked to help investigate the death of Bridget Hayes."

The effect was instantaneous. It was like being hit in the gut again, this time by a steel-toed boot. "Bridget's dead?"

"She was murdered on the beach not far from here, Mr. Corbett, and I understand you and she had been arguing. Is that right? Had you been arguing?"

"No, we weren't arguing. I thought she was hot, all right? I was just interested. I sure as hell didn't kill her."

"Where did you go last night after you were asked to leave the banquet?"

He looked somewhat dazed. "I was asked to leave the banquet?"

She could tell he wasn't acting. The memories of what he had done the night before had been successfully drowned in several quarts of expensive booze. She also knew that he had not been on the beach.

His shoes — one by the dresser, one across the room by the window — were where he had tossed them the night before, and they were nicely shined. No sand, definitely no salt water. His slacks were sharply creased near the cuffs. He hadn't been wading in the ocean with them. And the light-blue blazer on the floor was free of blood.

Wine stains on the pillow case and a half-empty bottle of cabernet on the night table completed the story. After being asked to leave the banquet, he had come to his room to drink. And that's what he had done until he had passed out.

She grilled him anyway, more to punish him for having pawed her than to shed light on Bridget Hayes' murder. Although it was certainly possible someone from Pierce Securities had killed the young woman, Dan Corbett wasn't a suspect and wouldn't be able to tell her anything worth knowing.

When she left Corbett's room a few minutes later, she looked down the hallway and saw Nazareth getting off the elevator. She smiled and gave him a thumbs up. He waited by the elevator door for her.

"Everything okay?" he asked.

"Complete waste of time. He was so drunk last night he couldn't have killed himself much less chased someone down the beach."

"Not surprising. Trott and his guys are interviewing other people from Pierce Securities, but we all know who did it."

"Same guy who killed the other two in exactly the same way."

"Yep, clearly. And this confirms my theory that he's going after tourists. We now have number three."

"You know, Melanie Seaward is also technically a tourist."

He nodded. "Yeah, I was just thinking the same thing."

The elevator door opened at the lobby, where guests huddled in small groups and spoke in low tones about the police presence. Two women, one of them sobbing, sat on a couch and tried to console each other. Jeffrey Pierce moved from employee to employee dispensing platitudes about fate, God's will, and being strong. It wasn't much, but it was all he had to offer at the moment. When he noticed Gimble by the elevator, he rushed over.

"How'd it go with Dan?" he asked.

"Still a little drunk from last night is my guess. No way he was on the beach with Miss Hayes."

Pierce looked relieved. "I didn't think he could do something like this, but ..."

"But anyone is capable of murder. As for Dan Corbett," she continued, "he would benefit from counseling."

"Understood. I'll make sure he gets a little help."

"You and I could use some help," Nazareth said to his wife as they walked across the lobby, "because we're getting nowhere fast."

Painfully aware that he and Gimble had done nothing to solve the mystery of Melanie Seaward's disappearance, he wondered how long they should wait before telling Bill Johnson that his faith in them had been misplaced.

32.

T ROTT WAS DRIVING N AZARETH AND Gimble back to Windfall when the call came over the radio. Shortly after 9:00 a.m. a man had noticed his neighbor's wide-open front door. When he entered the home, he found a lifeless body on the blood-soaked cot and immediately called 911. The senior officer on the scene was requesting Trott's presence.

"Why does he need me in particular?" Trott asked somewhat petulantly. He wasn't the only inspector in Bermuda, after all, and his hands were full at the moment. Did he really need a second killer dropped in his lap?

"He didn't say, sir," the dispatcher responded. "All he said is that you need to be there."

The inspector looked toward Nazareth, who said, "Not a problem. We're happy to go with you."

"All right, then," Trott told the dispatcher. "Give me the address, and I'll be on my way."

Trott made a U-turn on South Road not far from Tucker's Town and sped off toward Devonshire Parish in the heart of the island. The Upland Street address sounded familiar, but he couldn't quite place it. Not until he pulled in front of the rundown home fifteen minutes later did the ugly details come rushing back to him with a vengeance.

Like a number of other local police officers, Trott had on several occasions dealt with Delray Tankard, a petty criminal whose countless misdeeds had never been sufficient to keep him off the streets for good. He was a brawler, a gambler, a womanizer, and a drunk. But his worst alleged offenses, sexual abuse among them, had never been proven in court, mainly because key witnesses had either changed their testimony or refused to testify at all. Whether they had been bribed or threatened was anyone's guess.

"I've been to this place before," Trott told the detectives as he parked behind a waiting ambulance, "and I can tell you this guy's a bad one. His name is Delray Tankard, and I'm not surprised someone has finally killed him. Did us a favor actually, though I suppose I shouldn't say that."

"What was he into?" Nazareth asked.

"Pretty much anything you'd care to mention. I can't tell you how many times he was arrested, but I brought him in three times myself. One of those times he had severely beaten a woman he was involved with, and I thought for sure we'd be able to put him away for a long time. But before the case went to trial, the woman said it wasn't Tankard who had knocked out four of her teeth, broken her jaw, and left her deaf in one ear."

"She knew he'd kill her next time," Gimble commented, "so she kept her mouth shut. Happens all the time."

"Especially when judges keep giving wrist slaps instead of twenty-year sentences," Nazareth added, "as they love to do in New York City. Manhattan is the catch-and-release capital of America."

"I hadn't heard that," Trott said. "Must be awfully frustrating for the police."

"Even more for the public," Gimble said, "since that's who ultimately pays the price for judicial leniency. For every dirtbag who's put away for good, there are at least ten just like him who are released on a judge's whim. So I'm with you: if the bad ones want to kill each other off, I figure society wins."

A tall, barrel-chested police sergeant met Trott at the front door. He glanced at Gimble, then turned to the inspector. "I'm not sure the lady should be going in there, sir. It's an absolute slaughterhouse."

"The lady is a New York City homicide detective," Trott said loud enough for Gimble to hear. "I have no doubt she's seen worse."

"Oh, I beg your pardon, ma'am," the sergeant said. "I didn't mean to offend."

"No offense taken," Gimble smiled. "I appreciate the warning."

The warning turned out to be far tamer than the facts warranted. Tankard hadn't simply been murdered. He had been savaged beyond recognition.

"Good God!" Trott exclaimed. "I wasn't expecting anything like this."

"Yes, sir. This is why I wanted you here. It's another knife incident."

Incident hardly described the scene. Tankard had been stabbed dozens of times across the entire length of his body, from forehead to toes, with particular attention having been paid to what only with great effort and imagination could be called a face. What little of his blood hadn't soaked into the cot was now on the wall, the ceiling, and the floor.

Trott started to enter the bedroom, but Nazareth put his arm out to stop him. "We've already got a bunch of bloody footprints in there, mostly from what I'm guessing are police shoes."

Trott grimaced. Nazareth was right, of course. The first police on the scene had done a highly efficient job of contaminating the evidence. But in light of the circumstances, he could hardly blame them. You see a man like that, he thought, and, well, you're in a panic to do something, even if it's technically the wrong thing. Managing this sort of crime scene was hardly standard procedure for him and his colleagues.

Trott turned to the sergeant. "Did you and your men photograph the floor before tracking through the blood?"

The blank look on the sergeant's face answered the question for him.

"What's done is done," Nazareth offered. "We need photos of all the footprints, especially those." He pointed to a small section of distinct and seemingly undisturbed prints that had most likely been made by running shoes.

"The same kinds of prints we had out at Hog Bay Park," Gimble said, remembering the site of Charles Griffin's murder.

"That doesn't make much sense to me," Trott responded. "On the way over here you both said you're convinced we're after someone who's targeting tourists, and Tankard is most definitely a local. Furthermore, this crime looks nothing at all like the tourist killings."

"This one was personal," Nazareth told him. He stated it as fact, not theory. "He began the usual way, slashing Tankard's neck and then stabbing him through the heart. Then he lost control. He was no longer content to kill. He had to punish the victim as well."

Gimble had seen her husband's instincts at work many times, and she wasn't about to second-guess him. "You're thinking the killer and Tankard had a history?"

"No doubt about it."

"But he had already killed a woman on the beach," Trott argued. "Why would he come here and kill Tankard the same night? I really don't see it."

"I'm sure there are plenty of possible reasons," Nazareth replied, "but I'll mention only two. One: there's a connection between Tankard and Bridget Hayes. I don't think that's it, but I can't rule it out. Two: for some reason he just wasn't satisfied with only one kill last night."

"He's growing more confident of his abilities," Gimble reasoned.

"True, but I think it's more than that. His impulses are taking over completely. Some serial killers spread their work over years or even decades, but a few get so turned on by what they're doing that they can't take a break."

"So you believe he wants to pick up the pace?" Trott asked.

"I think it's a question of *needing* rather than *wanting*. He's becoming addicted to the feeling he gets while killing, so it's not surprising that he decided to squeeze in one more victim last night. The really scary part," Nazareth continued, "is that what he did to Tankard may have opened a secret door that had previously been closed."

"Mutilation on top of murder," Gimble offered.

"With victims he didn't know," Nazareth argued, "he simply killed and moved on. But with this victim, someone he knew, he completely lost it. And now that he's experienced this sort of thrill, I think he'll be craving it again. Sooner rather than later."

Trott studied the bedroom's bloody facts but still found himself unable to comprehend the ferocity of what had taken place. It was the aftermath of an act whose viciousness had gone far beyond anything he had ever expected to witness during his career. And now the homicide expert from New York was predicting more of the same.

Training, experience, and temperament had left him ill-prepared for this moment.

He swallowed his pride. "What do you recommend, Detective Nazareth?"

"First, have your forensics people compare the footprints from here and the Hog Bay crime scene. When they match, as I'm sure they will, have officers visit as many shoe stores as necessary to find out exactly what brand of running shoe we're looking at. And second, let Tara and me look at Tankard's police file, because that's where his killer is hiding."

For the first time since arriving in Bermuda, Nazareth felt as though he had done something to earn his pay.

He most likely hadn't gotten any closer to finding Melanie Seaward, but at this point a small victory on any front was most welcome.

33.

Like many Bermudians, Stephen Hinds had to hold down two jobs in order to cover the rent, put food on the table, and still have something left over toward buying his own home one day. His primary job was teaching high school math, something he had loved every day for the past five years. The other job, the one he loathed but couldn't do without, was cleaning the beach at one of the island's top resorts before the tourists came out to play each morning.

Juggling the two jobs was a challenge. In order to be in the classroom on time, he had to start raking the sand before sunrise. Fortunately, his hotel supervisor didn't care when the job got done as long as it was finished before the first guests arrived. So it was 4:30 a.m. and dark when he fired up the tractor, switched on the headlights, and began his first pass down the beach.

It was a boring, unrewarding job whose sole positive, aside from helping pay the bills, was that Hinds could do it half asleep, which he usually was. All he had to do was steer a reasonably straight line. The large raking machine behind the tractor did the actual work. Its steel conveyor swept up debris, deposited it in a large bin, and groomed the sand in one smooth motion. Cigarette butts, water bottles, seaweed, and even lost jewelry vanished instantaneously, and the beach was left flat and pristine, awaiting the day's first footprint.

He was nearly finished with his first pass when he noticed the motion up ahead of him in the dunes, and he immediately knew it was going to be one of those days. Technically, his only job was to clean the beach, and for what he was being paid, that should have been enough. But his supervisor had made it clear he was also responsible for making sure people weren't camping out on the hotel's private property.

"Homeless people don't get to sleep on our beach," the guy had told Hinds more than once. "You see them, you get off the tractor and tell them to leave. And if they don't leave, you plant your foot on someone's butt. If they stay on our property, I blame you."

But strong-armed tactics weren't part of Hinds' repertoire. Even though he was a big guy and a fairly competitive weekend athlete, he was not about to manhandle homeless people who had no other place to sleep. As far as he was concerned, half the residents of Bermuda were only one bad break away from being homeless, and those who had already hit bottom certainly didn't need him adding to their woes. He had come across homeless people four times while raking the beach, and on three of those occasions a gentle word from him had been enough to send them on their way.

Ah, but that other time. Yes, that had been a problem. The old guy had argued that the beach belonged to God, not the hotel, and that he was therefore well within his rights to be there. So Hinds had to call hotel security, wait until the man had been escorted from the property, and then resume his chores. He had gotten to his teaching job twenty minutes late.

No way did he need another one of those episodes today. He had gone to bed late after drinking a little too much with his friends, and he was in no mood for extracurriculars.

He put the tractor in neutral, set the parking brake, and climbed down onto the beach. The tractor's headlights threw only enough light for him to make out the shape at the edge of the dune, so he walked toward it. At first glance it had appeared to be a person leaning over in the shrubbery. But as he got closer, he saw that it looked more like the curved top of a small dome tent.

Oh, please, not a tent! It would be daylight by the time the camper took his stupid tent down and packed it up, and someone on the hotel staff would no doubt look down the beach and see what was going on. Then someone would blame him for not having gotten rid of the trespasser.

His supervisor's words echoed in his head: "If they don't leave, you plant your foot on someone's butt. If they stay on our property, I blame you."

Why me? Why today?

He walked closer and shouted over the rumble of the tractor's engine. "You can't stay here. Pack it up fast before the police arrive."

When he got no response, he took a few more steps, now unwisely placing himself between the tractor's headlights and the object. The object seemed to shudder, as though being shaken by the wind. But the air was perfectly still.

Had anyone heard him?

"Okay, enough games. The police will be here shortly. You need to leave the beach now."

He moved closer — too close, in fact — before realizing what he was looking at.

The tractor was still running when Hinds' angry supervisor came looking for him an hour later.

34.

Kane Swainson was in a nasty mood.

His day had begun shortly after sunrise with a speeding ticket that was going to cost him five hundred dollars, which was substantially more than he would make in tips over the next four days.

The delay had caused him to arrive late for his shift at the hotel, and for that he had received a long, threatening lecture from the bell captain.

Then his first job of the day had been unloading a van that had ferried a family of nine loud Americans to the hotel. After delivering a total of thirteen bags to four different rooms on three different floors, he received a total of nothing in tips. Zero. Nada. Everyone thought someone else would take care of him, so no one did.

Just when he thought things couldn't get worse, he had been confronted near the taxi stand by an angry and dangerous-looking driver.

"I almost lost my job because of you," the guy snarled.

Swainson pretended not to know what he was talking about. "What did I do?"

"You told your manager my cab was dirty, and now I have to pay for some rich American bitch's new pants. Three hundred dollars!" he screamed. "Why did you say my cab was filthy?"

"I didn't," Swainson lied.

The driver put his face close to Swainson's. "I know you did, boy, so now you owe me three hundred dollars. And I'll be collecting one way or the other." He patted the side of his waist. Did he have a gun under his shirt? A knife? Or was he bluffing?

Swainson didn't wait to find out. He raced over to help four more Americans — this time a husband and wife in their early forties, a twenty-year-old nanny, and a whiny five-year-old — with their bags.

"No, we're fine," the husband said brusquely. He and his wife rolled their large suitcases toward the lobby and left the nanny struggling with their brat and two more suitcases. When Swainson offered to bring the bags inside for the young woman, the husband looked over his shoulder and yelled, "Did you not hear me? We're fine!"

Then he muttered something to his wife about the money-grubbing locals.

And now, adding insult to injury, he was at the pub as thirsty as a dog but unable to drink because Dwayne was late. He looked at his watch for the third time in a minute. It was 6:10 p.m., and Dwayne should have been here ten minutes ago. They always met at 6:00, and Dwayne always bought. That's how it was. Yet today of all days Dwayne had chosen to be late. It wasn't right.

Dwayne finally walked in at 6:15.

Swainson greeted him with, "Been waiting for you, man."

Dwayne sat at the table his friend had picked out for them. As usual, it was close to the bar. Swainson always chose a seat by the bar because that way he could flag the waiter down more easily if the place got busy, as it generally did. This was a workingman's pub, and such men were powerfully thirsty after a long day of toiling for their meager wages.

"The traffic was bad," Dwayne apologized. "Really bad."

The waiter came by and took their order. Swainson ordered two pints for himself because he knew the first one would go down so quickly he might not even taste it.

"My whole day was bad," Swainson complained. "Listen, Dwayne, this hotel job of mine is killing me. You've got to talk to your boss man for me. His name's Jacob, right?"

"Yes, Jacob Brangman."

"Okay, well, you've got to tell Jacob Brangman you have a friend who's hurting bad. I'm not cut out to be a bellman who kisses butt for a living. You with me? I could be a gardener real easy."

"I can ask him."

"Good. You do that." Swainson drank half his first beer in one gulp. "And make sure you tell him I'm your ace boy, right?"

"I will," Dwayne nodded. As he took his first sip, he noticed the guy at the bar watching him. Swainson followed Dwayne's eyes.

"Hey, come on over," Swainson hollered when he saw who it was. Quincy Warner, the young guy from the laundry room, was drinking alone. He walked to the table. "Have a seat, Quincy. Fancy seeing you here. Hey, Dwayne, this is my friend Quincy Warner. He works at the hotel."

Dwayne and Quincy shook hands and found their grips evenly matched. Both men had been laborers of one sort or another all their lives, and they each possessed the raw power that comes only from hard work. It was the type of strength the muscleheads at their fancy gyms could only dream of.

"Are you a bellman?" Dwayne wondered.

"I should be so lucky," Warner growled. "I work down in the laundry washing sheets and blankets all day. The tourists make 'em filthy, and I have the privilege of making 'em clean again. Lucky me, right? So what's the celebration here?"

"We're finished working for the day!" Swainson shouted. "And Dwayne here is going to find me a new job. Aren't you, Dwayne?" Then to Warner, "Dwayne works at a mansion out on Billionaires' Row."

"Billionaires' Row, eh? Then you must be a rich man, Dwayne," Warner teased.

"Mr. Johnson is the rich man. It's his house."

"And where is this Mr. Johnson from?"

"The United States."

"Ah, of course. Another American slave master. Does he carry a whip to make sure his boys stay in line?" The sarcasm was lost on Dwayne, who couldn't remember ever having seen Johnson with a whip, but Warner and Swainson howled.

The waiter arrived, and Swainson ordered a round for the three of them.

"No more for me," Warner protested. "I've spent as much as I can for tonight."

"Dwayne's treat," Swainson told him. "Ain't that right, Dwayne?"

Dwayne shrugged. He didn't especially like the idea of buying drinks for someone he didn't know, but he didn't want to offend Swainson, who was one of his only friends.

"Sure, Quincy. My treat."

"So tell me more about Mr. Johnson," Warner probed. "Does he live here all the time, or does he just pop over now and then to make sure his boys are taking care of things properly for him?"

"He doesn't live here all the time. He comes to play golf sometimes."

"Well lucky us, then," Warner sneered. "The master comes to town, sprinkles a bit of cash around for the poor starving locals, then sleeps safe and sound in Tucker's Town so that he doesn't have to mingle with the likes of us."

"Typical American," Swainson said between sips. "If it was up to them, they'd probably make Bermuda one of their states. Everything's for sale as far as they're concerned."

"I don't like Americans," Warner confessed. "The ones I see at the hotel aren't worth spit."

"Well, at least their numbers are dropping," Swainson snorted. "Someone's been thinning the herd a bit, or so the newspapers say."

Dwayne didn't recognize the phrase. "Thinning the herd?"

"Killing them off," Swainson clarified. "Three of them now. It's not much, but at least we've got things moving in the right direction, don't we?"

"I hope no one kills Mr. Johnson," Dwayne said softly. "I'd be out of a job then."

"Oh, I'm sure he's nice and safe," Swainson replied, "living behind the big gate with his other rich friends. They should use all their money for some higher purpose."

"Like handing out free beer every night for the workingmen," Warner laughed.

"Yeah, just like that." Warner and Swainson toasted each other and drank. "What do you say, Dwayne," Warner asked.

"I need to go home now."

The annoyance registered on Warner's face. The free drinks had just begun flowing, and now the man funding the party was about to leave. He gave Swainson a puzzled look.

"Dwayne has a young wife at home," Swainson explained, "and she won't let him come home late for dinner. Ain't that right, Dwayne?"

"She's making fish chowder tonight," Dwayne replied. He carefully counted out a few bills and set them on the table. Then he placed his half-empty mug over them so that they wouldn't be disturbed. "She doesn't like me late."

"He's an odd one, isn't he?" Warner noted once Dwayne had left. "Is he always in a bad mood?"

Swainson shook his head. "He's actually in a good mood. It's just that he's got some parts missing upstairs. But he's good for some free beers, isn't he? So it pays to be nice to him."

Warner was thinking the same about Swainson. He had never particularly liked the guy but figured he might be of use sometime. And tonight he had been. "Then I'll be on my way, Kane. Thanks for the beers."

"No problem, Quincy. You know what? Give me your phone number, and I'll text you next time Dwayne's here buying."

They high-fived each other and traded phone numbers.

Then they left the pub on their scooters. Five minutes down the road, Swainson was pulled over and given a ticket for using his cell phone while driving. Just like that: another five-hundred-dollar fine.

His mood turned stormy.

God help the next person who got in his way.

35.

JENNA TUMBRIDGE WAS DELIGHTED THAT the detectives had finally called again. After several days of being chauffeured around the island by Inspector Trott, they had asked her for a ride into Hamilton.

"It's good to see you both," she said as they strapped in. "I was afraid you had fired me for good."

"Not a chance, Jenna," Nazareth assured her. "But so far all we've seen are crime scenes, so we just rode along with the police."

"You've had a bad time of it, haven't you? The newspaper articles are simply horrible. Between the disappearances and the murders, Bermuda hardly seems like Bermuda these days."

"I'm sure it's almost impossible for you to fathom so much ugliness in the face of all this beauty, but I guarantee you no place on earth is immune."

"I know that's true, but it still hurts. Are you making any progress?"

"Some on the murders," Gimble answered, "but I'm afraid we're not very far along when it comes to the disappearances."

"Melanie Seaward is such a lovely woman. I keep hoping she'll turn up, but I'm sure that the longer she's missing ... well, the less likely it is we'll see her again. Do you think the murders and the disappearances are connected?"

Tumbridge had asked a key question, but she wasn't going to get a straight answer. Neither detective was willing to discuss that particular issue with anyone other than Trott.

"Anything's possible," Gimble replied. "Now I have a question for you. After Pete and I spend a few hours at police headquarters, we'd like to have lunch in town. What do you recommend?"

"Fancy or simple?"

"We've had plenty of fancy food at Bill's place, so simple would be nice."

"Then here's what you do. Go over to Café 4 on Queen Street and have them make you up a couple of sandwiches. Then walk to Victoria Park, grab yourselves a bench, and enjoy the glorious local atmosphere while you eat."

Nazareth and Gimble agreed that was an outstanding idea. But first they had to spend the rest of the morning digging through Delray Tankard's arrest history. Tumbridge dropped them off at the police building, where Trott led them to the private room he had arranged. He ceremoniously handed them two thick file folders.

Nazareth's eyes widened. "This is all one guy?"

"He was a busy man, detective. There's no telling how many more folders we would have needed if someone hadn't killed him. Now, if you need anything at all," Trott smiled, "please let me know. Oh, and there's a coffee room just down the hall. Feel free to help yourselves."

Tankard's record was much like those of many career criminals the detectives had encountered during their NYPD careers. The minor offenses began when he was ten. Shoplifting headed the list, but there were also scattered complaints of bullying and trespassing. During his teens he graduated to aggravated assault, breaking and entering, and attempted rape. After reaching adulthood, he picked up the pace and added new crimes to his repertoire. A string of domestic-abuse arrests stood out. Six different women had accused him of assault, although three of them had ultimately refused to testify against him.

"Hard to know where to start, isn't it?" Gimble sighed.

"I vote to begin with the most recent crimes and work our way back. List the names of people who are likely to have held a grudge."

"That'll be a long list."

He nodded. "I'll go get us some coffee."

After two hours of scouring case files, they came up with the names of ten people who in their judgment were likeliest to have wanted Tankard dead. There were six men and four women. In eight cases the victims had been robbed, stabbed, or assaulted. The other two cases had been domestic disputes during which a woman had ended up in the hospital with broken bones.

Although the detectives still assumed they were looking for a man, they knew better than to rule out the possibility that Tankard had been killed by a woman. They agreed that at least one of his female victims might have been willing to cut him to pieces while he was passed out on his bed. But if that were true, did it mean a woman had also killed Chloe Pedersen, Charles Griffin, and Bridget Hayes? Unlikely but not impossible was their conclusion.

"What I find hard to believe," Gimble said, "is that he was still on the street after all this. Did someone really need more proof that he belonged in prison for good? He did a total of seven years, Pete. That's it!"

"He had no drug offenses, no armed offenses, and no murders, so I guess he always fell just short of being put away. I agree it looks bad, but New York City's no better."

"It's much worse. But still, I'm shocked he was able to do this much damage and not spend more than seven years in a cell."

"On the other hand, he'll now be spending eternity in a grave."

"True. Funny how that works, isn't it? So how do you want to handle these ten people?"

Nazareth wasn't entirely sure. All he knew was that he and his wife couldn't be the ones visiting all ten of Tankard's former victims. To begin with, they had only a limited amount of time remaining in Bermuda. Even Bill Johnson's political clout couldn't keep them here for more than another week or so. New York City had its own problems.

On top of that, they weren't here to investigate homicides. They had come to look into Seaward's disappearance, and their only justification for working the homicides was the possibility, however remote, that she was tied to them in some way.

"Maybe you and I can talk to a couple of these people," he finally said, "but Trott's team will have to handle the rest."

"In that case, I vote for these two." She showed him the files. In the first case, a man had lost his home, his fishing boat, and his wife after being swindled by Tankard. According to court transcripts, early in the trial the man had threatened to kill Tankard. In the second case, a widow who had been dating Tankard was beaten beyond recognition after telling him the relationship was over. Tankard had also abused her young son, and the woman had vowed in open court to stick a knife in him if he ever bothered her or her boy again.

"Why these two?"

"I can't imagine two more highly motivated victims than a man who's lost everything and a woman who fears for her son's life," she explained. "I'm not saying these are the only two who might have wanted Tankard dead, but to my eye they're at the top of the pack."

"All right, then let's go see if Trott can arrange for us to interview them."

When they got to the inspector's office, they found him reviewing photos with Inspector Judith Embry, head of the forensics department. "Perfect timing," Trott said excitedly. "Our forensics team has come up with something quite useful."

"The shoe prints found at the Hog Bay Park crime scene match those of the running shoe prints in Delray Tankard's bedroom," Embry explained. She showed them the photos and pointed out the relevant characteristics. "You can see there are small forward-facing triangles on the front part of the sole — nine of them, actually — and the prints taken from both scenes are identical."

"Men's or women's shoes?" Nazareth asked.

"The size suggests it could be either."

"Any idea yet what brand?"

"Yes, in fact. Saucony. Those little triangles on the sole are a dead giveaway. I haven't found another running shoe with a pattern that's even close."

"Do you happen to know how many stores in Bermuda sell that brand?" Gimble asked. "It's probably worth checking sales records."

"We can try," Embry replied, "but there's a problem. I believe this particular model of the shoe dates back to 2012, and I seriously doubt any store keeps records going back that far."

"Ah, too bad."

"But," Embry quickly noted, "there's one additional bit of information that may prove helpful. At the time this shoe was introduced, the most popular model had a lovely Bermuda-blue upper, a red tongue, and matching red laces. Quite striking, actually."

"And quite noticeable," Trott added. "I'm going to be asking officers to be alert for a pair of running shoes matching this description."

"Excellent work," Nazareth said. "We've got the same killer at two scenes along with a possible means of identification."

"Now all we need to do is find him … or her, I suppose," Trott offered.

"Which leads me to why Tara and I stopped by your office."

He showed Trott the list of ten names he and Gimble had compiled. "We were hoping that you, Tara, and I could interview these two while your team covers the other eight."

"Absolutely. I'll take you whenever you're ready."

Nazareth checked the clock on Trott's desk. It was shortly before noon, and he had Café 4 on his mind.

"Would 1:30 or 2:00 be okay? Tara and I are going to grab a couple of sandwiches and go eat at Victoria Park. Care to join us?"

"That sounds wonderful, but I'd better stay here and get things moving. I'll have addresses on these two people when you get back, and we'll pay them a visit."

As he watched them walk off, Trott wondered yet again how he truly felt about their presence in Bermuda. They were pleasant enough and highly competent, of course, but did it serve his career well to have two New York City detectives essentially directing the most high-profile investigation in Bermuda's history?

Part of him wished they would go home.

The other part realized he desperately needed them.

36.

CAFÉ 4 WAS LIGHT-YEARS AWAY from the delis and food carts where Nazareth and Gimble usually grabbed lunch in Manhattan. The place was bright and clean. The counter staff was friendly. And the patrons weren't throwing elbows or trading dirty looks.

Nazareth ordered a Vietnamese beef sandwich: beef brisket with pickled vegetables and sriracha mayo on organic ciabatta bread. Gimble went with the organic kale salad topped with grilled chicken.

"The chocolate fudge cake is talking to me," Nazareth said as their sandwiches were being prepared.

"And it's saying?"

"*You're on vacation!*"

"You call this a vacation?"

"This particular lunch is a vacation, isn't it?"

"You're right. It is. By all means get two pieces of chocolate fudge cake."

"We can just share one piece if you'd like," he teased.

"Don't make me shoot you."

Lunch in hand, they walked the three blocks to Victoria Park and found a bench in the shade of a tall palm tree. They were lucky to find a spot. Since it was a warm, sunny day, a fair number of locals had already claimed their usual lunch-hour places. Most of them appeared to be office workers from the buildings that surrounded the park, but there were also mothers pushing strollers, people walking their dogs, and tourists snapping photos with their cell phones.

"Kind of like Central Park," Gimble quipped, "except that it's about eight hundred and thirty-nine acres smaller."

"And probably eight hundred and thirty-nine times safer."

"Oh, come on. Central Park's not all that unsafe."

148

"You say that because you're a judo black belt and carry a gun."

"Very funny. How's your sandwich?"

"Wonderful. How about your salad?"

"Really good … but not as good as that cake is going to be."

"Eat slowly, Tara. We're on vacation for only another forty-five minutes."

They both took their time enjoying the food, the weather, and the people watching. Although Victoria Park occupied only one square block, it appeared that almost everyone in Hamilton had decided to stop by on this particular day. Yet even though the park was busy, the people who passed by were noticeably less frenzied than the New Yorkers that Nazareth and Gimble were used to dealing with. Folks might be in a hurry to get somewhere, but they weren't homicidal about it.

After her last bite of chocolate fudge cake, Gimble glanced at her cell phone. "Time to head back, I'm afraid."

"It is. But we can at least take the long way."

"Agreed."

Instead of going straight back to the police headquarters along Victoria Street, they briefly headed in the opposite direction. They walked down Dismont Drive alongside the Earl Cameron Theatre, then turned left on Church Street, where they passed the imposing Cathedral of the Most Holy Trinity, one of Hamilton's most beautiful structures.

"Maybe we can come back and look around inside the cathedral before we leave Bermuda," Gimble said wistfully. She was looking forward to wrapping things up and getting home to Kayla, but she was nevertheless a bit sad over missing out on everything the island had to offer. Bill Johnson's hope that they could squeeze in some vacation while working here seemed destined to go unfulfilled.

"Hold that thought, Tara. We'll be coming back here on a real vacation, and we'll see whatever you'd like."

"Promise?"

"Scout's honor."

They reached the corner and were about to turn left on Court Street when Nazareth noticed something odd diagonally across the intersection. A man was idling his motor scooter at the curb directly in front of a bank, and he seemed to be studying the lobby door. Because the guy wore a helmet, Nazareth couldn't be sure what he was looking at, but there was no doubt he was waiting impatiently.

Was he waiting for his passenger to come out of the bank? If so, where was the second helmet? Why would a passenger have carried his helmet into the bank with him when he could have left it with the driver? That didn't seem right.

"Give me a minute," he told Gimble. He darted across Court Street against the light and stood on the corner directly opposite the bank. From his new vantage point he could see the CLOSED sign hanging on the front door. No one was entering or leaving the lobby, yet the scooter driver sat there watching the door expectantly.

Nazareth waited for the crosswalk signal to turn green, then casually strolled across Church Street toward the bank. He was ten feet from the front door when a helmeted man came out of the lobby, a gym bag in one hand, a gun in the other, and began running toward the waiting scooter. As soon as the guy got within reach, Nazareth caught him flush in the face with a high roundhouse kick, one of his most effective taekwondo techniques. The robber's legs flew out from under him, and he hit the sidewalk unconscious.

Then Nazareth sprinted for the scooter. The driver revved the engine and began to turn into the traffic when he got slammed to the pavement by the detective's flying tackle. The scooter wobbled forward on its own before crashing into a parked car. The driver, meanwhile, found himself flat on his back with Nazareth's forearm against his throat.

By the time Nazareth dragged the driver to the sidewalk, Gimble had already picked up the robber's handgun and called 911. The police were on the scene in less than two minutes. The bank was, after all, only a block away from the headquarters building.

"What absolute gall!" Trott fumed when Nazareth and Gimble returned to his office and recounted the story. "Who tries to rob a bank that's just down the street from a police headquarters?"

"Happens all the time back in the States," Nazareth laughed.

"You can't be serious."

"I am. In fact, I know of three instances so far this year: Illinois, Texas, and Wisconsin."

"But why would anyone do that?"

Nazareth shrugged. "Stupidity would be my first guess. Anyway, Tara and I are ready to visit those two people if you are."

"Oh, right, those two." Trott looked discouraged. "I'm afraid we won't be visiting them, as much as I'd like to. The man you wanted to interview has been in a hospice for the past two months and doesn't have much longer to live. As for the woman, she died of a heart attack years ago. I'm sure she'd love to know someone killed Tankard for her, but she's no longer a suspect."

Two pitches, two strikes. This was new territory for Nazareth and Gimble, who were accustomed to following the right hunches, making the right decisions, and hitting home runs. Now they were striking out.

"I'll give Jenna a call," Gimble said disconsolately. "She told me to let her know when we're ready to head back to Bill's place."

"Yeah, I guess," Nazareth murmured.

Then Gimble paused. "Wait. The dead woman had a son who was abused by Tankard. Where's he these days?" she asked Trott.

"I didn't check on that. Give me a minute."

Third pitch coming up.

Trott tapped the keys on his laptop. "Yes, there was a boy named Deion. He'd be nineteen now. But here's the thing. The mother, Syriah Jones was her name, went to court and had his name changed after she brought charges against Tankard. I guess she was afraid he would eventually go after the boy."

"Probably a wise move," Gimble noted. "What's his name now?"

"Well, you see, for security reasons the name was never added to our files."

"You can get his name from the court, right?"

"Well, the court doesn't answer to me, of course. All I can do is ask and hope someone will lend a hand."

Nazareth decided that if he were going to strike out, he would at least go down swinging. "There's no room here for hoping, inspector," he insisted. "This needs to happen."

Trott squirmed uncomfortably in his swivel chair. He didn't like being ordered around in his own office by an outsider, but he understood that arguing with Nazareth could easily mark the beginning of the end of his long career. "Perhaps the police commissioner can lend a hand."

"There you go."

And if the police commissioner can't get the job done, Nazareth thought as he and Gimble walked out, Bill Johnson probably can.

37.

THE TWIN FORCES OF LOVE and hate waged war within him whenever he returned to Horseshoe Bay Beach. He could not set foot in the sand without remembering how wonderful his life had been. Yet those same memories fueled his anger over how all the good things had been ripped away from him when he was only a boy.

But he was a man now, and his pain was the fire that forged his deadly power and steeled him for the work that needed to be done. If he couldn't reclaim the past, he could at least punish those who had stolen it from him.

And that was his plan.

His parents had brought him here often when he was a child. He and his father had built sand castles and played in the waves together. His mother had served up the sandwiches and sweets she had carried to the beach in an old straw basket. And he had tossed bits of bread to the gulls as they swarmed overhead.

Life couldn't have been better.

Then it all vanished. His father, disgraced and broken, had taken his own life. His mother had dropped dead when she could no longer handle what the world dished out. And he had been left on his own, terrified that Delray Tankard, his mother's former boyfriend, would find him and make good on his awful promises.

But he had taken care of Tankard, whose mutilated corpse would soon be rotting in a cold grave, and he was now free to deal with the others.

Having three times tasted the sweet thrill of killing tourists, he was hungry to increase the body count. He wondered how many of them he would need to dispose of before the invasion of outsiders subsided. Would twenty be enough? No, he didn't think so. But perhaps a hundred bodies stacked on Bermuda's pink beaches would help convince tourists to go elsewhere. The word would spread in a hurry, and with luck the accursed cruise ships might stop coming here altogether. Before long, Bermudians would have their home back, free of the rich tourists who wanted to make it their own.

It was an ambitious design, but he felt equal to it. He was strong, clever, and dedicated. Moreover, he was surrounded by opportunity on all sides.

That plump, sunburned couple at the water's edge would do nicely — the husband with his butt crack peeking out from his baggy swim trunks, the wife with her flab slopping over the bikini meant for a woman half her size. He imagined himself following them to their hotel room and carving them like the pair of ripe melons they were.

The young brunette on the blanket was another delectable choice. Ordinarily he preferred blondes, but something about the arrogant set of this one's mouth made him want to kill her on the spot. A single glance told him she was a privileged tart whose rich parents and fancy college degree guaranteed her a life of luxury and excess.

Or maybe he would have more fun with the old woman who waded barefoot at the shoreline, rum swizzle in hand. Tan and leathery, she wore gaudy gold bracelets on both wrists and had a diamond pendant draped over her silk blouse. Her white designer beach pants were fashionably rolled at the bottom so they wouldn't get wet. Yes, without question she was the one he would choose if he could act right here and right now. Her smug ruling-class attitude cried out to him.

"Please kill me" is what it said.

But he wasn't here to kill this afternoon. He was here to observe, to perfect his ability to assess his enemy's weaknesses. The more he knew about the behavior of these foreigners, the more efficiently he could dispose of them. He studied the looks they gave each other as they socialized on his beach. Memorized gestures that spoke of pleasure, desire, or concern. Learned how to identify the weakest members of the herd.

If he were going to kill scores of them, he needed to know how to target the right ones. A single bad choice could put him in a prison cell for the rest of his life.

He picked up his beach towel and casually walked toward the spot where he had finished off that young tramp from the cruise ship. A mother sat on a blanket and watched her three children dig in the sand exactly where Chloe Pedersen had fallen. He wondered whether the mother didn't know the recent history of this place or simply didn't care. He also wondered whether the dead woman's troubled spirit might still be present. That's the sort of thing his mother had always believed, so he kept an open mind on the subject. But in the end it didn't matter.

Chloe Pedersen was dead. He was alive.

He glanced at the mother on the blanket and caught her venomous look. She didn't like him staring at her children, and her look told him so.

On a different day and in a different place he would have killed her for that look. At the moment, though, there was nothing he could do.

Ah, but tonight!

Tonight someone else would pay the price for her insolence.

38.

THE SUN WAS LOW IN the sky as Nazareth and Gimble walked Windfall's grounds, attempting to relax after their frustrating day in Hamilton. They had made some tentative progress, only to be thwarted by a judge who had flatly refused to reveal the name of Syriah Jones' son. Trott had asked and been shot down immediately. Then the police commissioner had called and gotten the same curt response: "This court doesn't answer to anyone."

On their way back to Tucker's Town they had called Bill Johnson and asked whether he could help break the logjam. He agreed to call Bermuda's premier right away though he was careful not to promise success.

"U.S. Supreme Court judges bow to political pressure all the time," he noted, "but Bermuda's court might actually do things the right way."

Johnson had sounded disappointed when they told him of their lack of progress on Seaward's case. How could they blame him? They had come here to help find his cousin, and all they had done so far was work on homicides that in all probability weren't connected to her disappearance. But he had nevertheless offered to help in any way he could. As usual, he had shown himself to be a loyal and supportive friend.

A mother duck helped the detectives forget about business for a few moments. She waddled from under the bougainvillea, five tiny ducklings in tow, and marched toward a small pond at the back of the mansion. Beyond them, back among the palmettos, a pair of bluebirds flitted to and from one of the nest boxes that had been placed around the property.

Johnson had been careful to respect nature when designing the estate's landscape. Except for a bit of lawn in front of the mansion, the property had a deliberately wild look about it. Box briar, sword ferns, buttonwoods, and paw paw trees thrived under the watchful eye of groundskeeper Jacob Brangman. The only signs of civilization were a small grove of fruit trees, an herb garden that Shaun Lightbourne tended, and a narrow path that meandered through the greenery down to the beach.

The tranquil surroundings had barely begun to work their restorative magic when Nazareth's phone rang. "It's Trott. Let's hope he has a name for us."

He didn't.

"We've had another person disappear," he announced without preliminaries.

He gave the detectives the few facts in his possession. Stephen Hinds had signed in for his job raking the beach at one of the island's most popular hotels. Some time later, his supervisor came looking for him and found the riderless tractor, engine running. Furious, the supervisor then called the high school where Hinds taught math, but Hinds hadn't reported for work. "This is highly unusual," the woman in the principal's office had told him. "Mr. Hinds has never even taken a sick day, so we're quite surprised he would miss school without calling in."

"Wife or family?" Nazareth asked.

"Neither. He lives alone, and officers have searched his apartment. He showed up for work, left the tractor running, and vanished without a trace."

"It's not possible for this many people to vanish without a trace," Gimble challenged. "If someone's killing them, the bodies are out there to be found."

"As I mentioned the other day," Trott answered, "there are places where people could, in fact, disappear without a trace and never be found. You really should have a look at our caves."

"I'd like to do that."

"I'll gladly pick you up in the morning and show you."

"Then let's do it."

"Will 10:00 be okay?"

"Perfect."

When the call ended, Gimble turned to her husband. "You didn't say much. Are you okay with visiting the caves?"

He shrugged. "No reason not to, but I doubt we'll learn anything worth knowing. When we first met Trott, he thought people were drowning themselves. Then he thought they were being eaten by sharks. And now he thinks maybe they're being murdered and hidden in secret caves. I mean, come on, Tara."

"Having two serial killers in Bermuda at the same time strains the imagination."

"As does a single killer with two entirely different MOs. Sometimes he leaves his victims on the beach, but sometimes he hides the bodies where they can't be found? No way."

"So where does that leave us?"

"It leaves us asking the wrong questions about the disappearances. If you and I are willing to rule out all the possible causes Trott has mentioned, then we're dealing with something that's outside our normal experience."

She frowned. "Please don't say it's alien abductions. I've had enough fantasy for one day."

"I rule out nothing," he laughed, "but I'm not arguing for aliens just yet. But there's something at work here that you and I have never dealt with before."

"Then let's hope we find it in the caves tomorrow," she joked.

"Be careful what you wish for," he grinned.

"The only thing I'm wishing for right now is dinner. I hope Shaun has something wonderful tonight because my mood could use a boost."

"Does he ever disappoint?"

"Hmm, no, he doesn't. I feel better already."

Nazareth didn't.

He was being hounded by his own words. *There's something at work here that you and I have never dealt with before.*

What had he even meant by that?

39.

MISTAKING HER FOR JUST ANOTHER ignorant tourist, cab driver Keith Naylor tried to overcharge Pam Bathgate for the ride from Hamilton to Southampton. Instead of setting the meter for a single passenger, he set it for five passengers, thereby increasing the fare by about twenty-five percent. As soon as she spotted the scam, she ordered him to stop the car and let her out.

The matter most likely would have ended there if he hadn't called her a "nasty old biddy" as she exited his cab. Incensed, she wrote his name down on a slip of note paper as he sped away. When she got home, she would make him regret his rudeness.

Her next choice of cabs worked out better. The driver was pleasant and talkative, and, more importantly, honest. Though she normally tipped only fifteen percent, she gave the guy twenty percent when he dropped her off at her condo. Her mood had brightened, and she had already decided she wouldn't report the first driver. She lived alone, after all, and didn't need any enemies.

Bathgate had bought her one-bedroom slice of paradise in 2017 after teaching literature at the University of Connecticut for thirty-nine years. For two hundred thousand dollars, she had gotten the right to use the tiny resort condo for five weeks each year, and each of those weeks met her definition of heaven on earth. An active seventy-year-old, she kept her daily routine relaxed but full. She read incessantly alongside the resort's pool, took long beach walks, and worked on her novel whenever the spirit moved her.

The novel, a serious and largely autobiographical work, had been a long time coming. She had thought about it for decades but had only recently begun writing. If all went as planned, *Alone in the Quiet* could easily be nominated for a National Book Award, and she already imagined what she might say in her acceptance speech. But she had eighty thousand words to go and sensed she should pick up the pace.

She dropped her handbag on the kitchen counter and opened the sliding door to a private patio surrounded by a hibiscus hedge laden with bright red blossoms. Her ground-floor unit was ideal for someone who liked to come and go all day long. The pool was to her left, the restaurant to her right, and the ocean straight ahead. No stairs, no elevators.

Also no oppressive relationships. She knew her neighbors well enough to say hello and trade a few words about the weather, but she was content to spend her days inside her own head. Marriage had come and gone decades earlier, and she had since learned that she was her own best company.

After spending the afternoon reading, she fixed herself a light dinner: fresh greens topped with a piece of leftover grilled chicken from the previous night's restaurant meal. Two glasses of chardonnay argued for a third, but she resisted the temptation because the weather was spectacular and she wanted to take an extra long walk on the beach this evening.

After trading emails with friends back in Connecticut, she laced up her walking shoes and set out for the beach. As usual, she left the patio door unlocked behind her because she had lost the key months ago. But she didn't worry much about locking doors here anyway. The resort had its own security team, and there had never been a hint of trouble from either residents or outsiders.

She spent nearly an hour strolling west at the water's edge, watching the sun slowly approach the horizon while she picked up bits of sea glass for her growing collection. Blue was her favorite color, but she gladly took whatever she could find. One day soon she would do something with all that glass back at the condo. Filling a small lamp base was the leading option, but if she got really ambitious, she might consider making her own necklaces. In fact, the resort offered a class on how to make sea glass jewelry. Why not? She still had three weeks left in this year's fractional-share visit.

On her way back to the condo, tired but happy, she paused to snap a few pictures of the magnificent crimson and orange sky show as the sun finally sank behind the ocean. She normally watched the evening's spectacle from her patio, but the view from the secluded beach was even better. Maybe this would become the new normal.

A text message from her sister in New Hampshire intruded on her thoughts as she began walking toward home again. Her eyes were on the cell phone, not on the shadowy figure that had emerged from the dunes behind her.

She was only a hundred yards from her condo when time stood still.

For Pam Bathgate, it would never start again.

40.

TROTT PICKED NAZARETH AND GIMBLE up at 10:00 a.m. sharp for the short drive to Crystal Cave, the most famous of Bermuda's one hundred and fifty known caves.

"No one knows how many caves there are," he told them along the way, "and I suspect we never will. All we know is that they were formed roughly a million years ago and that many of them are connected by a vast network of natural tunnels that eventually open to the sea."

"Are they explored much?" Nazareth asked.

"Some of them, yes, by divers. It's not something I've ever thought about doing, though. Too many things can go wrong."

"Such as?"

"Getting lost is what I'd worry about most. Take the Green Bay Cave out by Harrington Sound, for instance. I'm told it has nearly two miles of underwater passages. Can you imagine being underwater in total darkness and trying to find your way out?"

"Sounds like a nightmare to me," Gimble offered. "I'm mildly claustrophobic, and just the thought of swimming through underwater tunnels creeps me out."

"I'm also told," Trott continued, "that in many cases the passageways are so narrow you have to tow your air tank behind you in order to squeeze through. So I'm with you, Detective Gimble. I'll leave the cave diving to someone else, thank you very much."

When they reached the Crystal Cave, Trott asked for twenty-year-old Brijette Matthews, the guide who would be leading them on their private tour.

"We'll begin by walking down some stairs," she told them, "because the cave is about a hundred and twenty feet below us. Going down is a lot easier than coming back up, of course, but we'll take our time when we return." She looked mostly at Trott when she spoke since he appeared to be a bit out of shape. The other two looked quite fit even though by her standards they were fairly old.

A few minutes later they stood on a pontoon bridge that spanned a spectacular crystal-clear lake surrounded by complex gem-like formations that covered the cave's roof and walls. Though quite beautiful, the ancient cave was also a bit intimidating and seemed to touch some primitive nerve in both detectives.

"It's like visiting a prehistoric world," Gimble said. "The rock formations are kind of eerie, aren't they?"

"They certainly are," Matthews agreed. "The stalactites and stalagmites you see here are made of calcium carbonate and were formed very slowly one drop at a time. Rain water works its way through the ground, dissolves the limestone crust, and deposits tiny specks of calcium carbonate. Wait half a million years or so, and this is what you get."

Nazareth was even more impressed by the subterranean lake. The water was so clear he could make out a pair of sunglasses resting on one of the rocks far below the surface. "Looks as though someone got a little careless," he laughed.

"Oh, the sunglasses," Matthews answered. "Yes, visitors lose all sorts of things in here. Once or twice a year we have a diver come in to remove the cameras, cell phones, sunglasses, and even dentures."

"Dentures? Seriously?"

"You name it, someone has dropped it here."

"How deep is the water?"

"About twenty meters."

Nazareth was plainly shocked. "Sixty-five feet? I would have said fifteen or twenty at most."

"Perfectly clear water is like that. The water depth varies from cave to cave in Bermuda, but here it's generally twenty to twenty-five meters."

"And this lake connects to the sea?"

"Yes, but precisely where or in how many places we don't really know. What lies beneath Bermuda's surface is unimaginably complex, and it's changing all the time. Much of the change occurs naturally," she added, "but some of it is triggered by human activity."

Trott expanded on the idea. "Construction projects often have unintended consequences. It's quite common for caves to collapse or get sealed off when the surrounding limestone is disturbed. Sometimes we know when it happens, but I'm sure in most cases we don't."

Gimble noticed a narrow opening in the cave wall on the far side of the lake. "Are there smaller caves off this main one?"

Matthews nodded. "Some of them are no larger than a closet, but others are immense. You'll find them both above and below the waterline."

"And that," Trott added quickly, "is why I wanted you to come here today. In this one cave alone there are probably scores of hidden rooms where someone could, as we discussed yesterday, disappear without a trace. Now multiply that by the number of other caves in Bermuda, many of which we've never discovered."

Nazareth didn't need to do the math. He knew Trott was right. If Melanie Seaward had been taken to a hidden cave and murdered, no one on the planet would ever discover her body. It was a chilling thought.

"Ready to head back up?" Matthews asked.

They were.

As soon as they reached the surface, Trott found that he had three missed calls on his cell phone. He checked in with his office and had a short, cryptic conversation. "When? Who's in charge there? Address. Okay, I'll be there shortly."

Nazareth read the look on the inspector's face. "Bad news?"

Trott nodded. "They just found a woman on the dunes out in Southampton. Throat cut, twenty or thirty other stab wounds as well."

"Tara and I can go along for the ride if you want us. Your call."

"I'm feeling a bit lost right about now," he confided. "Your help would be most welcome."

During the drive to Pam Bathgate's condo, they got additional details from the sergeant in charge of the crime scene. A young couple walking along the beach had found the body lying among the dune shrubs. The police had arrived within minutes, but it had taken nearly an hour and a half to find someone who knew the victim and could provide a positive ID. Apparently the old woman had kept to herself and didn't have many friends at the resort.

The cell phone found in her pants pocket contained sunset photos that the sergeant assumed had been taken shortly before the attack. When they searched her condo, they found nothing unusual except for an unlocked patio door.

"Overly trusting," Gimble observed as they sped along South Road toward the resort. "Went out for a sunset walk by herself and didn't bother locking her condo. Two bad choices."

"A week or so ago I wouldn't have considered either of those actions unwise," Trott responded, "but my opinion is rapidly evolving."

"What's also evolving," Nazareth offered, "is the nature of the attacks. The butcher job this guy did on Delray Tankard obviously liberated his worst demons, and he's no longer content to kill."

"He also wants to inflict maximum punishment," Gimble said.

"Is that normal for cases like this?" Trott wondered.

"If you're willing to use the word *normal*," Nazareth replied, "then yes, it's normal. Psychopathic behavior has a reasonably standard trajectory. In our experience, the pace and ferocity of attacks both accelerate as killers become more accomplished."

"The more they kill," Gimble said, "the more invincible they feel, which feeds the impulse to kill again."

"One tiny bit of good news," Nazareth added, "is that at this stage these people also begin to take greater risks and therefore make more mistakes."

"But only as they take more lives," Trott said.

"Unfortunately, you're correct. With this particular killer," Nazareth reasoned, "we could easily have ten more victims before he makes the mistake that leads us to him. So far he hasn't left a single clue that means anything."

Trott couldn't find words to express what he was feeling. His beloved Bermuda was under attack, and he was powerless to stop it. He hadn't signed up for this sort of job, yet here he was.

When they entered Bathgate's condo fifteen minutes later, they found little evidence that someone had recently lived there. Bed perfectly made. No dishes in the sink. No clothes draped over chairs. Pam Bathgate had apparently been meticulous about everything but her own safety.

The only thing that caught Gimble's attention was the pocketbook on the kitchen counter. After checking to make sure the forensics team had finished taking pictures, she brought the pocketbook to the kitchen table, turned it upside down, and used a pen to move the contents around. The wallet, lipstick, and small bottle of hand sanitizer said nothing, but the slip of yellow paper had potential.

Keith Naylor. Coral Taxi. Overcharged. "Nasty old biddy." 11:15 a.m.

"Check this out," she said. "Looks as though she had a run-in with a cab driver and wrote herself a note about the incident."

Nazareth read the note. "Gets into an argument with a cab driver, then gets murdered."

"A cab driver," Trott said auspiciously. "Could that be it?"

"He comes into contact with people all over the island," Gimble said, "especially tourists. And except for Tankard, all the murder victims have been tourists."

Trott was feeling cautiously optimistic for the first time since meeting Nazareth and Gimble. Yes, a cab driver would be an ideal suspect. He met new victims every day, had ample opportunity to assess their vulnerability, and knew just the right places to attack them. Had a simple handwritten note from the latest victim identified the killer for them?

"Care to have a chat with Keith Naylor?" Trott asked.

The detectives couldn't think of anything they'd rather do.

Except, of course, find Melanie Seaward.

41.

MOST OF KEITH NAYLOR'S FACE was hidden behind a mug of honey ale when Trott, Nazareth, and Gimble walked into the Wet Whistle, a rowdy workingman's pub out in Somerset Village. It was 4:00 p.m. and the place was jammed, but the noise level dropped by eighty decibels when the drinkers spotted the newcomers. The young blonde was sizzling hot, but the two stone-faced guys with her had police written all over them. Several men nervously eyed the door, hoping they could get out before being arrested for their most recent transgressions.

Trott walked over to the bartender and flashed his badge.

"Please direct me to Keith Naylor," he said softly and politely. The bartender reflexively glanced at Naylor, who sat at the far end of the bar, then refocused on Trott's face.

"I don't recognize the name!" the bartender said as Trott walked away. The inspector had already found his murder suspect.

When four men seated near the door hastily finished their drinks and left the pub, Nazareth and Gimble grabbed the empty table and waited to see whether Trott needed assistance. They were outnumbered but confident they could handle a half dozen drunks each.

Naylor studied Trott's ID, set his mug on the bar, and looked over at the two detectives. If he was thinking about running, their presence had just laid that bad idea to rest.

"We need to ask you some questions, Mr. Naylor," Trott intoned in his best police voice, "either here or at police headquarters. Your choice."

"I didn't do anything."

"I didn't say you did."

"Then why do you want to talk to me?"

"Because your name has come up in an investigation. Here or at police headquarters?"

Naylor opted to chat with Trott and his colleagues in the Wet Whistle's familiar surroundings. His fierce scowl signaled his disapproval, but he grudgingly took the chair next to Nazareth.

"Detectives Pete Nazareth and Tara Gimble are on assignment here from New York City," Trott told Naylor, "and they're helping us with several investigations."

Naylor made brief eye contact with the two detectives, didn't like what he saw, and turned back to the inspector.

"So what do you think I did?" Naylor grumbled.

"Tell us about the woman you called, and here I'm quoting, a *nasty old biddy.*"

Naylor remembered watching from the rearview mirror as the old woman stood at the curb scribbling on her notepad yesterday. He had wanted to turn the cab around and run her down. Would have served her right for accusing him of being a crook.

"I don't recall ever using those words," he said flatly.

"Allow me to refresh your memory. Here's the entire message. *Keith Naylor. Coral Taxi. Overcharged. "Nasty old biddy." 11:15 a.m.* Your company's dispatcher has already confirmed that you picked someone up at 11:15 yesterday but immediately canceled the fare. So why don't you just tell us what happened?"

"What happened," Naylor snarled, "is that some old tourist bitch accused me of overcharging her, as though she'd know the difference. And when I didn't offer to kiss her American arse, she said she wanted to get out of the cab. So I let her out. That's what happened."

"But you don't remember calling her a *nasty old biddy?*"

"I told her to have a lovely day parading around Bermuda like a member of the royal family, which is what she was doing. Which is what they all do."

Gimble jumped in. "*They* meaning?"

"Tourists. All of them basically, but the Americans are the worst. And it doesn't matter to me that you two are from the States," he continued, "because I'm just saying what everyone here knows is true.

You come here with your pockets full of money and ruin everything for us."

"Ruin how?" Nazareth wanted to know.

"Treating us locals like servants is how, and also by driving up the cost of everything we buy. Listen, my wife pays eleven dollars for a gallon of milk and five dollars for a lousy loaf of white bread. All because tourists can afford the high prices. Leave the decision to me," he added, "and they'd all be gone today."

"Interesting you should say that," Nazareth replied, "because there's one less tourist in Bermuda today. Pam Bathgate, the woman you got nasty with yesterday, was found murdered this morning."

The blood drained from Naylor's face. "Hey, I don't know anything about that," he sputtered. "She was in my cab for less than a minute, and that's the last I saw of her."

Gimble pressed him. "You had her home address, am I right?"

"Of course I had her address. How else could I give her a ride? But I didn't kill her!" he shouted.

At the words *I didn't kill her*, most of the pub's remaining patrons set their drinks down and headed for the door. At least a few of the pub's regulars knew Keith Naylor to be a volatile, ill-tempered thug who was in all probability perfectly capable of killing someone, but they had no interest in testifying to that effect.

"You hate tourists, Pam Bathgate in particular, and you knew where she lived," Nazareth prodded. "Tell us something that will make us believe you didn't kill her last night."

"I was with someone all night," Naylor pleaded.

"Your wife's alibi isn't worth much to us."

Naylor hesitated, then took a deep breath. "My wife moved out a few days ago."

"So you weren't with your wife?"

"No."

"Okay, then give us the name of the person you were with all night."

Naylor squirmed in his seat. "Her husband will go crazy if he finds out."

"You're close to being charged with murder," Nazareth growled, "so you have bigger things to worry about."

"Okay, okay. Her name is Jasmine."

"Jasmine what?" Trott demanded.

"Jasmine Naylor."

"I thought you said your wife moved out."

"She did. Jasmine is my brother's wife."

"Your brother's wife," Gimble repeated. "You spent the night with your brother's wife?"

"He's in Jamaica on business."

"Thank you for that helpful explanation," she sneered.

Trott spent the next few minutes recording the sordid details. Naylor and his brother's wife had met at her place around 8:00 p.m., eaten dinner, shared two bottles of cheap red wine, and then enjoyed each other's company until 6:00 the next morning, when he had left for his cab shift.

"Get her on the phone for me," Trott ordered. "If anything she says doesn't match up with what you've just told me, you'll find yourself in a cell."

"She'll tell you the same thing, man. But you can't get my brother involved in this, all right?"

"One step at a time, Mr. Naylor. First let's talk to your sister-in-law."

Jasmine Naylor was alternately teary, confrontational, and frightened. She mentioned more than once that her husband would kill her and his younger brother if he found out about the affair. But in the end she confirmed all the relevant details her brother-in-law had given Trott.

"You're free to go," Trott told Naylor when the call ended, "but don't plan on leaving Bermuda anytime soon. Do you understand?"

Naylor said he did, then immediately thought about retreating to the bar for one more pint. But the looks he was getting from the New York City cops made him edgy. Local police had never bothered him one way or the other, but these two gave off a distinctly unnerving vibe. He decided to leave the pub thirsty.

"So what do you think?" Trott asked once Naylor was out the door.

"Serious dirtbag in every conceivable way," Gimble offered, "but not the person we're after."

"I agree," Nazareth said. "There's no way he'd offer up his sister-in-law as an alibi unless that's how things actually happened. Both of them are scared to death of Naylor's brother."

"Yes, I took note of that," Trott nodded. "I think I may have a look at what sort of business the brother is doing in Jamaica."

"Drugs maybe?" Nazareth asked.

"That's a reasonable guess. We have an ongoing issue with Jamaicans and drugs."

The bartender approached their table.

"Can I get you something to drink? I have nothing else to do now that you've shut the place down."

"That wasn't our intent," Trott replied evenly, "but I'm sure your regulars will be back once we leave."

He was right. Many of the patrons who had left the pub earlier were hanging out in the parking lot. As soon as Trott's SUV pulled onto the roadway, the drinkers filed back in.

"Well, that was interesting but not terribly helpful," Trott announced. "Back to square one yet again."

"We're doing all the right things," Nazareth assured him, "and the break will come along. It always does."

They were on South Road less than five miles from Windfall when the police commissioner called. After speaking with Bill Johnson, the premier had succeeded in convincing the court to release the new name Syriah Jones had chosen for her son.

Quincy Warner had just hit the radar.

42.

GABRIELLA HARRISON PARKED HER SCOOTER and hiked down the narrow cliffside trail to the Gravelly Bay shoreline. Watch Hill Park might be one of Bermuda's tiniest parks, but Harrison knew it also offered some of the island's most scenic overlooks, and that's why she had come here. She was a wedding photographer, and she wanted to add a few sunset photos of the park to her portfolio.

An old man fishing on the rocks at the water's edge looked up at her, smiled, and waved. She held up her camera and pointed to it, wondering whether he would mind if she snapped a few pictures. He motioned for her to wait a moment, then bent over and pulled a large rockfish from a cooler. He held it up for her as she memorialized his trophy.

She waved and moved on, searching for just the right alignment of rocks, trees, and horizon. The colors worked beautifully together in the subdued light, so now it was up to her to find the perfect composition. After twenty minutes of shooting from every conceivable angle, she walked back toward the parking lot. She looked down to the shore, thinking to wave goodbye to the fisherman.

Odd. His rod was lying in the sand alongside the cooler. Harrison had done enough fishing in her life to know how quickly sand could ruin an expensive reel. Why would he have dropped the pole in the sand instead of resting it atop the cooler?

She scanned the beach, studied the bushes along the shore, and looked up the trail ahead of her, but she couldn't spot him. So she surveyed the entire area again through her telephoto lens. Same result.

The old man was gone.

As much as she wanted to walk down to the beach for a closer look, she knew she shouldn't. Murder was rampant in Bermuda these days, or so the newspapers said, so she simply took a few photos from her hilltop vantage point and set off for home.

An hour later, after viewing all the Watch Hill Park photos on the twenty-four-inch editing screen in her studio, she called the police. The last two photos she had taken were frightening.

One of them clearly showed what appeared to be blood on the rocks where the fisherman had been standing.

The other revealed a mysterious grey shape beneath the surface of the turquoise water several hundred feet offshore. Trailing behind it was a long red stain.

• • •

Officers John Greaves and Oliver Beasley walked the beach with flashlights, doing their best to match the shadows to the scene depicted in the photos Gabriella Harrison had texted to the police a few hours earlier. But it was a lost cause. To begin with, the tide had come in and washed over the rock where the fisherman had been standing.

In addition, his fishing pole and cooler were long gone, either carried out to sea or picked up by someone who had walked the beach after Harrison left. There was no evidence that anything unusual had happened here.

"I think her imagination got a little out of control," Greaves concluded.

"It's the newspapers," Beasley agreed. "All they talk about these days is the murders and the shark attacks. Hardly surprising that people are half crazy with fear."

"But I'd still rather have people call us about nothing than not call us when they should."

"I think you're being overly generous in this case. Think about it. She imagines a shark jumping onto the rocks, snatching an old man, and swimming off with his bloody remains. Come on. I think she had one too many rum swizzles while she was looking at her pictures."

"But the photos do show something odd," Greaves countered. "I'm not saying it's what she thought, but it's something."

"Sunset is what it is. You've got a bright red sky reflecting in a puddle on the rocks and in the waves. It's a reflection, not blood.

That's what I saw when I first looked at the pictures, and I haven't changed my mind."

"And then there's that grey shape in the water."

"I think you're starting to see things too, Johnny. That shape is most likely a seaweed bed, but it could be rocks or a cloud reflection or a school of parrot fish. But a shark? Not a chance. It's a big blob of whatever, not a shark."

Greaves shrugged. "I still say it's good to have people call us when they see something that doesn't look right, especially with these murders happening."

"Hey, maybe a shark is the murderer after all," Beasley said sarcastically. "He climbs out of the water, tiptoes up to unsuspecting tourists, and cuts their throats with his pectoral fin." He drew his hand across his neck for emphasis.

Greaves wasn't amused. Although he didn't know whether a fisherman had been washed out to sea tonight, he knew only too well that people were being murdered on the island.

And that was nothing to laugh about.

43.

TROTT AND TWO OF HIS colleagues worked well past midnight learning as much as they could about the young man named Quincy Warner, formerly Deion Jones. There wasn't much to the story, but Trott called Nazareth and Gimble shortly after 10:00 a.m. to share what little he had.

Not long after his mother's death, Quincy Warner had dropped out of high school and taken a job as a deckhand on a commercial fishing trawler. Two weeks later he had been arrested for attacking a fellow crew member with a boat hook and spent a month in jail. Then his name had disappeared completely from all public records for several years.

"We have no idea what he was up to all that time," Trott reported, "but we finally found his name late last night through the employment records of a local hotel. He's been working there for the past three months."

"Do you have an address?" Nazareth asked.

"For the hotel, yes. For him, no. He and his mother were homeless at the time of her death, and for all I know he's still homeless. If you want to speak with him, I'll pick you up and take you over."

"Sounds good. Tara and I will be ready when you get here."

Twenty minutes later, Trott and the detectives were on their way to Paget Parish. The drive had barely begun when Gimble raised a subject that had been on her mind throughout the night.

"That cab driver we interviewed yesterday didn't bother disguising his hatred of tourists, particularly Americans. Pete and I haven't experienced any problems during our time here," she added hastily, "but in light of the recent murders, we're wondering how common that sentiment is among Bermudians."

Trott smiled. "Out of roughly seventy thousand residents, you'd have trouble finding a hundred like Keith Naylor. And even in his case, I doubt you're dealing with actual hate. Some people aren't meant to work with the public, but they're forced to take whatever jobs are available. In a different line of work, Naylor might be fine."

"If you don't like working with the public," she said, "you probably shouldn't be driving a cab."

"Well, you see, Bermuda is one of the world's leaders when it comes to insurance and other financial services, and that's where you'll find the best jobs. But our second largest industry is tourism. So if you're not qualified to work in the financial sector, there's a good chance you'll be driving a cab or working in a hotel."

"Okay, so a lot of residents end up in jobs they're not crazy about, but you'd say that resentment of tourists is not widespread?"

"I would, yes. But, for the record, I would also say that some visitors, whether here in Bermuda or in any other country, go out of their way to be obnoxious and rude. If you encounter enough people like that," Trott observed, "I'm sure you get sick of their behavior. But I doubt you'd get sick enough to begin killing them for it."

"Can't disagree with that," Gimble offered. "Any idea what this guy Quincy Warner does at the hotel?"

"Not really. But it all boils down to the same thing, I suppose. The hotel exists because of tourists, so that's who Warner works for."

The back-and-forth between Trott and Gimble triggered a thought that for some reason seemed relevant to Nazareth even though he couldn't say why.

"Do either of you remember what Quincy Warner's mother did for a living?"

"I didn't notice that in the police report," Gimble answered.

"It may have been mentioned in the court documents," Trott said, "but I don't remember it distinctly."

"Can you check?" Nazareth asked.

"Of course."

"And if there's anything in the record about the guy's father, that would be helpful as well. I know the mother was a widow, but I don't remember hearing anything about the father."

Trott phoned his office, explained what he was after, and got a callback just as he was turning into the hotel parking lot. After digging through old police records and court documents, his aides had succeeded in pulling together a few preliminary facts about Quincy Warner's parents.

The mother had worked at a hotel and was fired after being accused of stealing money while cleaning one of the rooms. She had died of a heart attack that same day.

The father, also a hotel employee, had committed suicide after being fired for stealing a valuable antique from a hotel guest. The antique in question, a medieval dagger, had never been found.

"I think we just found that dagger," Nazareth declared. He was halfway out of the SUV before Trott shut the engine down. "Now how do we find Quincy Warner?"

"The hotel manager's office is just off the main lobby. That's our first stop."

The general manager, Alex Basden, froze when he saw Trott's badge. Basden and his wife were in the midst of a nasty divorce, and she had already twice accused him of physical abuse. He was greatly relieved to learn the police were only looking for one of the hotel's employees. Why a couple of New York police officers were involved was of no concern to him. He simply pulled up Warner's record on his laptop.

"Yes, here it is. Quincy Warner, full-time employee for just over three months, works in the laundry as an equipment operator. No complaints of any sort from either his supervisor or guests."

"We need to speak with him," Trott said.

Basden reached for the phone on his desk. "I'll have him ..."

"No, we'll go to him."

"Oh, uh, okay. In that case, I'll take you there myself."

Trott nodded, and Basden led the way. They took the elevator to the hotel's lowest level, then followed the hallway to an immense room that was hotter than an August beach at noon. Lining the walls were banks of huge washing machines and dryers. The central part of the room was filled with large bins, each piled high with dirty sheets, pillow cases, and bedspreads. Folding tables and pressing machines took up what little floor space remained.

Three sweaty employees glanced at the manager when he walked in with his guests but didn't stop what they were doing. They worked on a deadline and didn't have time for anyone, including the general manager. But their supervisor set her paperwork down on her tiny metal desk and walked over.

"Can I help you, Mr. Basden?" she said. Emily Morris smiled despite the heat and the pressure of her job, a low-paid supervisory position that nevertheless directly affected the hotel's reputation every single day. A few dirty sheets would almost certainly translate into negative online reviews, something the hotel's management wouldn't tolerate.

Basden studied the woman's name tag. "Yes, Miss Morris, we want to speak with Quincy Warner."

"I'm sorry, sir, but today's his day off. He'll be in tomorrow, though, first thing. His shift starts at 8:00 a.m."

"Ah, I see. Well, Inspector Trott here needs to see him today. Do you know his home address?"

"No, sir, that's not something I would have. The human resources office would, though."

"Right. Okay, then. Sorry to bother you."

"No bother, sir."

The HR office wasn't able to help either. A flustered young woman who had never been in the general manager's presence apologized for not being able to provide Warner's address or phone number. "His record indicates he doesn't have a permanent home," she explained.

"What exactly does that mean?" Basden demanded.

"It usually means the employee is homeless, sir."

"But why no phone number?"

"I don't know, sir. If someone doesn't have a phone, we just note that in the file."

"Then how do you get in touch with him if there's an emergency?"

"I suppose he'd have to hear about it on the radio or TV," she replied wearily, "if he has a radio or TV."

Basden shook his head in dismay. It had never occurred to him that some of the hotel's employees might be living in abandoned homes, caves, or tents. They had jobs, after all.

"Please tell your manager that I want all hotel employees to have phone numbers in their files," he insisted. "No exceptions."

"Yes, sir, I'll be sure to tell her."

Once they were in the hallway, Trott turned to Basden. "My colleagues and I will be back tomorrow morning to see Quincy Warner, but under no circumstances should he be told. Is that clear?"

"Absolutely, Inspector. That won't be a problem."

Unbeknownst to Basden, a problem already existed. Laundry supervisor Emily Morris was about to have lunch with her boyfriend, bellman Kane Swainson.

What she told him about her morning was going to make his head spin.

44.

TROTT WAS PULLING OUT OF the hotel parking lot when the BPS dispatcher radioed him. Late the previous night a distraught woman had called to say that her grandfather was missing. But not until a few minutes ago had someone at police headquarters considered that the old man's disappearance might be linked to a similar report phoned in by a photographer who had been taking pictures at Watch Hill Park.

"The chief inspector has asked that you visit the photographer," the dispatcher said, "because she has pictures that might be helpful."

"Did no one look at her pictures last night?" Trott asked.

"Two officers did, but apparently they didn't find anything disturbing."

"Then why do I need to see them?"

"Uh, well, the chief inspector said that you're in charge of these sorts of things."

Trott took down the photographer's name and address, then vented his frustration to Nazareth and Gimble.

"So now I'm Bermuda's resident expert on both serial killers and vanishings," he grumbled. "How lucky can one man get?"

"We know the feeling," Nazareth sympathized. "Someone in New York City thinks Tara and I are in charge of all things crazy. The nuttier the crime, the more likely we are to get called in."

"And what do you do about that?"

"We solve the cases," Gimble said, "which guarantees we'll get another two just like them. So basically we're victims of our own success."

"Well, the key difference here," Trott noted, "is that I haven't solved anything yet. I haven't found a murderer, and I haven't found a single missing person."

"But you're getting there," Nazareth pushed back. "Quincy Warner looks like an awfully good murder suspect, and that's a crucial development. Whether the murderer is also responsible for the disappearances remains to be seen. In the meantime, you're making progress. Stay positive and do what you do."

"Good advice, detective, and I appreciate it. Care to visit a photography studio with me? It's on the way."

"We'd be delighted."

Gabriella Harrison was surprised to have a BPS inspector and two NYPD detectives at her front door, but she was also greatly encouraged to have someone taking her seriously. The officers she had spoken with the night before had struck her as either skeptical or downright dismissive of her report.

After detailing what she had seen at the shoreline, she put the two relevant photos on her screen. The effect was instantaneous.

"Good God," Trott exclaimed. "How did two officers look at these photos last night and not see anything disturbing?"

"Did the officers see the photos on this screen?" Gimble asked Harrison.

"No, I texted the images to police headquarters."

"Then there's your answer," Gimble told Trott. "You can't compare what they saw on a cell phone with what we're looking at on this large screen. To my eye, at least, one photo shows blood on the rock where the old man had been standing while the second shows a trail of blood in the water."

"That's exactly what I thought," Harrison said. "But I still have no idea what that grey shape is."

"Neither do I," said Gimble, "but it's big and it's definitely real. Now we need to identify it."

Like his wife, Nazareth had no idea what the grey shape was, but he thought he might know how to find out. He placed a phone call to the FBI Laboratory, and three minutes later Harrison's images were on their way to the bureau's photographic operations unit in Quantico, Virginia, for enhancement and interpretation. The unit's supervisor, Rebecca Ingram, said she wasn't sure how long it would take to analyze the photos, but she agreed to give the project top priority since the evidence was tied to an active murder investigation.

On the way back to Windfall, Trott stopped at Watch Hill Park so that he and the detectives could walk the trail down to the spot where Harrison had seen the old man fishing. What Nazareth noticed first was the similarity between this beach and the beach where Seaward had vanished. It was small and relatively isolated, unlike the most popular tourist beaches he had either seen or read about. Whether this meant anything was an open question.

What he noticed next, though, was unquestionably meaningful. He pointed to the rock where one of Harrison's photos showed what appeared to be a small pool of blood. "That's where the old man stood when she took his picture. Now look about fifty yards into the water. What do you see?"

Trott and Gimble studied the pale-blue water of Gravelly Bay.

"I see water," Trott finally answered. "What else is there?"

"Nothing," Nazareth smiled. "Which means that grey thing in Gabriella Harrison's photo is no longer there."

"Which means," Gimble nodded, "it was either an optical illusion or it was mobile."

"I'll keep an open mind," Nazareth responded, "but most optical illusions don't leave blood trails behind them."

Gimble shivered even though the day was quite warm. Was it her husband's words that troubled her? Or was it the eerie sensation of being watched?

45.

Kane Swainson sat in stunned silence as Emily Morris began recounting her brief interaction with the hotel's general manager and three police officers.

"I nearly fainted when I looked up and saw Mr. Basden walking into the laundry," she chattered while scraping the bottom of her yogurt cup with a plastic spoon. She had been eating light lately after deciding to lose weight in advance of the wedding she hoped was in her future. Swainson hadn't committed yet, but after nearly four years of dating, she was still confident he would get there. "The three police officers, they didn't say a word. Just stood there looking nasty and tough. But Mr. Basden said they were looking for Quincy Warner — he's one of the new guys in my department — and he wasn't happy when I said I didn't have his address."

"If they didn't say anything, how do you know the other three were cops?"

"Mr. Basden said *Inspector Trott* was looking for Quincy. I assume the other two people were police because they were with him."

"Why were they looking for Quincy?"

"No idea. Have you met Quincy?"

"I'm not sure," Swainson lied. "I can't know everybody who works in the hotel, can I? So are the police coming back?"

"Probably, unless they got Quincy's address from HR. That's where they were going next."

"Yeah, then maybe they already found him. I wonder what he did."

"Wasn't anything good, that's for sure. Quincy's an okay worker and all, but he's a little scary if you ask me."

"Why scary?"

"He hardly ever smiles and never says anything unless you ask him a question. And he looks like all he does is lift weights, you know? I can picture him beating someone up in an alley."

When Morris began jabbering about the engagement ring she had seen in a jewelry store window, Swainson cut lunch short.

"We have a lot of check-ins this afternoon, and I want to catch my share," he told her. "I'll see you tonight."

She watched him reach for his cell phone as he walked off. Hey, maybe he was looking up the number for that jewelry store she had just mentioned. Her birthday was coming up, and a ring would make the perfect present. She decided to make something extra special for dinner tonight.

Swainson found the phone number Warner had given him at the pub a day or so earlier and kept the text message short.

Police at hotel looking for you. What you do?

At the moment the message reached him, Warner was sitting on the edge of his cot admiring the news clippings about his string of murders. One newspaper had begun calling him the Bermuda Terror, and his skin tingled as he read the words. Another reported that several hotels had begun warning guests not to walk alone at night. Perfect! In time there would be no guests. They would either stay away entirely or have their throats cut. It wouldn't be easy, but he would rid the island of its plague.

The text message jolted him back to reality.

A few simple words from a person he hardly knew had turned his world upside down. *Police at hotel looking for you. What you do?* He fought the wave of nausea that swept over him and focused on the two problems he faced. The police were after him, and Kane Swainson knew how to get in touch with him.

He fixed the phone problem immediately by removing the SIM card and flushing it down the toilet. Now all he had to worry about was the police. Was it possible they had identified him as the Bermuda Terror? Unlikely, but why else would they be after him? And did it matter?

No, it didn't. If he met with the police for any reason, they would in short order figure out he was a killer, and he would spend the rest of his life in prison.

No, he would never let that happen.

What he would do instead was hide out in his basement apartment until he was able to flee the island. Some Jamaicans he knew could probably help on that score, but for the moment he simply needed to stay out of sight.

He heard the footsteps above his head. The old woman again. She knew it was his day off, so as usual she was wearing her hard-soled shoes and dropping oven pans on the kitchen floor. Anything to drive him out.

He suddenly realized she was more a threat than an annoyance. If he stopped going to work, he would no longer be able to pay even the small bit of rent her husband collected each month. In that case, the old woman would insist on evicting him, and her husband would no longer have a choice, even if Warner was his late cousin's son.

The plan wrote itself as he crept up the basement stairs. He waited patiently until she finished clattering around the kitchen and began lumbering toward the living room in her deliberately heavy-footed way. He opened the door as she passed, wrapped his powerful hands around her upper arm, and flung her down the stairs.

She was barely conscious when he cut her throat.

Her husband got home from work at 5:30 that evening and was shocked to find Warner sitting at the kitchen table drinking a beer.

"If my wife finds you up here," he said nervously, "she'll throw a fit, Quincy."

Warner didn't bother getting up. He just turned and plunged the dagger into the old man's chest.

As he helped himself to another beer from the well-stocked fridge, it occurred to him that he probably should have done this months ago.

Think of all the annoyance it would have spared him.

46.

"I'M DEFINITELY GOING TO MISS having a private chef," Gimble mused, "especially in the unlikely event I try to make fish chowder."

Chef Shaun Lightbourne was clearing the dishes after another of his stunning meals. "It's not hard," he said with a straight face, "as long as you can catch your own rockfish, sea bass, and red snapper just before you begin cooking."

"Is that all it takes?"

"That and a few hours," he chuckled. "Oh, and you'll also need Gosling's Black Seal rum. You can't make proper fish chowder without Gosling's."

Gimble turned to Nazareth. "Do we have any Gosling's at home?"

"Not that I recall. I'm also pretty sure we don't have any rockfish or red snapper in the Hudson River. Lots of PCBs, though," he grinned.

"So you're saying we need to come back to Bermuda whenever we're in the mood for fish chowder?"

"I already promised you we'd be coming back."

"And when you do," Lightbourne interjected, "you'll be having your fish chowder right here at Windfall. I already know that Bill Johnson would insist on that. Now, are you ready for dessert?"

"There's no way I can eat anything else tonight," Gimble told him. "Dinner was spectacular."

"I'm with Tara," Nazareth added. "Thanks for another great meal."

"My pleasure. Tell you what, though. The chocolate mousse will be in the fridge if you need a snack later."

That struck both detectives as a reasonable compromise, so they went outside, kicked their shoes off, and hiked barefoot down the beach trail. This was the third time they had come to the beach in time for sunset, and this was also the third time they had found themselves alone. Were the wealthy folks who occupied those fancy hillside mansions bored with gorgeous sunsets, or had they been frightened off by the recent disappearances and murders?

"If we lived here," Gimble mused, "I'd be on the beach every night for sunset."

"No, if we lived here," Nazareth countered, "you'd be on the beach 24/7 because Kayla would never leave."

Gimble smiled sadly. She had been away from Kayla too long already, yet she still didn't know when they would be going home. It seemed to her that they might be close to wrapping up the murder investigation, but her head was spinning on the subject of the disappearances. Was that grey shape in Gabriella Harrison's photo a legitimate clue, or was it simply one more scrap of nonevidence that would lead nowhere?

"I wish Kayla were here right now," she said softly.

"I miss her too, but she's having a ball with your parents up at Lake George. I hope she leaves at least a few fish in the lake."

"We'll have to take her fishing when we get home. I can't imagine how excited she must get when she catches something."

"Lake George isn't that far from Hastings-on-Hudson, so maybe your parents will let us go up for weekends now and then."

"Are you kidding? They're counting on it. And, for the record, I'm getting really excited about moving."

"So am I. As much as I like our apartment, I like the idea of being surrounded by trees even more. Commuting into Manhattan will take some getting used to," he added, "but it shouldn't be too bad."

"Less than an hour whether we drive or take the train. We'll survive."

Gimble suddenly spun to her right and stared at the massive limestone outcropping at the far end of the beach. For the second time in as many days she sensed she was being watched.

"You okay?" Nazareth asked. He followed his wife's eyes down the beach but saw nothing other than the rugged outline of limestone rocks against an orange and red sky.

"This is weird. Yesterday at Watch Hill Park I had a strong feeling that I was being watched, and it just happened again."

"Did you see something?"

"No, but that doesn't mean it's not there. The human brain often picks up things that don't register with your sense of sight."

"Okay, then let's go down the beach and take a closer look."

She grabbed his arm as he began to walk toward the limestone cliffs. "No," she said urgently, "I don't want to go down there, Pete. Let's just go back to the house."

Nazareth looked down the beach again, saw nothing unusual, and turned back to his wife. This was a woman who had met danger head-on many times in her life and not flinched. But her face showed that she was shaken. Some strange sixth sense had just sent her a priority message, and she wasn't about to ignore it.

"Okay, no problem. Rumor has it," he said brightly in an effort to lift his wife's mood, "there's some chocolate mousse waiting for us."

But dessert held no appeal for a woman who had just heard death whisper to her in the cool ocean breeze.

47.

TROTT PICKED NAZARETH AND GIMBLE up at 7:00 the following morning in an unmarked car. The plan had been set. They would rendezvous with two other unmarked cars at the hotel where Quincy Warner worked, and with luck they would have him in custody before his 8:00 a.m. shift began.

Technically they were picking him up for questioning, but Nazareth was already convinced they had their man. A disgruntled, abused, and possibly deranged individual whose parents had run afoul of tourists was an ideal suspect. The fact that he probably owned an expensive antique dagger made him look even better for the crimes.

Trott parked behind the hotel near the employee entrance. The other two unmarked cars had already been positioned by the main entrance and the parking lot exit. Alex Basden, the hotel's general manager, had agreed to call Trott as soon as Warner clocked in for his shift, and the trap would be sprung.

Piece of cake. All they had to do now was wait.

The waiting ended at 7:45 when the first of three TV news trucks raced up to the hotel. Next came reporters and photographers from two local newspapers. Within five minutes, the media circus was in full swing. Trott and his fellow officers did their best to clear the area, but it was hopeless.

An anonymous caller had told each news outlet that the island's serial killer had just been taken into custody at the hotel and had already confessed to the crimes.

Bellman Kane Swainson was loading suitcases into a cab when the storm hit. A frenzied young reporter ran over to him, microphone in hand.

"Did the police go in this way?" she screamed. She charged into the main lobby before he could answer.

A photographer shoved his way through a line of hotel guests waiting for the beach shuttle, nearly knocking an old woman over. Right behind him was the police officer who had just ordered him to leave. One of the hotel guests shouted something about a mass shooting, and several people were slightly injured in the stampede that followed.

Then it ended just as suddenly as it had begun. The reporters figured out they had been duped, and the police realized they weren't going to be arresting anyone this morning.

Swainson grinned as the police drove off in two of the unmarked cars. If Quincy Warner had set this whole fiasco in motion, more power to him. It was a small but highly refreshing triumph for the common man. Swainson didn't know whether Warner was a killer, but he recognized him as a fellow oppressed worker. To the rich people around them, he and Warner were nothing more than slaves.

Trott, meanwhile, was on the warpath. He stormed into Basden's office and accused him of tipping off the press. After Basden vigorously denied having told anyone, Trott went after Emily Morris, who swore she would never jeopardize her job by getting in the way of a police investigation. When Trott noticed the other laundry employees eyeing him, he realized that any one of them might have overheard yesterday's conversation and decided to make his life difficult.

"I find it hard to believe someone would deliberately undermine a police investigation," he complained as he pulled out of the hotel parking lot. "People just can't keep their mouths shut, can they?"

"Unfortunately," Nazareth said, "it gets worse. While you were inside the hotel, a reporter came over to Tara and me and asked why two New York City police officers were involved."

Trott's deer-in-the-headlights moment was the low point of a seriously bad morning. For half a heartbeat he wondered how the press had heard about the two NYPD detectives. Then he remembered.

"I introduced you to Basden yesterday." *I'm being assisted by Detectives Nazareth and Gimble from New York City,* he had said. One sentence delivered in less than five seconds. "But why would he tell the press?"

"As you said," Gimble replied, "people can't keep their mouths shut. When the reporters jumped him this morning, he blurted out whatever came to mind."

"The commissioner will hang me for this," Trott muttered.

"It's nothing to worry about," Nazareth said reassuringly. "The word has been trickling out ever since we arrived in Bermuda, so it was just a matter of time before the press picked up on the fact that we're here."

"And we're not here on vacation," Gimble added. "We're here in an official capacity, so there's no reason to hide what we're doing."

"What did the reporter ask you?"

"Why the Bermuda Police Service had brought in New York City police to work on a murder case," Gimble answered. "Pete told them we have experience with similar cases, which is true, and that we agreed to consult with you. End of story."

"And did that seem to satisfy his curiosity?"

"It did when Pete gave him a look that said he wouldn't be taking any more questions."

"Okay, good. Then maybe that's the end of it."

"That's definitely not the end of it," Nazareth replied. "I'm sure he'll call you or someone else for a comment, and then with or without a comment he'll mention Tara and me in whatever story he decides to write."

"I apologize to both of you for this."

"It's not a problem. What *is* a problem," Nazareth continued, "is that our man Quincy Warner didn't show up for work today. I'm assuming that means someone tipped him off about our visit yesterday. So now you need to go public with your interest in him."

"Do you have his photo?" Gimble asked.

Trott shook his head. "Not even one of him as a young boy. All we have is his name."

"Then it's time to get his name out and ask for help in finding him. Surely someone out there knows where he lives."

"I'm sure you're right. But will that someone actually tell us? Possibly not."

"*Probably* not," Nazareth said, "but you still need to try. At the same time, though, have your forensics people sit down with hotel employees and create a facial composite. Some of the computer-driven composites I've seen are nearly as good as actual photographs."

"I'll get them on it right away."

Trott was about to call in his request when Nazareth's phone rang. As promised, Rebecca Ingram of the FBI's photographic operations unit had put a rush on the analysis of Gabriella Harrison's photos. Unfortunately, their report was going to raise more questions than it answered.

Four different experts had studied the grey shape, she explained, and all they could say for sure is what it was not. It was not a school of fish or rocks or seaweed or cloud reflections. The object was definitely underwater, and the fact that it was casting a very faint shadow on the seabed meant it was midway between the surface of the water and the ocean floor.

"They're also certain the object was animate," Ingram added, "because it left a noticeable wake pattern behind it. We can't say for sure how fast it was moving, but it wasn't slow."

"What about the stains in the water behind the object?" Nazareth asked.

"Yes, I was about to mention that. It's almost certainly blood, and it appears to originate at the upper right side of the grey object. There's a slight distortion of the object in that area of the photo, and we think it might be the lower portions of two legs."

"*Legs* as in human legs?"

"Yes. We're not sure, but it's possible the photo shows the grey shape carrying someone out to sea."

"So wait. We have a large grey shape traveling underwater at high speed," Nazareth summed up, "and it looks as though it might be carrying a human body. But we don't know what this thing looks like."

"We don't know what it is," Ingram corrected, "but we do know what it looks like. It actually looks something like a hippo."

"Did you say *hippo*?"

"Yes, that's what the rough outline looks like when viewed from the angle shown in the photograph. Obviously it's not a hippo," she added, "but the rough shape and size are similar. Remember, though, that the object is underwater and the sky is quite dark. So I can't ID it for you."

"Who would be able to?"

"With the limited evidence we've got, probably no one. But it's possible a forensic biologist could take a more informed guess."

"Do you have one of those in Quantico?"

"Sure. Want me to follow up for you?"

"That would be great."

By the time Trott pulled up in front of Windfall, Ingram was calling back with an update on the mysterious grey object. The FBI's forensic biology unit couldn't provide an ID, but the unit's head knew someone at NOAA who probably could. The National Oceanic and Atmospheric Administration maintained the country's only lab devoted to marine forensic analysis, and Ingram's contact had already passed the photos along for assessment.

"I've asked them to contact you directly," Ingram said, "because that will save some time, but I hope you'll let me know how this all ends up. My husband and I are supposed to visit Bermuda in August, and I'd really like to know what that thing is."

"Whatever I get," Nazareth assured her, "I'll pass on to you. I really appreciate your help."

"That's why we're here, detective. Good luck."

Nazareth tried never to rely on luck to get his job done, but in this case he was willing to take whatever help he could get. It seemed possible, perhaps even likely, that a killer lurked beneath the surface of Bermuda's pristine waters.

But no one had any idea what it was.

48.

PERCHED ON THE FRAYED EDGE of the living room couch, Warner sucked down what little beer remained in the bottle, then leaned low over the coffee table and resumed sharpening the dagger's fine blade. *Take good care of what you have,* his mother had once told him, *because some people have nothing.* He thought of those words every time he removed the dagger from its wooden box. Although he didn't have much, he had this. And he had always taken excellent care of it.

While he worked, he listened to the evening newscast on the old couple's small TV. A Jamaican drug dealer had been convicted and sentenced to prison. A fire in a Hamilton restaurant was being called suspicious. The weather was about to turn unseasonably warm.

Then he heard his own name.

Late today the police named Bermuda resident Quincy Warner as a person of interest in their investigation into the recent string of murders. They are asking anyone with knowledge of Warner's whereabouts to call 911 immediately.

He was mildly alarmed but hardly surprised. Kane Swainson had, after all, told him the police had come to the hotel looking for him, and now they had gone public with his name. So be it. He was safe.

The only people who knew where he lived were presently decomposing in the basement of their tiny home.

A facial composite purportedly representing Quincy Warner popped up on the screen. He laughed uncontrollably when he saw it.

The police also released this computer-generated sketch of Warner's face and, again, ask that you call 911 if you have any information about him.

Only the name underneath the image was accurate. The face itself could have been that of ten thousand other men on the island.

Had his hotel colleagues deliberately misled investigators about his appearance? Or was it nothing more than sloppy detective work on the part of a police force unaccustomed to dealing with someone like him? That was a comforting thought. Yes, they had somehow stumbled across his name, but they knew nothing else about him.

What newscaster Alycia Humphries said next, however, was shockingly unexpected.

We have also learned that two homicide detectives from the New York Police Department have been brought in to assist with the investigation.

Humphries went on to explain that a reporter from one of the local newspapers had followed a vehicle driven by the person heading the investigation, Inspector Earl Trott, to the gates of an exclusive community in Tucker's Town, where he apparently dropped off the two NYPD officers. The reporter then spoke with someone at police headquarters in Hamilton and was able to confirm that Detectives Pete Nazareth and Tara Gimble were, in fact, staying at the home of Bill Johnson, a wealthy American whose cousin and property manager, Melanie Seaward, had been reported missing and was now presumed to have been murdered.

Warner didn't waste time pondering how the two New York detectives had been called to Bermuda or why they were staying at a mansion on Billionaires' Row. That was irrelevant. All that mattered was that they were here, that they presumably knew a lot more about serial killers than their Bermuda counterparts, and that they were after him.

He jumped to his feet and threw the empty beer bottle at the TV screen, producing a cloud of broken glass that filled the room. His anger had gone from simmer to full boil in nanoseconds.

The insult was unbearable. The same kinds of tourists who had killed his parents were now destroying Bermuda with their ostentation and sense of superiority. Yet who did the government call upon for help with the string of murders? Tourist police! And where did those tourist police choose to live while serving Bermuda? In a gated community where billionaires didn't have to mingle with Bermudians.

His entire body shook with rage.

He would soon flee Bermuda, but he vowed to take care of one final piece of business before he left.

The two New York detectives had to die.

49.

THE HUNT FOR THE GUILTY began shortly after 7:00 a.m. when Bermuda Police Commissioner Neville Whitmore stormed into his Hamilton office. He had watched in horror the night before as one of the local TV stations identified Nazareth and Gimble as "homicide consultants" and then proceeded to announce that they were residing at Windfall, the Billionaires' Row mansion owned by American Bill Johnson. According to the TV reporter, someone at BPS headquarters had confirmed all the details.

If that was true, someone was about to become unemployed.

An hour later, he had the guilty party: a secretary who had been on the job for less than three weeks. She had taken a reporter's call, found the information about Nazareth and Gimble in a press release, and, proud of her efficiency, provided the details without delay. When confronted by the commissioner, she showed him the document in question. She was right. It was a press release, albeit one the commissioner had ordered his staff not to distribute. Why it hadn't been removed from the active files would be the subject of another internal investigation.

Still angry over the episode but powerless to undo whatever damage it might have caused, he returned to his desk just in time to take a call from his New York City counterpart, Police Commissioner Ed Kelly. The Bermuda TV station that had broken the news about Nazareth and Gimble was an ABC affiliate, and someone on Kelly's public information staff had clued him in on the previous night's reporting.

Kelly was restrained but obviously displeased. "It's routine for the press to have the names of officers who are in charge of criminal investigations here in New York City, so it doesn't bother me that people know that two of our best detectives are working with you. But I don't think it was necessary to tell everyone, including the murderer, where they live."

The conversation was short and reasonably cordial given the circumstances, but it didn't change the landscape. Nazareth, Gimble, and Johnson had been exposed for their roles, however limited, in BPS operations. Whether this put them at risk remained to be seen.

Whitmore's next call of the morning came from the premier, whose mood was even worse than the commissioner's own. "I just got off the phone with Bill Johnson. I'm sure that name is familiar to you."

"Yes, sir, it is."

"He's unhappy, as you might imagine. Do I need to explain why?"

"No, sir. My staff had absolutely no business confirming his involvement in this murder business."

"You are absolutely correct, commissioner. I now wish to make two points. First, see that no harm comes to those New York detectives. As of this moment, their welfare is your most urgent priority. Second, see that you catch your murderer while at the same time determining why Bill Johnson's cousin disappeared. Once you've done that," he snapped, "the two detectives can go back home. Are we in agreement?"

They were.

Whitmore wasted no time in getting the word out. Effective immediately, there would be a 24/7 police presence at the gate outside Bill Johnson's private community. And if the rich residents didn't like it, they could call the premier to complain.

No one was going to harm Nazareth and Gimble on Whitmore's watch.

50.

THE DEAD COUPLE'S ANTIQUATED LAPTOP took forever to respond, but it was sufficient for Warner's purposes. He wasn't surprised to learn that Bill Johnson had no online telephone listing. Why would a rich American lower himself to socialize with anyone outside his small circle of wealthy neighbors? But Melanie Seaward's phone number and Tucker's Town address were prominently displayed on the screen, and that was enough.

What he needed next was to scope out the place where the two detectives were staying. Since getting past the community's guarded gate wasn't an option, he would have to take an alternate route — one that would require a credit card with someone else's name on it.

For that he went down to the basement and pulled a thin brown wallet from the old man's back pocket. The twenty-five dollars in cash would come in handy at some point, but more important at the moment was the Visa credit card. With that and a few hours of his time, Warner would be well on his way to ridding Bermuda of the two foreign detectives.

They would be going back to New York in separate coffins.

Shortly before noon, Warner reached the dock on Castle Harbour and used the old man's credit card to rent a thirteen-foot motorboat, snorkeling equipment, and fishing gear. Since his former landlord was buying, he also got a cooler filled with ice, two sandwiches, and three bottles of his favorite beer.

The leisurely four-mile cruise to the private beach on the south shore of Tucker's Town took only fifteen minutes, but what he saw on the hillside was worlds apart from the Bermuda he had grown up with. Each of the sprawling mansions — more like palaces, it seemed to him — was twenty or thirty times larger than the tiny home he had known as a child, back in that lost "other time" before his father's suicide. All of the structures were surrounded by towering trees and terraced gardens, and the sunlight shining on their immense windows made the homes sparkle like diamonds against the blue sky. These were the toys of the rich and powerful, priceless symbols of the fat, self-satisfied beings that dwelt within them, and Warner was disgusted.

If he had never killed before, this would have driven him to it.

Thousands of poor men and women like him slaved day after day, year after year, to keep food on their tables while the privileged class spent enough on gardeners to feed a thousand people for a week. He thought about Dwayne, Swainson's friend, who had bought him a round at the pub. How he wished he were Dwayne for just one day. He would come here to Tucker's Town with his dagger and make short work of the aristocrats, eagerly wiping out the lot of them. It would take no more than a few hours to rid Bermuda of this scourge forever.

He assumed that the gigantic home closest to the edge of the limestone cliff was the one he had heard about on the news the night before. The reporter had said it was both the newest and largest mansion on Billionaires' Row, a forty-million-dollar behemoth that looked east across Surf Bay. Warner shut off the motor and drifted on the afternoon tide a hundred yards from shore. As he scanned the landscape before him, he considered how easy it would be to come here at night, beach the boat, and do what needed doing. He would be gone long before anyone realized what had happened.

A woman high on the hillside caught his attention. Blonde and slender, she stood at the top of a narrow trail that led to the beach far below. Her tight shorts showed off her long legs. She held a cell phone in front of her face as though taking pictures of the ocean. He wondered if she was one of the New York detectives, then rejected the idea. She looked too young and, even from a distance, far too pretty for that. No, she was probably just another tourist filling her days with meaningless diversions while the people around her toiled to keep her happy.

Then he noticed a man kneeling at the far end of the beach tying his running shoes. When the man stood, Warner immediately sensed he had found one of the two New York detectives. The guy was tall, lean, and muscular, and his movements were relaxed but confident like those of a mountain cat. Then he began sprinting at a pace that Warner judged he would not be able to sustain for the entire three-hundred-yard length of the beach. But he did. He rested for one minute, then did it again in the opposite direction. Rest, sprint. Rest, sprint. Totally spent after ten repetitions, the man took some deep breaths, removed his running shoes, and began walking slowly down the beach.

When the man looked toward him, Warner smiled and waved. The man waved back. Then he began climbing the trail toward the mansion. When he reached the top of the hill, he walked over to the woman. She showed him something on her cell phone as they walked out of sight side by side.

Warner struggled to understand what he had just seen. If, as he suspected, the runner on the beach was one of the New York detectives, what was the woman to him? Had he brought his wife along while consulting with the Bermuda police, or was the blonde actually the second detective? And if so, why the obviously affectionate behavior?

In the end, he decided it was a mystery that didn't need solving. When he got inside the mansion, he would simply kill everyone he found and let God sort them out.

His next trip to Tucker's Town would be at night.

This time he would be armed.

51.

AS THEY WALKED BACK TO the house following Nazareth's intense beach workout, Gimble showed her husband a photo she had taken with her cell phone while strolling the grounds. It was a close-up of an orange hibiscus bloom framed by the blue sea.

"I was lucky to get this one," she said, "because a minute later there was a boat in the picture right behind the flower."

"That would have ruined the shot for sure. You need to blow this one up and hang it in our new home."

"You really like it?"

"I think it's great. What else do you have?"

She scrolled through a dozen photos, three of which showed a man in a small boat looking toward the shoreline. In the third of those images, he was waving.

"He must have been impressed with your running because he watched you the whole time," she said.

Nazareth nodded. "Yeah, he waved to me when I was finished. It looked as though he was putting on his snorkeling gear. This must be a good area for diving."

"You're probably right, but that's the first boat I've seen here."

"It had **RENT ME** written on one side. Next time we're here, I wouldn't mind renting a small boat and doing some snorkeling."

"First we figure out what that grey thing is."

"The grey thing in the photo, you mean."

"That would be the one."

"Well, I'm sure we'll know soon, so keep an open mind about snorkeling, okay?"

Gimble's face said her mind wasn't terribly wide open on the subject.

"Oh, and by the way," she said, "Trott called while you were on the beach. Not much to say other than that he's gotten two dozen calls about the composite sketch of Quincy Warner that was on TV last night. All dead-ends. One person claimed to know Warner and said the sketch doesn't look anything like him, but there's no way of knowing."

"It's a small island, Tara, and he'll turn up somewhere."

The detectives were about to go inside for lunch when head groundsman Jacob Brangman walked toward them from the workshed.

"Good afternoon, folks. May I ask you a question, Detective Nazareth?"

"Of course," Nazareth replied. He and Gimble hadn't spoken with Brangman since the conversation about his relationship with Melanie Seaward, but they didn't attach any meaning to that. He kept busy all day, and Windfall was easily the best maintained estate in the neighborhood thanks to his efforts.

"I'm sure this will strike you as a little odd given all that's going on these days, but here goes. It involves a young man who served under me in the Royal Bermuda Regiment." Nazareth immediately expected a tip relating to either the murders or the disappearances, but he was wrong. "My friend Miles Lapsley owns a taekwondo school in Hamilton, and he recognized your name when he heard it on TV last night. He tells me you're quite the martial-arts champion."

"I don't compete as often as I once did, but I still give it a shot now and then. How did your friend connect me with you?"

"He knows I work for Bill Johnson, whose name was also mentioned in the TV report. So he called me last night and begged me to ask whether you would consider going to his school some evening and giving a few pointers to his students. Apparently there's a major championship coming up in a few weeks, and your advice would be greatly appreciated."

Nazareth seemed dubious until Gimble weighed in. "You should do it, Pete. We've been free almost every night since we got here anyway."

"What night did he have in mind?"

"Any night," Brangman said, "including tonight if you're available. I can't tell you how excited he would be to have you at his school.

I'll gladly take you there myself and bring you back. The class runs from 7:30 until 9:30, so you'd be back here by 10:00."

"You don't mind?" Nazareth asked Gimble.

"I'm all for it. Go help train a few champions."

"All right, then. I'm in."

"That's wonderful," Brangman said. "Miles will be ecstatic. How about we leave here around 7:00?"

"I'll be ready."

Nazareth was energized by the thought of sharing some of his favorite fighting techniques with local students. His NYPD schedule didn't allow him to do much teaching anymore, and he missed working with younger students.

As for Gimble, she was content to sit alone and read.

It would be a true vacation for at least a few hours.

52.

NOAA RESEARCH SCIENTIST ROGER WINANT took one look at the photograph that Rebecca Ingram of the FBI had sent him and knew he had waded into uncharted waters. His knowledge of marine life was encyclopedic when it came to things like sharks, whales, turtles, or his favorite, the rare and critically endangered ornate sleeper ray, *Electrolux addisoni*.

But the odd grey shape pictured in Gabriella Harrison's photo was unlike anything he had ever seen swimming in the world's oceans.

He called Ingram and got her permission to pass the photo along to one of his grad-school friends, and a few minutes later Curt Earnhart found himself immersed in a mystery that had already left some extremely smart people scratching their heads. A paleobiology professor at Millheim University in Pennsylvania, Earnhart was one of the guiding lights of a relatively new field that married biological science with fossil research. Essentially, he used biological facts about living organisms to draw conclusions about how extinct animals might have behaved and evolved.

And the photo he looked at momentarily caused him to doubt his own eyes. Identifying the grey shape was the easy part. Figuring out how and why it was in Bermuda would be the challenge of a lifetime.

His friend Roger Winant had asked him to phone Nazareth directly with any thoughts he might have, and he did so even though he suspected the call wouldn't go well.

He was right.

The detectives had just finished lunch when Earnhart called. He explained how he had gotten involved, then identified the mysterious grey shape for them.

His words were met with stony silence.

"Are you still there?" he finally asked.

"Uh, yes, professor, we're still here," Nazareth replied coolly, "but I think we're both having trouble believing what you just told us. I mean, how could this be possible?"

"If you're a scientist long enough," Earnhart began, "you learn that just because something has an extremely low probability of occurring doesn't mean it cannot or will not occur. For example, the odds against life forming on Earth were roughly seven hundred quintillion to one. But we're here, aren't we?"

"We are, yeah, but ..."

"There's no *but*, detective. Against all odds, this thing is there. Now we need to figure out what to do about it. And for that I need to be in Bermuda."

"You're willing to come here?"

"Try keeping me away," Earnhart laughed.

"In that case, let me make a phone call and see if I can arrange transportation."

"If you can, great. If not, I'll get there on my own. But please promise me you won't tell anyone else about this until I arrive."

Now it was Nazareth's turn to laugh. "We may never tell *anyone* about this, professor."

"Trust me, detectives. This is one of the most important scientific discoveries of all time, and you'll be happy to have your names associated with it."

As soon as the call ended, Gimble opened her laptop and searched for the source of Earnhart's enthusiasm: *metoposaurus algarvensis*, a huge amphibian that according to conventional wisdom had disappeared from the planet two hundred million years earlier.

Except it hadn't.

Gimble's search produced dozens of artists' renderings based on fossil remains. Despite their differences, all the images were consistent on several points. The immense, lizard-like animal was about ten feet long, had wide jaws filled with sharp teeth, and weighed at least half a ton. The creature also had a tail like an alligator's, but that hadn't been obvious in Harrison's photo because of the angle from which she was shooting.

"How could something that went extinct millions of years ago suddenly show up in Bermuda?" she wondered.

"I doubt that it did," Nazareth replied. "The only thing that sounds remotely close to this was the discovery of the coelacanth."

"The prehistoric fish."

"Yep. It was extinct until a fisherman caught one back in the nineteen thirties. Now we know it hadn't been extinct at all — just MIA."

"But that was a fish. Why would anyone seriously think the same thing could happen with an animal this big?"

"I have a feeling the professor is seeing what he wants to see. To a man with a hammer, everything looks like a nail, right?"

"And to a paleobiologist, every grey blob looks like a living fossil."

"There you go."

"So you don't think we should tell Trott?"

"That an extinct dinosaur is snatching people off the beach? No," he shook his head, "I don't. All I'm going to do is call Bill and see if he can have the professor flown here. If Earnhart still thinks we've got a metoposaurus on the loose, he can be the one to break the news."

Gimble looked concerned. "But what if this thing really exists?"

"For Melanie Seaward's sake, let's hope it doesn't."

53.

IT WAS A FEW MINUTES before 7:00 p.m. when Nazareth, outfitted in a T-shirt, lightweight sweatpants, and flip flops, climbed into the passenger seat of Brangman's two-month-old Toyota HiLux pickup. Despite the fancy dashboard and fifty-thousand-dollar price tag, this was plainly a workingman's truck. The floor in back was littered with muddy boots, several pairs of leather work gloves, and an open bag of plant fertilizer.

"Sorry for the mess," Brangman smiled, "but I didn't have time to clean up in here."

"Why in the world would you want a clean pickup?"

"You're quite right. I wouldn't. But I'm still glad you're not wearing a nice white taekwondo uniform."

"I didn't bring my dobok with me, but this outfit will work fine. So tell me something about your friend Miles Lapsley."

"He's a good man. Twenty-five now, just out of the Royal Bermuda Regiment, and trying hard to get his taekwondo business established. If his students do well at the upcoming championships, that will certainly help him grow the school."

"Is he a competitor himself?"

"Yes, he is, though he has already told me he's not in your league. You've won quite a few major tournaments, have you?"

"Some big, some not so big. But I really enjoy competing, and it's excellent on-the-job training. The martial arts have come in handy quite a few times for both Tara and me."

Brangman seemed surprised. "Your wife is also a taekwondo expert?"

"Her specialty is judo, actually. But her taekwondo is coming along."

"So you're something of a deadly duo."

"Only if necessary. We always prefer talking our way out of trouble. It's safer that way."

Safety went out the window when Nazareth began working with six of Miles Lapsley's top black-belt students. They were all between eighteen and twenty years old with skills ranging from above average to borderline world class. After demonstrating some of his favorite fighting techniques, he sparred one-on-one with each of them so that they all had an opportunity to apply what they had just learned.

Going up against six highly motivated young black belts in a row was a stiff challenge even for someone at Nazareth's elite level, and by 9:00 he was worn out and ready to let the students spar with each other.

"Class ends at 9:30?" he asked Lapsley.

"Or however late you'd like to go. My students won't get this kind of coaching again anytime soon."

"All right, then let's have everyone pair off. Your guys will fight each other, and I'll offer critiques. Sound good?"

It did.

The first two students began trading kicks as though the big tournament had already begun. Showing off for someone with Nazareth's reputation was a rare treat.

When the clock reached 9:30, the training session was still in full swing. Nazareth was having a great time and in no hurry to leave.

54.

THE MOON SHIMMERED ON THE placid waters of Surf Bay as Warner reached the beach directly below Windfall. He had originally planned to return another night, then decided it would be foolish to wait. If the two detectives were called back to New York, he would lose his opportunity to kill them. Far better to strike while he had the chance.

So instead of returning the rented boat, he had taken it to a beach not far from his home and waited until after sunset. Then, dagger in hand, he had set out on his deadly mission. He had drifted offshore several miles away from Tucker's Town waiting for the full darkness of night before pointing the bow toward Windfall.

At 9:25 he stepped onto the sand, dragged the boat up the beach, and tied it to a large rock. Then he made his way up the trail leading to Johnson's mansion and began stalking his prey.

A light went on at the left end of the house, and he crept closer. It was the kitchen, and the young blonde woman he had seen earlier in the day opened the refrigerator door and removed a pitcher. After pouring herself a tall glass of what appeared to be lemonade, she turned off the light and walked toward the opposite end of the building.

He watched through the living room window as she turned on a floor lamp next to the couch. She put her bare feet up on the coffee table, took a sip of her drink, and picked up a book from the end table. She was soon lost in whatever fantasy had captured her imagination.

Breaking in and killing her would be an easy matter, but Warner wanted two trophies, not one. Where was the man he had seen running on the beach? He scanned the mansion's upper windows, found all of them dark, and concluded the woman was alone. Should he settle for what was being offered tonight, he asked himself, or should he wait?

Once again, the pressure of time weighed on him. Waiting might mean losing the opportunity altogether. In the end, he decided that one kill was better than none.

He began by testing the basement windows and soon found one that had been recklessly left unlocked. He squeezed in, lowered himself to the floor, and carefully moved through the darkened space toward the staircase.

As he reached the top of the stairs, he heard the woman's cell phone ring, and he gently opened the door when she began speaking.

"Hi, Mom," she said. "So what have you guys been up to today?"

He didn't bother listening to the rest of her meaningless conversation. She was distracted, and that's all that mattered. The dagger and his right hand had fused into a living, death-dealing force he could no longer control. His heart pounded and his skin tingled as he moved closer. She began laughing at something her mother had said, and when she tossed her head back, he saw the inviting curve of her soft neck.

Before he could strike, though, she dropped the phone and jumped away from the couch. She had seen his reflection in the living room window.

"Who the hell are you?" she yelled.

Warner leered but said nothing. He knew what she was thinking. She was about to become the Bermuda Terror's next victim, and there was nothing she could do about it.

As he moved slowly toward her, he raised the dagger in front of him and twisted the blade from side to side, allowing its keen surfaces to catch the light from the table lamp. The fear he read in her eyes excited him, and he was lost in the feeling.

Gimble's back was nearly against one of the living room windows when he finally spoke to her. "Now I'm going to cut you up into little pieces."

From behind him he heard Gimble's mother screaming into the phone that had fallen to the living room floor. "Tara, what's wrong? Tara! Tara!"

The thought of his victim's mother listening to the assault, hearing her daughter beg for mercy as her throat was cut, intensified his euphoria. This, he knew in that moment, was the purpose for which he had been born.

He swung the dagger at her throat.

Gimble instinctively grabbed his forearm with both hands, pivoted quickly to her right, and flung him over her shoulder in a flawlessly executed *ippon seoi nage*, the same technique she had used in winning numerous gold medals in judo tournaments. Warner flew through the window and landed on his back amid a shower of broken glass. The largest of the shards landed on his face, slicing open his left cheek from the bottom of his ear to the corner of his mouth.

While Gimble ran for the phone to call 911, Warner hobbled toward the beach path. He was gone by the time the police arrived.

His dagger, however, was still on the lawn where he had fallen.

If Quincy Warner chose to kill again, he would need a new weapon.

55.

PROFESSOR CURT EARNHART WAS UNPREPARED for the celebrity treatment. First he was picked up at his home near the Millheim University campus by a stretch limo. Then he found himself the sole passenger on a gleaming private jet. Shortly after Bill Johnson's Gulfstream lifted off from University Park Airport at 8:30 a.m., Earnhart was sipping freshly-brewed coffee and chowing down on a bacon omelet.

This was far outside the boundaries of his quiet academic life. So, too, was the mystery that awaited him in Bermuda. In two hours he would begin an inquiry virtually guaranteed to make him one of the world's most acclaimed scientists. Harvard, Princeton, and Yale would come calling. His future was assured.

His only regret was the way he had handled the conversation with those two detectives. What he should have done, he now realized, was tell them that the grey shape in the photograph might be a rare creature of some sort but that he would not be able to confirm its identity without on-site study. He could have left it at that, and they probably would have been satisfied. Why on earth had he told them it was a creature that had been extinct for millions of years?

How naive!

By now they had probably passed his theory along to everyone involved in the case and perhaps to the local press as well. He pictured himself at the airport in Bermuda surrounded by reporters clamoring for a few quotably nonsensical lines from the crackpot dinosaur hunter. How easy it would be to make him sound like some UFO nut claiming to have been abducted by little green men. Just one newspaper article like that could be enough to derail what so far had been a promising academic career.

But he knew what he had seen.

Well, at the very least he was *almost certain* he knew what he had seen.

No, it was worse than that. Alone in the private jet's opulent cabin, he finally told himself the truth. He *thought* he was sure he knew what he had seen.

Doubt was creeping in.

By the time the pilot announced they were on final approach to Wade International, Earnhart was wondering whether he should cancel the whole thing. He could call the detectives, fabricate a family emergency, and have the plane take him back home. That's what a reasonable man would do.

But he couldn't. If, in fact, there was a metoposaurus swimming the waters of Bermuda, he needed to be the one to find it. He was gambling with his entire future, but he had no choice.

He got off the plane and entered the terminal, where Jenna Tumbridge was the only person waiting for him. After loading his small suitcase into the limo, she chatted with him all the way to Tucker's Town. Among other things, she told him that he would be staying at Johnson's home along with the two detectives.

"There's plenty of room, as you'll see," she told him, "and the accommodations are among the finest on the island."

Sharing a house with two NYPD detectives struck him as odd, but he was no longer master of his own fate. He had agreed to come to Bermuda to help with their investigation, and the rest was up to them.

He was mildly shocked by what he found waiting for him at Windfall. It was smaller than a hotel though not by much. And the two people waiting for him at the front door looked like anything but street-tough New York cops. They both wore T-shirts, shorts, and running shoes, and they were smiling.

"Thank you for coming so quickly, Professor Earnhart," Gimble said as she stuck out her hand. "I'm Tara. Pete and I are looking forward to working with you."

"I'm happy to be here. And please call me Curt."

"Welcome, Curt," Nazareth responded. "How was your flight?"

"I'd be happy to commute like that every day for the rest of my life," he joked, "but I doubt the university would approve the expense."

"Yeah, Tara and I know what you mean. Bill Johnson's world is a little different from the one that we inhabit, but it's nice to live in fantasy land once in a while."

"Which is what you'll be doing here at Windfall," Gimble added. "It's a pretty amazing place."

Nazareth and Gimble waited downstairs while housekeeper Chelsea Butterfield guided Earnhart to a bedroom that was slightly larger than his entire apartment back in State College. The two Andrew Wyeth paintings on the wall were originals, and the ocean views from every window were stunning. For the moment, at least, his fears of a disintegrating academic career faded. He would enjoy his time here no matter what came next.

When he went downstairs, he noticed a workman replacing the living room window but didn't bother to inquire about it. He simply followed the detectives into the kitchen, where they introduced him to Shaun Lightbourne. The chef had laid out some fresh fruit and coffee for them.

"Just a light snack, folks. Let me know when you're ready for lunch, and I'll get things moving."

"Shaun is the main reason Tara and I will be chaining ourselves to the fireplace shortly," Nazareth joked. "We're not going home."

"I suspect our daughter might miss us, though," Gimble added wistfully.

"I'm sure Bill will fly her down for us. Right, Shaun?"

"Absolutely. And it would be a pleasure to cook for Kayla. Maybe I could do pancakes shaped like dolphins and starfish. What do you think?"

"I think I'd like some of those myself," Gimble teased.

"Tomorrow, then. I'll see to it."

The lighthearted banter ended when Nazareth said, "So, Curt, how about we sit out on the deck and talk about that photograph?"

"You bet. I'm sure you both have some questions."

Truer words had never been spoken.

Nazareth launched the first question as soon as they settled into their chairs. He was tactful but direct.

"Someone at the FBI photo lab said the grey thing in the water looked like a hippo, and I have to say it looks more like a hippo to me than a dinosaur."

"The head was my primary clue," Earnhart began, "because it's extremely broad and triangular. A hippo's head is a lot narrower than its body, and it's also rectangular. The creature's tail is foreshortened in the photo because of the camera angle, but if you could view this animal from above, you'd see how long the tail is."

"I think the chief problem," Gimble said, "is that you're willing to see something that the rest of the world believes has been extinct for millions of years. Aside from the coelacanth, which Pete and I talked about yesterday, no extinct creature has ever been found."

"It's worth remembering that the most recent extinction event, which occurred about sixty-six million years ago, did not wipe out all life on Earth. Lots of plant and animal species disappeared, but a lot didn't. Otherwise, we wouldn't be here, right?"

"That's certainly true," Nazareth replied, "but it doesn't convince me that something this large could have remained hidden until now."

"Are you familiar with the name *Mokele-mbembe*?" Earnhart asked.

Neither detective was, so Earnhart provided a brief overview. In the early nineteen hundreds, European explorers became fascinated with an African legend about a creature called *Mokele-mbembe* that supposedly inhabited the Congo River Basin. Natives who claimed to have seen it said the creature was the size of an elephant, had a long, flexible neck, and a tail like that of an alligator.

Then during the nineteen eighties, a retired University of Chicago biologist, Dr. Roy Mackal, led two expeditions into the vast and extremely isolated Likouala Swamp area of the Republic of the Congo in search of what sounded like a living sauropod dinosaur.

"In 1987 Dr. Mackal published a book entitled *A Living Dinosaur? In Search of Mokele-mbembe*, Earnart said. "Although he never saw or photographed the animal, he couldn't rule out the possibility that something awfully strange was living in the swamp. And, for the record, we're talking about an area that covers about fifty thousand square miles of almost impenetrable wilderness."

"And you believe there's a dinosaur still living someplace in that wilderness?" Nazareth asked.

"How can I rule it out? Every living thing there is — all the trees, all the flowers, all the birds, all the fish in the ocean, and the three of us — has beaten the odds against life springing up on this or any other planet. So if a coelacanth was able to survive our planet's five mass extinctions," Earnhart challenged, "why not a metoposaurus? Bottom line: saying that something is highly improbable isn't the same as saying it's impossible."

"Okay," Nazareth said, "we'll keep our minds open. What's next?"

"Let's take a walk to the beach," Earnhart grinned. "I want to see where this thing lives."

56.

QUINCY WARNER STUDIED HIS FACE in the bathroom mirror. The long cut was raw, jagged, and oozing blood despite his having kept it bandaged overnight. That he needed stitches was obvious, but going to the hospital was out of the question. If that blonde had seen him get cut, the police would be on the lookout for a man with a vicious facial wound.

That blonde, he now realized, was unquestionably the female New York cop he had heard about. Who else would have been able to handle him so easily? He had been only inches away from slitting her throat when she had picked him up and flung him through the window like a toy.

When he leaned over the sink and poured rubbing alcohol on the open wound, his screams were almost loud enough to rouse the dead couple in the basement. But the humiliation Gimble had caused him burned far deeper than the alcohol. She had not only thwarted his attack but also taken his dagger.

His father's dagger.

The symbol of his manhood.

The penalty for her sins was death. Killing her and her partner was all that mattered to him now.

He spent hours rummaging through the house, but the knives and garden tools he discovered would be of no use against his intended victims. Finally he found a suitable weapon in a kitchen closet. It was a large plastic jar of lye crystals the old couple had used for cleaning out clogged drains. The label told him what he needed to know: *Causes severe damage to eyes, including blindness.*

His ugly mood turned brighter.

Blind detectives would be no match for him.

All he needed for his next mission were the sodium hydroxide crystals, two large plastic cups, and a bottle of water.

The pieces of his plan came together smoothly as he gathered the necessary equipment. Just before breaking into the house, he would load the two plastic cups with drain cleaner and fill them with water. Whichever detective he met first would then get sixteen ounces of liquid fire in the face. When the other one heard the screams and came running, he or she would get the same. Then while the two detectives fumbled blindly about the mansion, Warner would take his time butchering them.

He spotted a pair of rubber gloves under the sink. Yes, he'd bring those as well. And sunglasses! He needed to protect his own eyes while attacking the two cops.

By noon, when it was time for him to see what food remained in the fridge, all of his weaponry was arrayed on the kitchen counter.

The only thing he needed now was darkness.

57.

AS HE STEPPED ONTO THE pink sand for the first time, Earnhart focused immediately on the immense limestone cliffs that bookended the beach like ancient guardians from another world. Even though he had never been to Bermuda before, he knew a fair amount about limestone. He knew, for instance, that it can gradually dissolve in rainwater to create spectacular caves like those he had visited in Pennsylvania, the largest of which, Laurel Caverns, had more than three miles of intricate passageways. And it was the presence of so much limestone that gave him reason to believe a prehistoric animal could against all odds still be alive in Bermuda.

"Have you taken a close look at these limestone cliffs from the water?" he asked the detectives.

Nazareth shook his head. "Actually, I think this is the first time we've been on this beach at low tide, so we wouldn't have been able to do any exploring until now."

"Not that we had planned to," Gimble added quickly. The limestone outcroppings had a raw, primitive appearance that she found menacing. She couldn't explain why, either to her husband or herself, but that's how it was. "And that was before we thought there might be a prehistoric beast out there."

"I'm going to take a peek," Earnhart announced gleefully as he kicked off his sandals.

"Then I'll go with you," Nazareth said.

Gimble gave her husband a hard look that invited him to change his mind, but he simply unlaced his running shoes. Against her better judgment, she did the same.

"You sure?" he asked her.

"No, but I'll go anyway. Let's do this before the tide comes in."

The three of them followed the narrow beach as it meandered along a wall of ancient limestone whose jagged surfaces were as dangerous as razor ribbon. It was obvious to them that being thrown against these rocks by an errant wave could prove deadly, so they kept a safe distance even when it meant wading up to their knees in the cool water.

They had traveled no more than a hundred yards when Earnhart stopped and stared at a ragged fissure in the limestone cliff. Located a few feet above the waterline, the opening was roughly eight feet high and seven feet wide, but far more interesting was the fact that it appeared to be quite deep. How deep was impossible to judge from where he stood.

"Now you know why I asked whether you had explored the area from offshore," the professor exclaimed. "This is precisely the sort of place a prehistoric creature might inhabit." He leaned into the opening with his cell phone and turned on the flashlight. "There's a tunnel that goes back maybe fifteen feet then turns to the right. I really can't tell from here."

Earnhart appeared ready to climb in.

"If you plan to do that," Nazareth warned, "you better get something on your feet."

Earnhart studied the sharp limestone rocks that littered the tunnel floor, then looked at his bare feet. As much as he wanted to go in, he had to agree that doing so without proper equipment was a bad idea. And maybe, it briefly occurred to him, going in even *with* the right gear was stupid. He snapped a few photos of the opening and reluctantly began walking back to the beach.

"So what are you thinking?" Gimble asked.

"I'm thinking about what you told me over the phone when we first spoke," Earnhart replied. "You said that within the past week or so two people have disappeared from beaches right near that tunnel entrance while others have disappeared within a mile or so. So the question is this. If prehistoric creatures are responsible for those disappearances, why have they only recently become active? Shouldn't they have been attacking people for as long as Bermuda has existed?"

Gimble looked stricken. "You said *they*, plural."

"Well, sure. You couldn't have a lone metoposaurus that's been alive for millions of years, right? So we can assume there's a colony of them. But why haven't they attacked humans until now? That's the puzzle."

"Let's back up a step," Nazareth suggested. "Before we talk about a whole colony of these things, can we talk about how even one of them could have survived the extinction event we talked about earlier today?"

"Of course. Please come into my office." Earnhart smiled and sat down in the sand alongside his sandals. Nazareth and Gimble followed suit. "I've given this a good deal of thought since looking at that photograph you sent, and now that I've seen the tunnel entrance, I believe my theory is even stronger. Here goes."

The professor began by describing characteristics that most scientists were willing to assign to metoposaurus. To begin with, it was an amphibian, meaning it could survive on land as well as in water. Although the creature's four small limbs caused it to move clumsily on land, it was primarily an aquatic animal that dined on fish. It almost certainly would have eaten land-dwelling animals, however, if they came within reach, and Earnhart didn't rule out the possibility that metoposaurus was a reasonably adept ambush predator.

"The most important fact at the moment," he emphasized, "is that it's a strong swimmer. This is something that could easily travel up and down the coast in search of prey. And, as distasteful as this may sound, there's no reason to believe it wouldn't eat humans if they made themselves available."

Beyond the limited facts, though, were certain assumptions that Earnhart believed might account for the creature's ability to survive in modern-day Bermuda. For example, while almost all amphibians are freshwater creatures, he assumed that metoposaurus could have adapted to salt water over time. At a minimum, he said, no one could prove it was impossible. He also assumed the animal was largely nocturnal. By hiding in caves all day and hunting mostly at night, the creature would have the best chance of going unnoticed by humans.

"But I come back to the question I asked before," he said. "Why has the creature only recently begun attacking humans? And I have an idea."

The case he laid out struck the detectives as unlikely but marginally plausible. Millions of years ago, his argument ran, a tunnel leading to an underground cavern collapsed, trapping a number of the creatures inside. Some died, but a few lived, surviving on the small fish that generously populated the cavern's subterranean river. With each new generation, metoposaurus grew more comfortable with its environment and readily became the apex predator of its lost world.

"I'm assuming the first generations lived in fresh water aquifers — lakes, if you prefer — but over time the water became brackish as the ocean found its way into the space. If this happened gradually enough," Earnhart posited, "this would have allowed the creatures to adapt to a marine environment. Most amphibians can't handle salt water, but a few can. Why not this one?"

"What about sunlight?" Gimble wondered.

"Not a problem. In the U.S. today there are more than a dozen salamander species that live in total darkness. Why not metoposaurus, which is basically a gigantic salamander? Give evolution millions of years, and miracles sometimes happen. Apes become humans, for instance."

"If this is all true," Nazareth said, "let's get back to why this thing is only now beginning to hunt for humans."

"Just reverse the process. Millions of years ago, a wall collapsed and trapped the creatures in a cave. This time a wall collapsed and released them from captivity. But to confirm that part of the story," Earnhart said, "I'd like to speak with someone who knows about construction."

"As in constructing buildings?" Nazareth asked.

"Exactly."

"Then you're in luck."

58.

Jacob Brangman had explained the difficulties associated with building a mansion atop limestone when Nazareth and Gimble first arrived in Bermuda, so he seemed the logical choice to address whatever construction questions Earnhart had. They found him in the living room, where he had just finished replacing the window that Quincy Warner had flown through the night before with Gimble's able assistance, and he said he'd be happy to help in any way he could, though he didn't consider himself an expert on the subject.

Brangman repeated the construction facts he had shared with the detectives, then told Earnhart, "The little bit that I know is based on conversations I had with the man whose construction company built Windfall. He stopped by to say hello a few weeks ago while he was in the neighborhood for a new project, and he told me about some of the problems his people had faced when building Windfall."

"Do you know whether the construction crew used ground penetrating radar as part of the process?" Earnhart asked.

"The man I spoke with never mentioned it, but that doesn't mean they didn't. Why do you ask?"

"I'm interested in knowing whether there are any large voids deep in the ground beneath the mansion."

"Voids meaning caves?"

Earnhart nodded. "Precisely. If the construction people had a radar map of this property, it might help with a theory I'm working on."

"Well, I don't know what sort of theory that might be," Brangman replied, "but I doubt you'd need a radar map to conclude that there are caves under our feet. This entire area, from Tucker's Town out to

Castle Island and all the way over to the causeway, is riddled with caves. No one knows how many, but they're basically everywhere."

It wasn't a scientific answer, but it was sufficient to prompt Earnhart's next question.

"If you build on top of a cave, don't you need to worry about a sinkhole forming at some point? I mean, if the cave roof collapsed, you'd have a real problem on your hands."

"I suppose it depends upon how far below you the cave is. If it's hundreds of feet, maybe it's not a problem, but you'd really need to ask an expert about that. All I can say is they've built lots of mansions here in Tucker's Town, and not a single one has been swallowed up."

"Good point. By the way," Earnhart continued, "you said the contractor was here a few weeks ago working on a new project. Do you happen to know what it was?"

"Yes, they're adding a guest house at the property just down the road," Brangman said. "They've already sunk the pilings and built the foundation, so the home will be going up fairly quickly now, I should think."

"Where exactly are they building?" Earnhart asked.

"You can see it from the window." Brangman pointed. "Right over those hedges."

He was pointing to a location about one hundred yards from Windfall.

Earnhart smiled and turned to the detectives.

"If you draw a straight line from that spot to the shoreline directly below it, you'll be within a few feet of the cave entrance we saw earlier."

"Which suggests," Nazareth added, "that maybe a new construction project triggered a change in the architecture of the limestone far below."

"Thereby opening a tunnel that had previously been sealed off," Gimble concluded.

"It's only a theory," Earnhart noted, "but all the pieces seem to be fitting together, don't they?"

"And what's this theory?" Brangman asked. "Or should I not ask?"

"It's okay to ask," Nazareth said gently, "but it's too soon for us to answer."

What he really meant was, *I'm pretty sure this is crazy, but it's seeming slightly less crazy all the time.*

If a simple construction project had accidentally opened a tunnel through time, Nazareth wanted to see the hard evidence.

59.

WARNER WAITED UNTIL 11:30 P.M. to fire up the outboard. He had convinced himself that the two New York detectives would not expect him to attack two nights in a row, especially given what had happened the first time. This was precisely why going after them now made perfect sense.

It would be nearly midnight by the time he reached the mansion. They would be asleep, safe and warm in their luxurious nest, when he broke in. And after dousing their faces with lye, he would slaughter them. The newly sharpened butcher knife he carried with him didn't feel as comfortable in his hand as his father's dagger, but it would get the job done.

A bright moon lit his way to Tucker's Town, and the strong incoming tide helped push him ashore. He dragged the boat up the beach, grabbed his tools, and hiked cautiously up the trail to Windfall. The night was gloriously still except for the sound of waves splashing onto the sand, and the mansion was completely dark.

Conditions were ideal.

He sat quietly in the bushes for fifteen minutes and studied his surroundings, ready to flee at the first hint of trouble. But he was alone. The detectives, it was clear, had already dismissed him as a threat, and for that indiscretion they would pay the ultimate price.

He stuffed the water bottle in his back pocket, set the two empty plastic cups on the ground, and poured lye crystals into each of them. Only after entering the house would he fill the cups with water, transforming them into terrifying weapons against which his victims would be defenseless. No matter how skilled they might be, Nazareth and Gimble would not be able to fight what they couldn't see, and they were only minutes away from never seeing again.

Warner was no more than ten feet away from the back of the house when he triggered the motion-sensing floodlight that Brangman had installed earlier that day. He froze momentarily as a five-thousand-lumen explosion of light transformed night into day, then turned and sprinted for the boat. But he stumbled near the top of the beach trail and lurched forward, losing his grip on one of the plastic cups, which instantly released a small cloud of lye crystals ahead of him. Several of those crystals lodged in his right eye and immediately began burning their way through the cornea.

His screams were loud enough to awaken Nazareth, who looked out the window, spotted the intruder, and raced downstairs. He was barefoot when he bolted through the back door, Glock 19 in hand.

Warner screamed all the way to the beach, but his screaming stopped abruptly just as Nazareth approached the bottom of the trail. Wary of an ambush, Nazareth ducked low in the dune grass and prepared for an attack that never came.

His eyes were drawn to Warner's beached boat. Beyond it, slipping under the moonlit waves, was an immense animal with a human body in its jaws.

60.

It was 5:15 a.m., and the sky had barely begun to brighten when Nazareth rapped on the door to Earnhart's bedroom. The professor had slept through the previous night's commotion, but he was ready to move in less than five minutes once he heard the story. He met the two detectives in the kitchen for a quick jolt of coffee before heading down to the beach.

"Why didn't you wake me up last night?" Earnhart said somewhat irritably. "I should have been down there."

"In the dark?" Nazareth replied. "To see which one of us got eaten next? No way."

"But we might have found important evidence."

"The most important piece of evidence is in my head. I can't say for sure what I saw, but it was big and it was real. All I want to do this morning is take some pictures of the scene."

"You haven't told anyone else about this, have you?"

"I'll do that when we get back. There's no reason to drag the police out here this early when we still don't know what we're dealing with."

"I know exactly what we're dealing with," Earnhart insisted. "You may not be sure yet, but I am."

Gimble cut the debate short. "None of this helps us figure out how to find Warner's body if, in fact, it's still findable," she declared. "And, for the record, I'm not sure that the three of us should be going down to the beach without some serious firepower behind us."

Earnhart looked shocked. "Firepower? My God, you're not going to shoot this animal. It's a living treasure, one of the most significant finds in the history of modern science."

"You'd just put a leash on it maybe?" she scoffed.

"No, I want to find out where it hides and then bring in a team to capture it."

"Even though it might eat a few more people in the meantime?"

"It won't. We can block the entrance to the cave, if that's where it's living, and wait for a team to arrive from the States. I can have the right people here within twenty-four hours."

"Let's talk about next steps later," Nazareth fired back. "All I want to do now is go to the beach and take some pictures."

Earnhart set his empty coffee cup on the counter.

"Then we should get going," he grumbled. He eyed Nazareth's Glock. "But please don't bring that gun."

"If Tara and I go, this goes too."

"Even though we'd probably need an elephant gun to kill that thing," Gimble added.

"You won't need to kill it," Earnhart replied. "The sun is just coming up, and I seriously doubt the animal will be out hunting now."

"It's probably full anyway," Gimble observed as she picked up the flashlight she had found hanging in the pantry. The professor couldn't tell whether she meant the comment to be funny, but he knew she was right. In all likelihood, metoposaurus was comfortably digesting its latest meal.

The first thing they did upon reaching the beach was inspect Warner's boat, which was high and dry now that the tide had gone out. Congealed blood on the boat's gunwale and outer hull provided a strong clue as to what had happened the night before. After running to the beach half blind, Warner must have attempted to pull the boat into the water. But the beast, perhaps aroused by the screaming, had crept from the water, clamped its jaws on the intruder, and dragged him off.

Nazareth looked down the beach toward the tunnel entrance they had visited the day before. "How fast do you think this thing can move on land?"

"Not fast at all," Earnhart said, "because its legs are short and stubby."

"So to hunt on land it would have to rely on stealth?"

"Absolutely. It would most likely hide in the seagrass and wait for prey to walk by. There's no way it could catch a healthy person who saw it coming."

Gimble suddenly realized why her husband was curious about the animal's speed.

"We're not going after this thing, Pete. So if that's what you're thinking, forget it."

"Let me tell you what I'm thinking."

"I already know what you're thinking."

"What I'm thinking," he said as though he hadn't heard her, "is that Bill Johnson asked us to find out what happened to Melanie Seaward, and I don't want to leave here without knowing."

The plan he described was well outside Gimble's comfort zone. Since the tide was dead low and since they now had a flashlight, he reasoned, this would be the ideal time to take a closer look at the tunnel and see what clues might be lying in plain sight.

"If we're lucky, we might actually see evidence of victims," he said.

"If we're *really* lucky," Gimble countered, "only one of us will get killed."

"That won't happen. The tide is out, Tara, and this thing moves like a tank on land. Outrunning it won't be a problem."

"He's right!" Earnhart blurted. "This is the ideal time to have a look inside the tunnel, and the risk is minimal."

"Plus," Nazareth told her, "I'm armed."

"Stupid idea, Pete," she insisted. "Going into that tunnel is nuts."

"It may be the only way we can tell Bill what actually happened. We owe him an answer."

"No answer is worth dying for."

"No one is going to die, Tara. I have to do this."

"But I'll go in first," Earnhart declared. "I don't want you shooting the animal."

"Curt, I never shoot anything that doesn't need shooting. If the animal doesn't attack, I won't use the gun."

"I have your word?"

"You do."

Nazareth turned to his wife. "You wait here, and if …"

"Not a chance, Pete. If you're doing this dumb thing, I'm going with you."

He gave her a disapproving look but knew it wouldn't do any good.

Both detectives could be dangerously stubborn when they wanted to be.

61.

NAZARETH PAUSED AT THE CAVE entrance and peered into the darkness. Then he turned to Gimble and smiled. "Can I borrow your flashlight?"

She glared as she handed it over. "You've done some really stupid things," she told him, "but this goes right to the top of the list."

Before Nazareth could respond, Earnhart grabbed the flashlight from him. "As I said, I'll go in first. This is a research project, not a hunting expedition."

"If you change your mind in there, just let me know. I'll be right behind you." Then to Gimble, "Are you sure you don't want to wait out here?"

She was in no mood for debate. "Let's just get this over with, okay?"

One by one they climbed over the limestone ridge at the base of the tunnel's entrance and stepped back in time. The flashlight's narrow beam exposed a prehistoric chamber with rough, menacing walls and sharp stalactites that hung low from the ceiling. The tunnel's floor alternated between expanses of pink sand and limestone rocks whose ragged edges threatened their every movement.

"Look at this," Earnhart said, pointing to the tunnel wall. "The algae is only on the lower three feet. This tells us that the tunnel doesn't normally flood completely at high tide."

"And we care about this why?" Gimble demanded.

"Well, it means we don't have to worry about the tide change while we're in here."

"We don't have to worry about the tide change," Nazareth corrected, "because we're only going to be here for another few minutes. So let's keep moving."

With Earnhart leading the way, they carefully worked their way almost to the point where the tunnel made a sharp right turn into the darkness.

"Move very slowly," Nazareth warned the professor, "because you have no idea what's around that corner. I'll cover you."

"You can put the gun down," Earnhart replied coolly, "because nothing is going to be there. Our voices would have frightened the animal off as soon as we entered the cave."

"Why do you think that?" Gimble wondered.

"Because it didn't charge us. An animal either attacks or flees, and this one is apparently smart enough not to attack multiple threats."

Nazareth wasn't convinced, so he kept his gun pointed toward the bend in the tunnel.

"Stay to the left, Curt. If that thing goes after you, I'll be shooting to the right."

The professor showed his scorn for the idea by deliberately moving to his right. He held the flashlight up and turned the corner.

"God Almighty!" he yelled.

Nazareth sprang ahead ready to fire, but he didn't need to pull the trigger. He found Earnhart standing at the edge of a huge cavern whose interior stretched at least one hundred feet in all directions. At the base of the cavern was a clear lake so deep that the flashlight's beam was unable to penetrate its depths.

To the professor's left and slightly above the lake's surface was a large, natural shelf measuring perhaps ten feet by fifteen feet. The limestone in this area was relatively smooth, and it was empty except for several small piles of bones.

Gimble finally said what Nazareth and Earnhart were thinking: "Those are human bones."

"They appear to be, yes," the professor allowed. "I don't see any skulls, but what's here is almost certainly human."

Nazareth began moving toward the nearest collection of bones, but Gimble grabbed his arm.

"What do you think you're doing?"

"Bones will give us DNA evidence."

"And trying to get that evidence could get you killed. The thing lives here, Pete. It's probably watching us right now from the water. We're leaving."

Earnhart broke the tie for them. He simply walked over to the nearest pile of bones and stuffed several of the smaller ones in his pocket. Then he moved to the second pile and did the same.

"Curt, for God's sake," Nazareth yelled. "Get back here."

Earnhart held up another bone, pocketed it, and said, "All finished."

He had begun walking back to the detectives when the creature raised its head above water near the middle of the lake.

"Curt," Gimble shouted, "it's in the water!"

The animal might be slow on land, but its speed in the water was frightening. It was at the edge of the lake before Earnhart could rejoin Nazareth and Gimble, and it began slowly raising itself onto the feeding platform. When it opened its massive jaws and revealed rows of long, razor-sharp teeth, the professor screamed.

"Shoot it, shoot it!"

Nazareth complied. He squeezed off ten 9mm rounds in rapid succession, and each bullet ripped into the animal's midsection at nearly twelve hundred feet per second. A single shot would have brought down most animals, but ten seemed to have no effect on this one. All it did was turn toward the shooter and study him with tiny eyes that seemed far too small for its wide, flat head.

But the animal's face presented a compelling target, and Nazareth emptied his remaining five rounds between the beast's eyes.

The creature turned back toward Earnhart, seemed to consider what it should do next, then quietly slipped back into the water. It swam halfway across the lake before diving under the surface.

Earnhart was already running for the exit when the first deafening crack rang out. The barrage of gunshots, each of them louder than a fighter jet taking off with full afterburner, had destabilized the limestone ceiling. A huge chunk of ancient rock fell into the lake, sending a wave of water over the platform and knocking the professor from his feet. He lost the flashlight and would have lost his life had Nazareth's iron grip not yanked him to safety.

"We need to run, Pete!" Gimble yelled.

"Right behind you, Tara. Move!"

The three of them raced through the tunnel toward the cave entrance, which still seemed a thousand miles away when they heard the roar of the cave ceiling collapsing behind them. They failed to reach the opening before a high-speed wall of churning water overtook them and flung them around in the dark like rag dolls. By the time they were washed onto the beach, Nazareth and Gimble were bleeding from their arms, shoulders, and legs after bouncing off the limestone walls.

Earnhart, on the other hand, was motionless on the sand with a large gash on the side of his head.

He appeared to be dead.

62.

WHEN CURT EARNHART OPENED HIS eyes late the following morning, he thought he saw an angel standing over him.

"Am I dead?" he asked.

"No, but you gave a pretty good impression of it," Gimble replied. She and Nazareth had taken turns stopping by the hospital since the professor had been admitted for treatment of his fractured skull and broken left arm. "The doctors say you'll be fine, though."

"I don't even remember coming here."

"You were unconscious when they brought you in, and then they kept you sedated for the pain."

"Yeah, I hurt all over. Are you okay?"

"A few scrapes and bruises, but nothing broken."

"Good, I'm glad. How about Pete?"

"Battered but not broken," Gimble laughed. "He was here earlier, but he went back to Bill Johnson's place to meet with the police. They have divers going in to see what's left of the cave."

"I doubt they'll find anything. For that much water to have been pushed into the tunnel," Earnart reasoned, "the entire ceiling must have caved in."

"Probably so."

"And the most important scientific find of my life may be gone forever."

"Hey, Curt, you were almost eaten by your important scientific find, so look at the bright side."

"You're right. But if I hadn't gone in to collect those bones ..."

"But you did, and what you found was really important. The FBI sent an agent here late yesterday with a device that does rapid DNA tests, and thanks to you they've identified three of the people who disappeared recently. One of them is Bill Johnson's cousin, Melanie Seaward, so Pete and I can now head back to New York."

"Who were the others?"

"Quincy Warner, who was wanted for murder, and the old fisherman who disappeared a few days ago."

"The guy in that photo?"

"Correct. A couple of other people vanished recently as well, and I assume they met the same fate. So thanks to you, Curt, we can close the books on this."

He shook his bandaged head gently. "The animals are still an open issue."

"But if the tunnel is sealed off ..."

"The one tunnel we knew about was sealed off, Tara. But that doesn't mean there aren't others. It's always possible the cave collapse created new openings. And, just to be clear," he added, "there's no chance we're dealing with a lone animal. There has to be a colony of them somewhere."

"Well, Pete and I will leave that problem to you. We're heading home tomorrow."

"Did the doctors say how long I'll be here?"

"A few days. After that, you need to go back to Pennsylvania and take life slow for a while."

She could tell from his grin that going back to Pennsylvania wasn't in his plans.

Somewhere out there among the island's complex network of caves and tunnels was a colony of prehistoric creatures, and he was determined to be the man to find it.

63.

IT WAS NEARLY NOON AND the tide was full when three police officers in scuba gear waded into the water and swam off to explore the tunnel. Inspector Trott had asked them to bring back any evidence they could gather without undue risk. If possible, he had added, they should also assess whether the cave collapse had truly sealed off the area.

"We don't need any sea monsters creeping out of there, do we?" he had laughed. Despite everything the detectives had told him, Trott was unwilling to believe Bermuda was home to a species of extinct dinosaur. Had they seen something unusual? Of course. But in the cave's dim light and amid the eerie confines of an ancient cave, Nazareth and Gimble had allowed their imaginations to run wild. It was that simple.

Trott walked up the trail to Windfall and found Nazareth relaxing on a blue Adirondack chair with a bottle of beer in his hand.

"Drinking alone, are we?" Trott teased.

"Since today is the first and last day of my Bermuda vacation, I figured I owed myself one."

"I'm sorry you didn't get any time off while you were here."

"Tara and I came here to work, and we worked. Plenty of time to relax next time."

"I hope you'll be coming back soon."

"We will."

Trott studied Nazareth's face and seemed to weigh his words carefully.

"You know, I wasn't terribly pleased when I was told you and your wife were coming here," he said, "but you've done some fine work, and I'm in your debt."

"We were glad to help out. And it's definitely a lot nicer chasing bad guys in Bermuda than it is in Manhattan."

"I've never been to Manhattan."

"You're not missing a whole lot," Nazareth assured him, "but if you decide to come up sometime, please let us know. We'd love to have lunch or dinner with you."

"Thank you. I appreciate that."

After a half hour of trading small talk with Nazareth, Trott decided it was time to see how his men were doing.

"Care to join me?" he asked.

"Sure. One last beach walk before returning to the real world."

When they got to the beach, Nazareth walked over to the boat that Warner had used on his ill-fated mission.

"I assume someone will be coming for this," he said.

"Yes, I notified the rental company. They were glad to know the boat wasn't gone for good."

"Did you tell them what happened?"

"No, I didn't. The commissioner has made it clear he wants nothing said about dinosaurs or sea monsters or whatever it was that was attacking people. I'm assuming rumors will leak out, but they won't come from the police. I'm hoping you and your wife will consider not sharing all the details with anyone."

"Tara and I can keep a secret, but I assume Professor Earnhart will let the whole world know what he found."

"But he has no evidence other than the accounts of two eye-witnesses," Trott noted, "both of whom would be doing Bermuda a great service by not fanning the flames of his speculation."

"As I said, Tara and I don't plan to spread the word. But, for the record, this isn't a matter of speculation. We know what we saw. The only reason we can keep quiet about this is that I put fifteen rounds in the animal before the cave roof collapsed on it. It's dead."

"Gone and all but forgotten, eh?"

"That sums it up."

Trott glanced at his watch. His divers had been gone for forty-five minutes already, and he was surprised they hadn't returned yet.

"You said the tunnel was about a hundred yards from the beach, didn't you?" he asked.

"About that, yes."

"Then I don't know why it's taking them so long."

Trott said the same thing fifteen minutes later ... then thirty minutes later. The divers had been in the water for an hour and a half, and they should have returned already.

Nazareth read the concern on the inspector's face. "If you're worried, let's take the boat out and see what they're up to."

Trott didn't hesitate. "Wonderful idea. I'd like to do that." After removing his shoes and socks, he helped shove the boat into the water. The outboard started on the first pull, and they headed toward the tunnel entrance.

Because the tide was in, the entrance was under water, and Nazareth had to estimate its location.

"Should be right about there," he told Trott. "I can't get much closer because of the waves. Do you see anything?"

"No, I don't."

They explored the area for another fifteen minutes before heading back to land.

Nazareth saw it first as the boat drew closer to the beach. It was a shiny black object being pulled back and forth across the sand by the waves.

"What's that?" he asked Trott.

"Not sure." And then, "It looks like a swim fin."

When they got close enough, the inspector leaned over the side of the boat to grab it.

It was, in fact, a swim fin.

And inside it was a bloody foot that had been bitten off at the ankle.

64.

BILL JOHNSON FLEW TO BERMUDA the following morning to preside over a memorial service honoring his cousin, Melanie Seaward. Knowing how much she had loved Bermuda's natural beauty, he arranged for the ceremony to be held at Windfall in her favorite garden overlooking the sea.

The guest list was limited to the household staff, a few close friends, and a small but distinguished delegation of local officials, including the premier, the police commissioner, and the minister of tourism. Johnson had also asked Nazareth and Gimble to attend since they had played a leading role in solving the mystery of his cousin's disappearance. His private jet would take them back to New York late that afternoon while he stayed in Bermuda for a few days.

When the service ended, the premier took Johnson aside to express his condolences ... and to ask for a favor.

"I'm hoping very much that you and the detectives can keep this sea monster story to yourselves until we've had time to confirm what's actually going on here."

"Pete and Tara have already told me they consider this whole thing a local matter," Johnson replied, "and I certainly don't know enough about it to comment. So you don't need to worry about us. I can't speak for Professor Earnhart, of course. I allowed him to stay at my place for a few days, but that's the extent of our relationship."

"We've reached an agreement with the professor. He'll be on retainer as a science consultant while we look further into the matter, and he has agreed to remain silent on the subject of this alleged creature until the issue has been resolved."

"I'm not sure how you resolve something like this."

The premier grinned. "We find it. We kill it."

When all the guests had finally left Windfall, Nazareth and Gimble went to the airport and boarded Johnson's Gulfstream for the short hop to Teterboro. At 6:30 p.m. they walked into their Manhattan apartment, where Gimble's parents and daughter Kayla were waiting for them. Kayla welcomed them back to the real world by launching herself from the couch to her father's waiting arms like a flying squirrel.

They were all eating dinner when Gimble got a text message from real estate agent Jill Sheppard who was helping them with the property in Hastings-on-Hudson. *Please call me when you're back in NYC.*

"Oh, please don't tell me there's a problem with our new home," she said nervously.

"Did you tell her we were going to be away?" Nazareth asked.

She thought back on her most recent conversation with Sheppard. "No, I'm sure I didn't. I remember thinking about telling her, but I decided not to. So how does she know we were away?"

"Not from us," her mother said. "The only calls we got were from you."

"A real estate detective," Nazareth joked. "I didn't know we had any of those in the department."

"This isn't funny, Pete. What if there's a problem?"

"What if you call her and find out?"

Gimble took a deep breath and dialed Sheppard's number.

"Hi, Tara. Thanks for calling. Are you guys back from Bermuda?"

"We are, Jill. I've got you on speaker. Pete and my parents are here."

"Oh, is it okay to talk business?"

Here it comes, Gimble thought. *The sellers have taken a better offer.* "Yes, it is. What's wrong?"

"*Wrong* isn't exactly the word I'd use. I got a call late yesterday from an attorney representing Bill Johnson," Sheppard explained, "which is how I learned that you guys were in Bermuda. Anyway, he presented me with an unusual — well, I guess you'd call it a situation. But I was able to pull the appropriate parties together today, so we're all set."

Gimble gave her husband a puzzled look.

"We're lost, Jill," Nazareth told her. "We have no idea what Bill Johnson has to do with this."

"He bought the house for you."

Her statement was met with profound silence.

"Are you guys still there?" she asked.

"We're here but in shock, I think," Gimble replied. "How could he buy a house for us?"

"With cash and one of New York City's top attorneys. Long story short: Bill Johnson bought the house and gifted it to you. He'll pay the gift tax, so the place is yours free and clear."

"We can't let him do that," Nazareth protested.

"It would be awfully difficult if not impossible to undo this, Pete. If you want my advice, you and Tara should just call him and say thank you."

That's what they did as soon as Gimble's parents had left for their home in Brooklyn, and Johnson listened patiently while they complained that his gift was excessive. Then he closed off further debate.

"To you it's a big gift, but to my accountant it's 0.00002 percent of my net worth. You dropped everything to help me in Bermuda and never asked what was in it for you," he told them. "This is my way of saying thank you. End of story."

When the call was over, the detectives sat on the couch scrolling through online pictures of their new home and talking excitedly about all the things they could do with it now that the burden of a big mortgage payment had just been lifted from their shoulders.

"I still can't believe this is really happening," Gimble finally said. "It all seems like a dream."

Nazareth nodded. "Yeah, life is pretty much perfect, isn't it?"

Fifteen blocks away, a white van exited the Lincoln Tunnel and turned onto 12th Avenue.

The weapon it contained would soon prove that life is anything but perfect.

EPILOGUE

CURT EARNHART COULD SCARCELY BELIEVE his luck. Because Millheim University's spring semester had ended on May first, he had an entire summer in which to locate the colony of "extinct" creatures he knew was out there waiting for him. And now the government of Bermuda had agreed to pay him fifty thousand dollars to serve as a science consultant and to keep his mouth shut unless or until he had definitive proof of the animal's existence. The minister of tourism had even agreed to put him up in one of the island's finer hotels for the duration of his visit.

Life was indeed good.

After two days in the hospital, he was released in late afternoon and returned to Windfall to pick up his things, intending to take a cab to the hotel where he would now be staying.

Bill Johnson wouldn't hear of it. "It's silly to go to the hotel tonight when you're already here. Spend another night at Windfall and let Shaun fix us something great for dinner."

"I don't want to put you out," Earnhart said.

"Hey, there's plenty of room and plenty of food. Enjoy one more night with us."

That settled it. The good news just kept coming.

Dinner that night was fish chowder followed by grilled yellowfin tuna, and Earnhart helped his host finish nearly two bottles of expensive Silver Oak sauvignon blanc from Johnson's well-stocked wine cellar. The men went their separate ways after dinner — Johnson to make some business phone calls and Earnhart to savor the sunset from the mansion's spectacular hilltop vantage point.

But as the sun began to sink below the horizon, Earnhart found himself in the mood for a seaside stroll. It was his last night at Windfall, so why not make the most of it?

He followed the trail down to the beach, where the bay was beginning to glow red and orange in the fading light. He took off his shoes, walked halfway to the water's edge, and snapped a few magnificent photos.

Then he saw it. Metoposaurus was no more than thirty yards down the beach to his left, struggling to pull its enormous bulk onto the sand. He took a dozen photos of it lumbering toward him on its laughably small legs, then shot a video. Even walking backwards, he could easily outpace an awkward beast that hadn't been built for life on dry land.

The words *Nobel Prize* popped into his head. He knew there was no Nobel Prize for biology, but surely the committee would consider honoring him with the prize for physiology and medicine. At the very least, his discovery would garner an International Prize for Biology, something only one paleontologist had ever won. And that was for studying fossils! Imagine how the science community would react to his discovery of a living, breathing "fossil" that had managed to survive one of the most devastating extinction events in Earth's history.

He was overwhelmed by the miraculousness of the moment. Here he was alone on a Bermuda beach with an animal that hadn't changed in millions of years, and now he now had incontrovertible proof. Two dozen undoctored, high-resolution photographs and a thirty-second video would be more than enough to convince even the greatest skeptics.

He took one last photo and smiled. This was the best day of his life.

When he turned toward the trail, he looked into the open jaws of the second creature that had quietly crept up behind him.

A fleeting question crossed his mind. *They were pack hunters?*

It was the last question he ever asked himself.

The police searched the beach the following morning. They found the professor's shoes but failed to notice his cell phone lying in the shallows, rocking gently to and fro in the gentle waves.

When the tide went out, all of Curt Earnhart's dreams went with it.

Made in the USA
Columbia, SC
26 December 2019